# Hannah's Dream

### Jerry Eicher

Book List of Published Novel Titles

*A Time To Live*
*Sarah*
*Hannah's Dream*

Hannah's Dream

Fiction/Contemporary

Published by Horizon Books
768 Hardtimes Rd.
Farmville VA 23901

www.readingwithhorizon.com

Editor – Janet D. Miller

This story is fictional. All persons, places, or events are either fiction or, if real, used fictitiously.

Cover design by www.KareenRoss.com

ISBN   978-0-9787987-3-4

# DEDICATION

*In dedication to dreams and to dreamers.*

OUTSIDE HER UPSTAIRS window it was springtime, the earth awakening from a Northern Indiana winter. Her dark hair already secured beneath the head covering she wore for work, Hannah Miller was taking one last glance at the piece of paper on which she had scribbled down the words. Her almost seventeen-year old hands trembled as she held the writing in front of her.

Breakfast was over, and her mother would soon call for help from downstairs. Her cousins were coming to visit tonight. But for now, she merely had time for another quick read and that would have to do. The words she had read last night for the first time still gripped her. It was a poem by E.S. White, written in 1908.

A Ballad of Spring

It's Spring, my love
Bowed down with care,
Your branches stripped and bare.

Old Winters past.
Its snow and cold,
Has melted long and lost its hold.

The earth it waited.
With bated breath for something more.
For life renewed called from its core.

It opens wide its arms.
For strength, for vigor, for its best.
It stirs its creatures to their nests.

All around it lies the warmth.
Because the sun has drawn near,
Touching, caressing, there and here.

Arise, it calls.
The pomegranates bloom,
They yell that life has room.

Will you come, my Dear,
Hold my hand, touch what I bring.
Because, my Love, it's Spring.

She paused, standing there, thinking about the words. *Could it be true? Was there really something like that? This feeling?* Her mother called from downstairs, "Hannah, time to start the day."

"Yes," she responded, placing the poem on the dresser as she reached for the knob of her bedroom door. However, turning the knob did not shut off the thoughts, nor did going downstairs and into the basement to start the laundry.

The old tub vibrated with its load of pants and shirts, the motor slowing and speeding up as the center tumbler turned, dragged and then lost its hold on the clothing.

As she reached inside the washer to check the progress of things, her mind formed a picture of James in the seventh grade. His grin was lopsided, as it always was. She turned her head to follow its outline, but then decided that wouldn't look right if someone saw her.

"*Un dumm kopp*" (a stupid head)—that's what they'd say. So she did the calculation in her head, without turning anything. His grin appeared again, not clearly, but she remembered it well enough. Now it didn't look nearly as cute as she thought it had in the seventh grade. She almost caught herself smiling, but caught it in time. Another *dumm kopp* moment if someone were watching.

It had been a pleasure to watch his eyes light up when she looked at him, but did it fit what she wanted? This love, this drawing on her heart, this moment that stopped time? She shook her head. *No, it wasn't. Not quite the fit.*

What other choice was there? There was Sam, at the end of the eighth grade when you just had to have someone you liked. The other girls would have thought her a true *dumm kopp* if there had been no one. So she had picked Sam. At random, it seemed now, because he sat across the aisle from her. Well, not quite across, but one row over, and then it was right across.

He had freckles, red hair, and a horrible habit of opening his mouth when he was puzzled or surprised, which was much of his life. During the lunch hour on the ball field, catching a high ball caused that famous drop, followed by an astonished yell.

The other girls greeted her revelation with admiration, she noticed. That was when she decided, back then, that the choice had been the right one.

"He needs someone," Mary had whispered to Ruth, not afraid that Hannah overheard. Mary was blond and sweet on Laverne who was truly a wonder in the Amish world, the picture of good looks.

In fact, Hannah would have picked Laverne if he had not already been taken by Mary. For some reason, it did not bother her that Annie, who was in the sixth grade, had her attention on Sam.

Maybe it was because Mary was her friend and talked with Laverne outside the schoolhouse when they got the chance, and the teacher wasn't around. Annie just blushed when Sam walked by, but said nothing to him.

*No,* she decided, *Sam did not fit for her.* Maybe Laverne would, but he had never stopped looking at Mary. Hannah supposed Laverne and Mary would soon be dating.

"Hannah," her mother, Kathy, called from upstairs, "are you done yet?"

Her mother was always busy and good at what she did. *Wonder if Mom ever had to figure this all out?*

"Coming," she called out. "This old washer is going as fast as it can."

"Well, hurry up. The clothing needs to be on the line before too late. The sun is already well up."

"Yes," Hannah called out again. "I'm getting it out now."

Dragging the basket up the basement steps, Hannah pinned the wet clothes on the line and they hung heavy in the morning air. Only later as they dried and the breeze picked up would they flap in the wind. Her mother would insist on bringing them in if the wind became too strong. That rarely happened, but washdays had to be when they were, and the wind had a mind of its own.

She watched the first of the wash begin to move slightly, as if it were trying to overcome the heavy inertia of earth and gravity. *Just like me,* she said to herself, watching a piece of blue shawl. It didn't move again. *Maybe I'll get myself going someday in this love thing, but I doubt it.*

That evening the buggies started arriving for the family gathering. Others could come, too, if they were in any way slightly connected to someone who was coming.

There would be three sets of parents. Two sets had brother or sister connections, the others were cousins.

It made for spontaneity while maintaining some of the structures formed by the natural family. That was how it came about that Sam came. One of the cousins took the notion to invite him.

After supper all of the young people went outside to play. Since so many younger children were involved, a game at their level must be initiated. At the age of sixteen, almost seventeen, Hannah pondered whether to join in the game of wolf that was chosen. It involved running at full speed in the darkness. Since all of the cousins and Sam were playing, she decided to join in. Time would bring changes, but not quite yet as Hannah was still playing children's games.

That was how it came to be that Hannah found herself a little later rounding the corner of her parents' home in hot pursuit of someone. She was not sure who she was chasing. The moon had already set, and the only light came from the stars. This corner of the house was devoid of any beams from the hissing gas lanterns in the living room and kitchen, making it particularly useful as a getaway exit.

Just as she passed the corner of the house, Hannah's

world exploded into a deeper darkness than the evening around her. Sam, coming from the other direction, missed the person being pursued by Hannah and now flew backwards after colliding with her. Hannah went flying sideways in a crumbled heap. Two children were behind Hannah and managed to avoid running over either her fallen body or that of Sam's. He crawled slowly up to a half sitting position. Hannah was not moving.

Young Mose, one of the children following Hannah, immediately ran to the kitchen door, stuck his head in and yelled in his loudest little boy voice, "Someone bring a light! There's been a hurt!"

Roy Miller, as the resident parent, was the first up. He rose from his seat in the living room and grabbed the kitchen lantern from its hook. This left the kitchen in darkness where the three women were, but no one cared as all were heading out the kitchen door anyway.

"What's going on?" Roy called outside from the kitchen door, holding his lantern aloft.

"She's hurt, over here," Sam said, resting on his left elbow and pointing towards Hannah's unmoving body.

Sam was slowly getting to his feet holding his head. Seeing Hannah on the ground he went over to her before Roy could get there with his lantern. Pushing her gently and getting no response, he pushed again. Under his watchful eye, Hannah moved her hands first, and then lifted her head and slowly began sitting up.

"You okay?" Sam inquired, tilting his head sideways to look down at her. His eyes sought her face in the darkness without success. Then Roy, still looking at her, brought his lantern closer as the light from it bounced up and down the

12

walls of the house, the sidewalk, and skyward. He waited to see. A burst of illumination shot skyward and then fell full on Hannah's face.

"Oh no, I broke her!" Sam yelled as he jumped to his feet. "Her head, her head!" And then he stood there unable to say anything more, his mouth wide open.

Roy got there quickly, glanced briefly at Sam, but his attention focused on Hannah. Her head looked dented in the forehead to a depth sufficient to produce a bulged eye on that side. Dizzily Hannah swayed back and forth, still seated on the ground. Gathering her up in his arms, Roy spoke to the closest adult beside him. "Take care of him," motioning with his head towards Sam before heading to the kitchen with Hannah in his arms.

Kathy met them at the door. "How bad is she hurt?" she asked, holding open the kitchen door.

"I don't know," Roy told her. "Let's get her over to the couch."

Putting her down gently, Roy stepped aside as Kathy got her first good look at Hannah's forehead.

"We have to take her to the doctor," was Kathy's instinctual response at the sight.

"Are you sure? Let's make sure it's bad enough first," Roy told her.

"Bad enough?" Kathy's voice was horrified. "Roy, her eye is bulging out!"

Roy looked for himself and nodded his head. "Can someone run down to the neighbor's and call for a driver?" he asked.

"I'll go," Roy's brother told him. "It shouldn't take too long."

Ten minutes later he was back with the news that it was not necessary to make a call; the neighbor would drive them.

❧

The neighbor, old Mr. Bowen, brought his car up to the front porch. Roy was waiting and placed Hannah in the back seat. "Get in with her," he told Kathy.

Kathy needed no telling, as she climbed in on the other side and held Hannah against her side. When Roy got in the front seat, they drove out of the driveway.

"Is she hurt badly?" Mr. Bowen asked in a concerned voice.

"I can't tell," ventured Roy in a low voice. "Her head seems to have a dent in it. The eye doesn't look normal."

Driving as fast as he dared, Mr. Bowen drove down their gravel road until he reached the blacktop. Here, he sped up considerably. "If the cops stop us, we can explain," he told Roy.

Roy nodded his head. "Just don't go faster than the car can take."

Mr. Bowen chuckled, "It's not the car. I'm the one to be concerned about."

"You're doing okay," Roy said, not wanting to insult the old man. "Better to get there in one piece."

Pulling into the hospital parking lot, Roy got out, opened the back door and took Hannah out. Carrying her inside he wasted no time in making his presence known to the woman at the check-in desk. "Just a minute," she said. "Fill out these papers and we will be right with you."

"I will not fill out any papers," he told her firmly. "My daughter is hurt, and I want her examined right away. My wife will stay with her while I fill out the papers."

She looked at him in surprise. He looked at her, a glint in his eye, his full Amish beard flowing down to where it touched Hannah as he held her in his arms. "You will take her in right away!"

"Ah, yes sir," she said. "I guess if you had brought her in with an ambulance we would have taken her right in."

Roy said nothing, but made it abundantly clear that he was ready to start walking. Following the woman back into the room she indicated, he left Hannah with Kathy while he went to fill out the papers. Ten minutes later when he was done and had walked back into the room, Kathy was alone.

"Already gone?" he asked Kathy.

"The nurse took one look and rushed her right in," Kathy said. "I haven't seen her since."

Two hours later the doctor walked into the room. "Dr. Benson," he said as he introduced himself. "Your daughter is resting now. There is really not much that we can do other than keep her under observation. We can't let her sleep for awhile, of course."

"What happened?" Kathy asked.

"A serious concussion from what I can tell. The bone structure of the skull has actually been damaged. That is what caused her left eye to protrude. We used suction to pull some of the damaged skull back into place, but there really is not that much more we can do. Nature will have to take its course. Some of the dent will fill in with time. The eye will return to normal now that we have taken the worst of the pressure off. We will have to keep her in the hospital for a few days, just to be sure."

"Well, thanks, doctor," Roy said. "Can we see her now?"

"Sure, the nurse will take you. You folks have a good night now."

With that Roy and Kathy followed the nurse two floors up and into a room occupied by two patients. Hannah was lying there, being kept awake by a watchful nurse. In the other bed was another girl whose face was turned away from them. She moved slightly when they walked in, but did not turn in their direction.

"You're in good hands," Kathy whispered to Hannah. "We'd better leave now. I'll come back tomorrow first thing."

Hannah simply nodded her head in understanding.

Let's go," Roy said.

With that, they left the room, hoping Mr. Bowen was still waiting for them in the parking lot. When they found Mr. Bowen he was seated in the front entrance waiting area watching television.

"How is she?" he asked when they walked in.

"Banged up with a concussion," Roy told him. "But she will be okay. She's staying for a few days."

"Sounds good," Mr. Bowen said. "Are you folks ready to go home?"

"We are," Roy told him.

When Mr. Bowen drove in their driveway he asked them about a driver for the next day.

"We still have no one," Kathy told him. "I have to go in first thing in the morning."

"Just count me as your driver until this is over," Mr. Bowen told her.

"That's awfully nice of you." Kathy was overjoyed.

"Think nothing of it," Mr. Bowen told her. "I am glad to help out."

SUNLIGHT STREAMED IN the window the next morning as the nurse came to pull the blinds. Hannah woke up, groggily looked around, and wondered where she was. She had been kept awake until the wee hours of the morning. Her thin body now shivered under the covers.

"Are you cold?" asked the nurse.

"No," she shook her head. "Where am I?"

"In the hospital, dear. You got your head banged up pretty bad last night. Your mommy will be in soon, okay?"

Hannah said nothing, but she felt a lot better with the explanation. Recollections of the previous evening and of being kept from sleeping during the night by the attending nurse began coming back slowly to her tired and bruised brain. A stray sunbeam that got past the blind played on Hannah's face. She squinted her eyes and moved to escape its brightness. As the nurse walked out of the room, Hannah noticed the English girl in the next bed for the first time. The girl was looking at her.

"You're Amish, aren't you?" she asked

Hannah nodded her head, not overly inclined to get into the subject, but not wanting to be rude. One never knew where that conversation would go with English people.

"I thought so," the girl said. "My name's Alice. I live in town. My mom owns the dry goods store in Nap. You Amish come in there all the time."

Hannah nodded again.

"What are you in here for?"

"Got my head banged up last night in a game."

"Must be a rough game."

"Not usually." Hannah held her hand to her head. "Just a running game, and I didn't see the person coming the other way."

"Must be a big person to put that dent in your forehead." It was more a statement than a question.

"Ya, a boy," Hannah told her, making a face.

Alice grinned, "Your boyfriend?"

"No," Hannah said in horror, her hand flying to her head from the sudden movement. "Sam? I would not say that."

Alice was still grinning. "Sounds like the ones you usually marry. Hate 'em, then love 'em."

Sam's mouth dropping open and his freckled face formed a picture in her mind and must have made a frightful picture on her face, because Alice laughed out loud. "Right, oh, aren't I? Some boy, hey?"

Hannah would have glared at her if she had been Amish, but this was an English girl, so she smiled. "I don't think so. Sam is not my type at all."

"Whatever you say, darling, just hope it turns out all right for you." Alice paused, a startled look on her face, her eyes fixed on the door of the room that led to the hall.

Hannah found her own gaze turned there, but she saw nothing more unusual than the glimpse of a boy in a wheelchair going slowly past. She could tell little of what he looked like other than that he had blond hair and looked English. "You know him?" she asked Alice, seeking an explanation for the look.

Alice seemed busy composing her face, for which Hannah could fathom no reason. "Oh, a little," she said. "I have seen him around town."

"You looked startled."

"Oh, it's nothing," Alice assured her with a smile. "Just seeing somebody I know is kind of surprising in here. I mean, what are the chances of them getting sick the same time you do?"

"I guess," Hannah said, not sure at all that this explained it, but she did not see what else it might be either.

Alice reached over and pushed the call button. When the nurse appeared, she asked whether she could go move around in the hall a bit. "I need some exercise," she offered as explanation.

"Sure, we encourage that here," the nurse told her. "Let me go see what I can do for you," she said and disappeared.

"Just need some air," Alice said in Hannah's direction.

Before Hannah could respond, a wheelchair appeared in the door opening. Hannah was sure it was the same boy who had passed earlier. "Can I come in?" he asked cheerfully.

What was she to say — "No"? "I guess"? So Hannah said nothing.

He smiled and gave the wheels of his wheelchair a push and rolled up between the beds.

"Hi," he said to both of them.

"Hi, Peter," Alice said, then added in Hannah's direction, "He's the boy that just went by."

Hannah nodded in Peter's direction, not paying that much attention to him. If Alice knew him, she would take care of him. It did occur to her that he had blue eyes and was quite good looking. With him sitting in the wheelchair she could not tell how tall he was, but his hair was, in fact, blond. She was also sure now that he looked quite English.

"You going home soon?" he asked in Alice's direction.

"This afternoon," she told him. "Mom's coming, and Dad, too, if he has the time. I should be up and about in a few days. Nothing serious, you know. Why it took them this long to figure it out, I'll never know."

"I'll be out tomorrow afternoon." Then in Hannah's direction, "You're Amish, aren't you?" he asked.

She looked at him without answering right away, reluctant to get into another English person's questions about the Amish.

"I know," he said, when she said nothing, "because your parents were in here last night after they brought you in. I saw them check on you. I am Amish, too. We live over in Goshen. What is your name?"

This got Hannah's attention and her reluctance immediately melted away. If she had been looking at Alice, she would have seen her glaring at her. "Hannah," she said.

Peter ignored Alice. "I am in here because I had my appendix taken out. They took it out yesterday. Like I said, I should be here 'til tomorrow, I think. You look like you might be out soon, too," he added, looking at her from across the space between them.

Hannah found herself looking back at him and she felt quite weak inside. Now that the English thing had been taken care of, it occurred to her that he was much better looking than even Laverne. She had never thought such a thing possible, but the impossible was right here in front of her. It was all a little too much.

Slowly, against her will, she felt her face becoming hot all over. Her body shivered under the robe, but not from the cold. Peter was smiling. She thought it the sweetest smile she had ever seen on a boy, as his high brows rose even higher and his mouth was extended with expressive warmth. Against the light hospital gown his blond hair looked even blonder than it really was.

"Is your mother coming back in soon?" he asked her, his blue eyes shining.

Looking into them, she found no strength to answer.

Alice solved the problem by saying sarcastically, "You are a bad boy, Peter." It also broke the spell Hannah was under.

Peter laughed, a deep manly sound emanating from deep in his throat. "That's something coming from you. You are quite a judge."

For Hannah, the powerful feeling was threatening to return.

To Hannah's astonishment, Alice was glaring at Peter. Hannah wondered how she dared.

At that moment, the nurse walked in and ended Hannah's utter embarrassment at this new world of feelings.

"Oh, you came in here," the nurse said to Peter. Then to Hannah, "Your mother is here." Turning back to Peter, the nurse asked, "Have you been behaving, Peter?"

He grinned at her. "Of course, I'm a good boy."

She glanced at him. "I've seen better, but I suppose you'll do."

Peter just kept grinning as the nurse took the handles of his wheelchair and wheeled him away.

Kathy entered then, with a "Good morning" for Hannah and a "Hi" for Alice. Kathy seemed to know Alice and chatted with her until the nurse came back.

"Time to go, Alice," the nurse told her. "We are to meet your parents in the lobby."

"I didn't know they were coming," Alice protested.

"Sudden change of plans, but the doctor has released you, so get your things."

Hannah and Kathy waited while the nurse helped Alice gather her things and got her ready to be discharged.

Hannah was sure there were tears in Alice's eyes as she left, and that she was making a point of not looking at her. *Maybe she's so glad to leave and go home.* But that didn't really make sense.

Hannah brought her thoughts back to her mother as Kathy asked, "Think you can leave the day after tomorrow? The doctor says you're doing real well."

"I'd be ready to go right now," Hannah told her.

"I know, but it's best to follow the doctor's orders. It will be over soon enough."

Hannah nodded grimly.

"I brought you something," Kathy said, producing what was obviously a homemade card.

"Oh," Hannah's face brightened, "a card."

"Ya, guess from who."

Hannah made a face. "How should I know?"

Kathy chuckled as she gave her the card.

Hannah opened it, then shrieked, giving the card back to her mother as if it were poison. "Not from him! After he did this?" she pointed to her head.

Kathy was laughing out loud now. "He didn't mean it, poor boy. He was so cute when he brought the card over. You can't help but love the bumbling fellow. The way his mouth dropped open when I told him I would be glad to give you the card."

"How could you, Mom? That horrid boy is beginning to be a pox on my life."

Kathy was still laughing. "You did say you liked him in the eighth grade."

"Only because we had to have someone, and there was no one else."

"We should always be careful what we say," Kathy said wisely.

"Well, I wasn't thinking," she said, "and I didn't mean it."

"You should at least look at the card," Kathy told her.

"I already did."

"You sure?" Kathy held up the card, opening at the centerfold so Hannah could see both sides. Sam had drawn a rough sketch of flowers; half of them looked like they were dying, the others were on life support. Over the top he had written, "So Sorry. Hope you get well soon. Yours Truly, Sam Byler."

Hannah shivered, and again it was not from the cold, but from an entirely different feeling. "Oh, don't make me look at the thing," she said turning away. "Take it home and put it in my room. If I get enough courage I will set it up some day just to be nice. Maybe I'll get some more to hide this one behind."

"Well, just be nice to him," she concluded. "Who was

that boy in here who left just as I was coming down the hall?"

"His name's Peter. Amish he said. Was in here for an appendix operation. He's from the Goshen area. That's about all I know of him."

"I see," was all Kathy said on the subject and then went on to catch Hannah up on all the news from home. When Kathy was done, she promised to be back to take Hannah home the day after tomorrow. With her departure, Hannah was alone, as Alice's bed was now empty.

Later in the evening, Hannah was lying awake as the last rays of the sun hung in the sky and weakly worked their way into the hospital room. She was wondering what these strange emotions from earlier in the day were all about.

Then suddenly she knew. Suddenly out of the clear blue sky, she knew. This was what love was. It felt the same as when she was reading the poem. She closed her eyes and let it all sink in. Who would have thought it possible, and so soon? "Peter," she said, moving her lips without any sound coming out. She said it again, "Peter"; it sounded better the second time than the first.

Then she wondered, *Does it feel like this forever?* She thought on that for a while, turning the feeling over in her mind. *Was it lasting?* She felt and then she was sure. It did feel like forever. She felt for his name again, and hung on to the memory.

"So this is love," she said softly in wonder, before dropping off to sleep. *Will it always be this beautiful?*

At home, Kathy was telling Roy about her trip to see Hannah. "And," she added, "when I came in she was talking with a boy."

Roy was not too happy. "Already? I wish she wouldn't get involved with boys yet. She's only sixteen."

"I didn't mean it that seriously," Kathy explained. "They were just acting sweet with each other, I think."

"She's too young for it," Roy told her. "What exactly were they doing anyway?"

Kathy smiled, "Well, I walked in and I could tell right away that Hannah was acting different. You know, you can tell. She had that first little flush on her face, even sick as she was, with her head banged up. I could just tell it was there. His name is Peter. He's Nathaniel's boy, one of your cousin's friends. Hannah didn't know, but I think that is who it was."

"So exactly what were they doing?" Roy repeated. "Don't give me this feelings thing. I want to know what they were doing."

Kathy chuckled, "Nothing, really. I think Peter was talking to her. I mean, he was in his wheelchair. Another girl, Alice, was with them, too. Her mom owns the dry goods store in Nap."

Roy was not really mollified. "You know anything more about this boy?"

Kathy lifted her eyebrows and ignored his question. "Like any of us can do anything about it. Nature has its own ways, you know."

"It may or it may not," Roy replied, "but we can stop a lot of things if we really want to."

"Just remember that she is still sixteen."

"I will," Roy told her. "What really concerns me is not just that she's sixteen but that she will soon be seventeen. That's already almost a year into *rummshpringa* (running around). She hasn't started anything yet, and I hope she doesn't. Depending on the boy, this might give her ideas. You know if the boy is running around in town, she might want to also. I just don't want her getting into things like we did."

"I know," Kathy sighed, "the thought had crossed my mind." Then a little grin crossed her face. "Maybe you'd rather have her go out with Sam. He's sweet on her, I think."

Roy laughed, "That boy? Well, he might at least be decent. His dad has his place paid off. He wouldn't be too bad a choice in that respect."

"I don't think he's right for her," Kathy said, "but I guess she will make up her own mind."

"Well, yes," Roy said, "but we are her parents and need to help her where we can.

"I agree," Kathy told him.

# CHAPTER THREE

T HE NEXT MORNING at the hospital, Hannah awoke with the first rays of the sun. She gently rubbed her head, which ached from deep within. Turning her head as the door to her room opened, she watched the nurse enter. Hannah's eyes followed her form as she checked some monitors and then stood in front of her. "How are you feeling, dear?" she asked.

Hannah shrugged her shoulders slightly. "My head aches."

"I imagine it does after what you've gone through. Let me get you some pain medication, okay?"

Hannah watched the nurse leave the room. Covered in her bed sheet, she lay in bed wondering when breakfast was coming and whether it would taste any better than the food had so far.

The wheels of a wheelchair appeared at the edge of her door and gradually she could see the rest of the wheelchair with Peter in it. With a sudden jolt, the memory of him and her thoughts from the evening before came back in a rush. Again she felt the warm feelings his words had unleashed in her the day before.

"Hi," he said by way of introduction. "They let me take a roll on my own, and I thought I'd stop by."

Hannah found herself struggling to find words.

"It's sure a nice morning," Peter said.

She simply lay there, letting the pleasure of his presence wash over her. It soothed her head, in a strange sort of way, until she was startled out of her reverie by the sound of his voice again, and the sudden thought, *He's a boy.*

"Mom and Dad should be by this afternoon," he told her. "I'm feeling better all the time. Well, I guess I must be for them to let me go to the waiting room on my own." He paused, looking at her.

Half-formed visions were flashing in her mind. Words and fragments of thoughts ran together, boys running faster than she did on the playground at school, the way they stood when the teacher called on them to answer a question: Sam, Laverne's eyes, and now Peter's look.

*Is that what the big girls saw when they left the singings with their boyfriends?* Suddenly she felt a little scared and uncertain, as if dangerous ground were under her feet. Alarm bells were going off inside of her. She didn't like the feeling. It felt a little like hearing the clanging wind-up alarm clock going off in her parents' room in the morning. Even though Hannah slept at the other end of the house and upstairs at that, the noise was never pleasant.

Cautiously she looked down at Peter's feet. She froze as they moved, sliding around on the wheelchair foot support. Glancing up, she saw that there was a slight smile on his lips and he held his head still against the head support without moving. Looking into his eyes, she was surprised that the fear stopped. In its place her heart grew warm and she felt cared for. Little shivers fluttered in her chest. Hannah dropped her eyes again. His voice came from across the room, "Are you having a little trouble?"

"My head aches," she told him, finally finding her voice.

"I heard the nurse say she would get you something," he said softly.

When she said nothing he asked her abruptly, "How old are you, Hannah?"

"Sixteen," she told him.

"I'm seventeen," he volunteered. "I started *rummsh-pringa* last year. You're old enough for that, so I was hoping to see more of you."

When she said nothing, he smiled, "Well, maybe we'll see more of each other somewhere. You are a really nice girl."

Hearing footsteps in the hallway he quickly jerked on the wheels of his wheelchair and pushed it down the hall. The nurse came in right after him with the pain medication and handed it to Hannah with a glass of water. Helping her sit up the nurse watched as Hannah swallowed the pills. Looking at her, the nurse said nothing, but Hannah was sure she had seen Peter leaving.

As the pills slid down, Hannah knew that something else was taking the pain in her head away faster than these pills. She wondered how such a thing was possible. Was this how love worked? If it did, she knew she liked it a lot.

The day continued without Peter making any more

appearances. She could feel his blue eyes still looking at her, whether they were actually there or not. The nurse who had seen him stop by her door that morning came by soon after lunch to tell her Peter would be discharged from the hospital before long.

By mid-afternoon both of his parents had walked by her door. She assumed it was Peter's parents since they were dressed as the Amish did. Not many chances of another Amish person being in the hospital with them. Hannah saw Peter's father walk by, nervously turning his straw hat in his hands.

"There we are," she heard the nurse say. "All better and ready to go home."

Hannah watched them go, Peter in his wheelchair, his parents on either side of him. Peter made no further attempt to look in her door. She assumed he did not want to greet her in front of his parents, but it would not have been necessary anyhow.

Watching the last of his wheelchair disappear, she felt a strange feeling of emptiness inside of her. It was different from the pang of hunger for food, yet, in a way, it was the same. It was as if two different people were trying to use the same buggy for different purposes. Hannah had never known before that one could be hungry for something like words. Nor had she known that words could so satisfy when spoken and could leave one so empty when they were gone.

Was this love, too? She drew in her breath deeply. The world was a strange place indeed. Not at all like she would have thought before this.

That evening the hospital room settled into a humming silence. People seemed to be continually coming and going outside her door. Eventually, even that subsided and Hannah finally dropped off into a troubled sleep.

The first thing the nurse told her in the morning was, "You're going home today. The doctor stopped by early while you were sleeping."

Hannah smiled weakly, fighting to become fully awake. "Is Mom coming?" she asked.

"We'll let her know when she comes this morning that you are ready for release."

"I want to go home now," Hannah told her.

The nurse smiled sweetly. "Doctor's orders. We all have to follow them."

❧

As planned, Kathy came that morning with Mr. Bowen for the official release. Hannah arrived safely at home and was now seated on the couch. Everything still looked the same in the room even though it seemed to her as if she had been gone for a long time.

"How long was I gone, Mom?" she asked.

"Only a couple of days," Kathy told her.

"It seems like a long time."

"Well, your head was banged up pretty badly," Kathy said softly.

Roy found her still sitting there when he came in at suppertime and decided now was as good a time as any to talk with Hannah. "That boy," he cleared his throat, "that stayed in the room with you. I hope you haven't got your heart set on him or something like that. You are not to get into such things."

Before Hannah could answer, Kathy came rushing out of the kitchen. "Now Roy, she's just home from the hospital and only sixteen. Nothing happened. You shouldn't be bothering her."

Roy ignored her and continued, "Your Mom said his name's Peter. It's just that I'm really concerned about it. Some boys just aren't right for you or us. This might be that type of boy. I think it would just be better if you stayed away from him."

Kathy gave up and was silent, waiting for him to finish. Hannah looked at the hardwood floor where her father's feet were firmly planted. "He told me who he was," she finally ventured. "They live in a different Amish district from us."

She knew better than to say nothing. That would only make things worse. Why all the fuss? Hannah was greatly puzzled by this. How did the feelings she felt in the hospital room about Peter relate to how upset her father was?

With her father looking at her, and apparently because he wanted more, she ventured in a quiet voice, "He said I was a nice girl." Her thoughts were going all over the place. *If good feelings like this were such a bad thing, then what was one to do? Hide them? Have it in secret? Deny they existed?*

Her father's voice cut through her thoughts, "That's just the problem. He shouldn't be saying things like that."

"Why not?" Hannah asked, the sincerity of the question on her face.

Roy saw the look and responded accordingly, "That is a very brazen thing to say to a girl you have just met. It takes a certain kind of boy to do that. A kind," he paused searching for words, "that it would be best to stay away from."

Hannah said nothing, because she did not know what to say.

Her father continued, "Let me tell you this. They don't make good men with just talk. It takes a lot of work to produce good character. This Peter may not have it yet."

Kathy tried to soften things a little. "We can't be absolutely certain of that, do you think, Roy?"

Hannah was hanging on every word.

"I think I'm pretty close," Roy told her, looking at Hannah for her benefit. "It would just be better, Hannah, if you have nothing to do with this boy. My guess is he won't be coming around since you're only sixteen, but even if you were older I would want you to stay away from him. Okay?"

Hannah answered by looking at the floor again. What else was there to say? She had no idea things were this complicated. It all started without her looking for it, and seemed determined to take its own course without her permission.

Roy took her silence as consent and was satisfied. He left to get cleaned up for supper. After he had gone, Kathy looked at her with concern. "You want any supper, you think?"

Hannah thought about it and decided that the feelings inside of her were somewhat related to food, but not entirely. "I think so," she nodded her head.

"Okay, then," Kathy brightened, "I will bring some out to you."

Afterwards, lying there waiting, Hannah decided that if this were all true, then the whole world must be bad. For something this good to be so wrong required a misalignment of major proportions. She found herself wishing Peter were here. The memories of his voice brought back the desire for his words. They would taste better than supper, she decided. She also decided she would listen to her father, but that she wanted to see Peter and could not do anything about that. Love, she was sure, was good. How it had gotten this bad was a mystery. Softly she lay back on the couch, feelings and senses blending in her mind, until she was not sure whether she was awake or dreaming.

"Peter," she said softly out loud and the sound of his name seemed to fill the whole room.

## Chapter Four

IT WAS AFTER breakfast, a few days later, that Hannah asked abruptly, "May I go riding, Mother? I miss being on Honey."

Kathy turned to look at her. "Are you sure you are well enough? It was not that long ago that your head was banged in."

"I think so. I don't get dizzy anymore."

After considering a moment, Kathy nodded, "Well, it might do you good. And I know Honey has missed you."

Hannah left for the barn immediately and five minutes later was holding on tightly to the reins of her pony. Although she would soon outgrow him, for now he could still carry her. Honey had been a childhood pet for years now and had given her hours of wholesome fun and pleasure.

It felt good to be out again after being laid up in the house for so long. Honey was a faithful little beast, not given to any excesses, and Hannah trusted him completely. Astride him, she was ready to ride in the usual bareback fashion. Looking across the field, a deep sense of joy filled her as the wind brushed softly against her face and stirred loose wisps of hair not restricted beneath the Amish head-covering she wore.

"Come on old boy," she said softly. "Are you ready to go?"

At the point of releasing the reins, her attention was caught by the sound of horse's hooves on the pavement out on the main road. She paused, waiting to see who it was. It could be anyone, but at this hour it was probably one of the womenfolk coming to see her mother.

To her surprise when the single buggy appeared it was being driven by a boy. A greater surprise was when the red hair and distinct features of Sam came into view. *What is he doing on the road at this time of the day?*

She had no idea why Sam would be on the road this time of the day until he turned into their driveway. Then she realized he must be there to see her. Briskly he brought the buggy up to the hitching post, jumped out and tied the horse. Seeing her on her pony, he headed in that direction.

"Good morning," he said, when he was close enough for her to hear.

"Good morning," she said, making no move to get off of Honey.

Sam rubbed his freckled face, a rueful expression on it. "I'm so sorry," he began, "for what happened, with me running into you."

"It couldn't be helped," she told him, wishing he would go away. *Where was her mother?*

"It was dark," he said, "I couldn't see anything. I didn't mean to do it, especially to someone like you." He blushed and looked like he regretted what he had just said.

"It's okay," she told him, keeping her eyes on Honey's feet. If she looked up, she just knew Sam's mouth would drop open. That would be a little too much at the moment.

"I just had a chance to slip away for a moment, in-between the field work," he said as explanation, assuming she wanted one.

*At least he's conscientious. I guess that is one point in his favor. Still, why did I ever bother with this guy in school?* Looking up, Hannah decided to at least be polite. She owed him that much. "Mom allowed me to ride today. She wasn't sure if I was well enough, but I think I am." She was careful not to look Sam in the eyes.

A look of grateful surprise crossed Sam's face, but his mouth did not drop open. *Maybe that's because he's using it to talk with at the moment.*

"Well, you should be careful," he said. "But it's plucky of you to be out and about so soon. Why don't you go for a ride and I'll watch, since I'm here?" His freckles fairly vibrated on his face with eagerness.

*Oh, how long will this creature haunt me? Now he's impressed by my good wife qualities of being up and about so soon.* She was careful, however, to control her outward appearance and made herself smile, although not in his direction. There seemed no option but to humor him, since her mother was still not making an appearance. Turning Honey around she got ready to speed away.

The open field of short stubble hay stretched out in front of her. At the house, behind her, Kathy had come to the living room window at that moment. She saw Sam and guessed Hannah's intended actions. Reaching for the living room door, she was at the point of opening it when Hannah started across the field. Then there was nothing to do about

JERRY EICHER

it as everything seemed in order, anyway. Kathy decided to return to the kitchen for a moment and then check on the two of them later.

As Honey started across the field and then increased his speed, Hannah let him have more of the reins. Glad to be out of the stall, Honey laid deep into the gallop. His legs hit the ground in a rapid concussion of sound, and his breath soon came in sharp jerks. Even knowing that Sam was watching, Hannah threw her head back and laughed in deep pleasure of the ride, nearly losing the head-covering in the process. Quickly lowering her head, she pulled the head-covering forward again as she hung onto the pony's mane and slowly tightened up the reins. The end of the field was rapidly approaching.

"Slow-boy," she said softly. "Honey, let's turn around."

Gently she brought the pony around, still at a trot, and then let him have the reins again for the round back towards the barn. Tears stung her eyes from the wind, but her body felt alive right down to the bare toes. The barn came into view much too quickly as Hannah tightened the reins again and slowed Honey down to a walk by the front board fence. Kathy walked out to the living room window to check and found a smile playing on her own face. *It's good to see her play again,* she thought. *There must be no lasting damage if she can ride like that. I'd better go out to see if Sam is leaving, though.*

Stepping out onto the walks, Kathy headed towards the barn. Neither Sam nor Hannah had noticed her yet.

"Shall we do it again, Honey?" Hannah asked the pony, still out of earshot of Sam. "Maybe you need to rest a little bit first? Concluding that he did, she guided him towards the gate. The water tank was there, too. She intended to let him catch his breath and get a drink of water. At this slow walk, Hannah was not paying attention to the ground. In their path was the hole left from a recently deceased ground hog. The pesky critter had escaped many times but had finally succumbed to Roy's 22-long shot rifle. However, the groundhog's legacy had not been filled in. A little dirt had fallen in around the top of the burrow, and a few small tufts of grass concealed the depth of the hole. The remaining groundhog hole was still plenty big enough for a pony's slim foot.

Into this hole the foot went. If Honey had been going at a run, he would never have been able to extract the foot in time before the forward motion of his body snapped the leg. Now, however, sensing the mortal danger he was in, Honey threw himself violently to the opposite side from the endangered leg. Honey's actions were guided purely by his instincts to survive. He succeeded in saving his leg, but Hannah lost her grip on his mane and went airborne. She struck the ground a few inches from the front gatepost and Sam's feet, and crashed into the post with the full force of her shoulder. Hannah felt a sickening crunch of bone and flesh hitting each other, and then everything went black.

How long she lay there, she was not sure. Honey's muzzle on her chest was the first sensation she felt. Her shoulder burned like fire. Through the haze of pain, she still noticed that Honey was trembling. He whinnied and jerked his neck up and down sharply.

"It was not your fault, Honey," she told him. "I should have been watching where we were going."

Honey's head bobbed and he nuzzled her chest again. He whinnied loudly.

"Honey, are you okay?" she asked him, and then winced when she tried to move her hand to touch his leg. "I must be hurt," she told him.

The hand of her mother appeared on the pony's neck, pushed him away, and reached for her. Kathy's voice was full of concern, insistent: "Hannah, can I do something? Where does it hurt?"

Hannah could not find her voice now that her mother was here, and the attention was on her.

"Hannah, are you hurt?" Kathy asked quietly.

"This hurts," Hannah said, pointing to her shoulder.

Kathy helped her gently to her feet and guided her towards the house. A wincing Hannah went slowly, each movement threatening to recreate the sickening sound deep inside her shoulder. Sam followed behind them, his mouth wide open.

"Sit on the steps," Kathy told her. "Sam, can you go get Roy? He's in the backfield."

Sam did not need to be asked twice and immediately headed down the dirt lane towards the Miller's farming fields.

When Sam found Roy, he was surprised to see him there. His next response was shock. "Hannah is *what*?"

"Hannah hurt her shoulder while riding her pony," Sam told him, although he offered no explanation as to his own presence on the scene. He stood there waiting in the middle of the hay field as Roy pondered this news.

"Is it bad?" he wanted to know.

"I can't tell," Sam answered. "She was holding her shoulder."

"Well, I can't come in right now. I have to finish cutting

the field. Just tell Kathy to go across the road and see if the neighbor can take her to the doctor's office. Don't take her to the hospital. The bill last time was way too high. We can't afford any of that."

"I can finish the field for you," Sam offered.

Roy looked at him in surprise. "You have time for that?"

"I don't need to be back 'til after lunch."

Roy shrugged his shoulders. "I'll go up and see that they get off then. It shouldn't take too long, then I'll be back."

Sam said nothing more, as he expertly took the reins and climbed up onto the hay cutter. Roy watched him go a few steps with the horses. Satisfied the boy knew what he was doing, Roy headed for the house. Arriving there he repeated his conclusions to Kathy.

"What if the doctor says we have to go?" Kathy responded.

"At least tell him to do what he can before you go to the hospital," was Roy's reply.

"I will see," she said. "Are you going to get Mr. Bowen?"

"Yes," he nodded and turned to Hannah. "How bad does it hurt?"

"Mostly it only hurts when I move," Hannah said.

"Try not to move then. I am going to find a ride to the doctor. I'll be right back."

With that, Roy left and was back quickly with Mr. Bowen, whose concern was evident when he got out of the car. "You're hurt again?" he asked.

Hannah numbly nodded her head and got up and climbed into the back seat under her own power. Kathy was soon out of the house with the things she needed and they were off. Roy walked back to his hay field to relieve Sam.

JERRY EICHER

"Is she okay?" Sam wanted to know.

"They left for the doctor. She was walking by herself, so I think she is."

"I am so sorry about all this," Sam told him.

"Well, these things happen," Roy said. "Thanks for keeping the team going."

He slapped the lines and the whirling blades started up with the first movement of the horses. Sam watched for a few minutes before heading back to his open buggy and back to his responsibilities on his father's farm.

An hour later the doctor was looking at the x-ray. "A nasty little break in the collar bone," he said. "The good news is we can tape you up and you're out of here. Just take care of it for a few weeks and you'll be okay."

"No cast for a broken bone?" Kathy wanted to know.

"Kind of hard to put a cast on the collar bone," the doctor explained. "A neck support just rests on the collar bone, so that would make it worse. Sorry, but that's what we do in these cases."

At home that night Roy found Hannah sitting on the couch again in silent despair. "You've got to quit hurting yourself," he told her. "Can't you be more careful?"

"Well, if you'd keep that Sam away from me."

Roy burst out laughing in spite of himself. "He had nothing to do with it this time."

She made no comment, big tears gathering in her eyes and slowly spilling down her cheeks. "We were only walking, Honey and me," she said. "I don't know what happened."

"That's why you need to be more careful," Roy told her. "These medical bills are getting expensive."

She nodded numbly, her shoulder throbbing, as he walked towards the kitchen and supper. "I wish I were a good girl," she said to herself after her father left. "I try to be."

## CHAPTER FIVE

IT WAS A week later and Kathy was getting ready for a trip to Nappanee when Hannah asked if she could go along.

"You sure you are well enough to go along to town?" Kathy looked sharply at Hannah. "It has not been that long since your collar bone was broken from the pony fall. The doctor just took the tape off yesterday."

"I'm fine, Mom," Hannah assured her. "I want to go to town with you."

"Okay," Kathy agreed reluctantly, not wanting to keep the girl indoors longer than necessary. "But you have to be careful."

"I will," Hannah said emphatically. "Surely I won't get hurt in town. I just need to get out."

"We hope not. Is there another reason you want to go?" Kathy asked.

"Of course not, Mom. What else would there be?"

"I don't know. Get yourself ready then. We'll go in half an hour."

Hannah smiled gratefully at her mother and went to get ready.

Kathy soon left for the barn, where she opened the back door and called to the horse. Bobbitt was his official name on the papers, but they just called him Bob. Half-hearted as the usual buggy horses are, Bobbitt was not bad or good, just lazy. He could be persuaded to some sort of speed, if needed. Not that Kathy cared for any speed other than to get to town and back quickly.

Kathy and Roy had never experienced the fast rides of some of the other young Amish people, done mostly after dark on the way home from the singings. They had been among those young people who were deeply involved in *rummshpringa*, and such times required cars, not horses. Some of the young people did *rummshpringa*, and some didn't, depending on many factors, including parental consent and the prevailing opinion of a particular district. Roy and Kathy had experienced a strong confluence of both parental willingness to see their children participate and the order of the day. They had both taken up what they would have called "full English ways." That would be in dress, cars, music, and parties, and all of these while living at home in Amish families. Marriage was the line in the sand, though, and could often bring an overnight transformation back to the Amish ways.

Kathy called to Bob again and he apparently thought better of running away and went towards the barn. Taking him inside, Kathy tied him up, got the harness, and expertly swung it onto Bob's back. Neighing, Bob let it be known he would appreciate a little grain as his reward for coming in.

"Later," she told him. "You eat too slowly. You can have it when we get back."

Bob must have understood or been used to the routine, for after jerking his head back and forth a few times, he settled down. With the horse hitched up, Hannah hopped in and held the reins while Kathy got in. Not that Bob would have made any problems, but there was always that moment between leaving the front of the horse and mounting the steps behind the wheel when a horse could make a dash for it. With Hannah holding on, there was no chance of that, even if Bob had wanted to. On the way home, maybe he would think of it, anticipating the grain, but not now when leaving for town.

"Off we go," said Kathy, slapping the reins slightly to get going.

The trip into town across the northern Indiana landscape went smoothly, the twenty minutes passing much quicker than one might have expected. With the clip-clop of the horse's hooves on the road, the gentle sound of the buggy tires on pavement, the slow scenery passing by, there was plenty to occupy the mind and soul of any man or woman.

Arriving in town, Kathy parked in front of the town's small farm supply store. "I'll be right out," she told Hannah. "This won't take too long."

"I don't want to see anything in there anyway," Hannah told her.

"I figured that," Kathy said. "I'll still tie Bob, though, so you don't have to worry about holding him."

Hannah nodded, glancing along the dusty sides of the farm supply building. Several old trucks sat out in front, as farmers went back and forth to them. A bright looking blue sports car sat over on the right, its rear end jacked up with over large tires and shocks. No one seemed to be around it. *Wonder who owns that?* thought Hannah, as Kathy made her way across the gravel parking lot to the front door of the feed mill.

As if in answer to her question, a side door opened to the loading dock. Out came a blond-headed boy. *I wonder who he is?* Hannah thought involuntarily, memories of Peter coming back to her.

Glancing around as he pushed the cart, the young boy caught sight of Kathy as she headed for the front door. The cart paused momentarily, then resumed moving. As Kathy disappeared into the mill, the boy looked towards the parked buggy, his face fully visible to Hannah. *It is Peter!* She drew in her breath and her hands suddenly gripped the reins she was holding even though Bob was securely tied to the hitching post. *I hope he didn't see me.*

Pulling her head back to the point her vision was blurred through the flexi-glass windshield, Hannah hoped it would also dim the view into the buggy. Gently she slid farther back on the seat, her legs coming tight up against the front edge. Peter was walking towards the buggy.

"Hi," he said, pulling the door of the buggy open and standing right next to the buggy wheel. "I was hoping it was you, when I saw your mom walk in." He nodded his head towards the mill doorway. "Is she staying long?"

"No," Hannah told him, trying to keep breathing. "She will be right back out."

"Then I had better not stay too long," he grinned. "You are looking better than you did in the hospital. Are you all okay now?"

Hannah just nodded, her voice gone. Peter did not seem to be bothered by her silence. "I'm *rummshpringa* you know. Did you see my car over there?" His head indicated the direction of the blue, jacked-up sports car. "She's a beauty. An old MGC with an incline 6-cylinder engine, all repainted and ready to go. Built in the late sixties, got it reasonable from a friend who works at the car dealership. I'll give you a ride sometime."

Hannah found her voice. "I couldn't do that. I'm not doing *rummshpringa*. I may never do it."

"That's too bad," he responded. "But what does that matter? A few more years and it will all be over for us anyway. Then we have to settle down like the old folks. Why not? I can still give you a ride. A pretty girl like you, in my beautiful car — I would love to have you along at one of the Saturday night gatherings."

"I don't think so," she told him. "Dad would not like it."

"Oh, so he's one of those, is he? Old-fashioned? Plans to keep you from having any fun? That's too bad." Peter's brow furrowed, as if pondering the situation. "Maybe you could sneak out? *Ya*? Let's see, I know where you live. Where is your bedroom window?" Pausing, he looked at Hannah, waiting.

She felt herself growing red all the way through. Her face, she was sure, was burning brightly, but what was there to do? This boy was asking her where her bedroom window was. Should she tell him? At the speed of light, a thousand questions suddenly chased themselves around in her head. *Why did he want to know? What would Dad say if he found out? Do I want to chase him away?*

Hannah covered all her bases by asking, "I don't date yet, so why do you want to know where my window is, and what would we do anyway?"

Peter's grin began slowly, starting at the corner of his mouth, spreading sideways until his blond hair was accented by the boyish glee on his face. "I could park the car out by the road, where your dad would not see me. Then I could sneak in the back way by the way of those bushes." She wondered suddenly how he knew so much about her place. "Then I could throw some pebbles or something up against the glass. You could come out, and we could go to the party."

"I don't think so," she said in response to his enthusiasm. "I don't want to go to a party."

"Okay, we don't have to," he said. "I'll just come in and we can talk for a little. That would be fun, right?"

She drew in her breath, words chasing themselves through her mind again. *Don't be silly and throw away your chance. He's a nice boy. Don't you want to feel like this again? Dad said to stay away from him. You should listen.*

He was looking at her, waiting. "Your mother will be back soon."

"I don't think I will," she said quickly, dropping her eyes to the floor of the buggy.

"Okay," he said without the tone in his voice changing. "I will see you then sometime, lovely girl."

*What did that mean? I just told him "No."* Hannah sat in stunned silence.

With that Peter was gone as he walked briskly back to the grain cart he had left by the loading dock. Pushing it before him, he never looked back at the buggy. He disappeared inside a little before Kathy came out the door of the mill. Walking up to the buggy, she looked at Hannah whose face now bore traces of red streaks on the throat and cheeks. Then she looked back at the loading dock of the mill. "Was that Peter?" asked Kathy.

Hannah only nodded. "Did he talk to you?" Kathy wanted to know. Hannah nodded again. "What did he say?" Kathy was still standing outside by the buggy wheel.

"Nothing, Mom, just get in, okay? Well, he told me about his sports car. It's the blue one over there."

Kathy was not convinced. "That's all he told you?"

"Come on, Mom. He did say some other things, but they aren't important."

Kathy shrugged her shoulders, distracted by the urgency of her day's schedule. "You are kind of young to be talking to boys, you know, especially Peter. Remember what your father said."

Hannah nodded, "I remembered. Besides, I didn't start this thing. He did."

"I know," Kathy sighed. "That's how boys are. I was just hoping you wouldn't get started this soon."

Hannah wanted to say many things, ask many things, but she dared not. *Had her mother ever felt like this? Did it always feel this good, to have a boy talk to you? Could this be an answer to a dream?*

So Hannah said nothing while Kathy drove along the streets of Nappanee. "You know I'll have to tell your dad about this," she commented.

"Please don't," pleaded Hannah. "He talked with me — I didn't start it."

"Dad must still be told. It wouldn't be good if he found it out from somewhere else."

"I guess so," Hannah said, resigned to her fate. She still wondered why a good feeling like this caused so much trouble. Life looked mighty strange to her.

True to her promise, Kathy raised the subject after all the

other children were in bed that night. As the eldest, Hannah already was afforded special privileges, but staying up late tonight was not something she would have chosen.

"Sit down, Hannah," Kathy stated to start the conversation, then turned in Roy's direction. "While I was in the mill today, Peter, who apparently works there, came out and talked with Hannah. I thought you should be told."

Roy looked up, mildly focusing on the comment. "What did he have to say?"

"Well, he had his sports car parked there, and I guess he told Hannah about it. He's *rummshpringa*, of course."

"Anything else?"

"I don't think so."

Roy now stirred more fully. "Hannah, we can't keep you away from boys forever, I guess. I had just wished it wouldn't be this quick. You are still very young. Then there is the matter of what boy it is. Sweet talkers like Peter are not as good as they seem. They come and go as the wind, and leave a lot of broken hearts. Good men are made through the trials of life, and I hope you pick that kind of boy someday."

Hannah was not sure what to make of this and sat there looking at the floor. She had been expecting an outburst for sure. *How did her dad know about the sweet talk thing?*

Roy continued, "I know that *rummshpringa* is probably coming up for you. I guess we can't keep you from that either, although I don't like it at all. I've been thinking what we could do about it."

"You can't forbid her," Kathy interrupted him in surprise.

"I know," Roy told her. "That's not what I was thinking."

Now Kathy was even more surprised. "What have you been thinking?"

"I'll tell you some time," he said. "Not right now, though. Let's let Hannah go to bed, and it's our bedtime too, I think. We'll talk about it later."

With that Hannah got up to leave and opened the door to the stairs from the living room. Climbing up step by step, she opened her own door at the top of the stairs. Going in, she walked over to her window from which she could see the sunset. Opening it, she breathed in the night air deeply. Tonight it was too late to see any sunsets, but not too late to think about Peter and the day's events. *What was Dad talking about? Did he really know how she felt? How could this be wrong?*

Dreamily she stood by the window looking out. The night sounds filled her ears and the thoughts of the day filled her heart. *I told him he couldn't come, but wouldn't it be wonderful if he did?* "Peter," she said the name again. *What would it be like to be with him all the time?* She wasn't sure how that would be, but it sure felt like it would be great. Maybe there would be other things involved she did not like. *What will I do if he does come to the window?* She didn't know that answer either, but she shivered, not from the cold, as she stood there in the night air thinking about it.

## CHAPTER SIX

HANNAH RARELY GOT to go to the Sunday evening hymn singing, unless her parents went. Having no older brother to take her, and not yet being up to driving herself, she was at the mercy of whatever chauffeur was available. Because of the location of the singing tonight, her cousins, James and Silvia, had picked her up.

"It's just a mile out of the way," Silvia had assured her that morning at church. "James won't mind."

When Hannah hesitated, not wanting to be an inconvenience, Silvia insisted, "You really need to get to the singings more often. There aren't enough of us decent ones the way it is."

Hannah nodded, knowing what Silvia meant. The young folks involved in *rummshpringa* showed up at times, but the staple of the Sunday night hymn singings were the ones whose parents disapproved of the practice.

"There's less of us all the time it seems," Silvia emphasized the point again. "When the others do come, it turns rowdy — sometimes with all the laughter and talk during singing."

"Okay, I'll come if you'll pick me up."

That was how Hannah found herself in the living room

of Wally Troyer's house, sitting on the third row. The singing was going well, their voices rising and falling in unison. She wished Sam would quit looking at her. As far as she was concerned, it was entirely a useless expenditure of his efforts, but he engaged in it anyway.

Hannah was sure that three girls over on the same row she saw Annie watching Sam, but she never saw him look in Annie's direction. *Why doesn't he go for someone who likes him?* She thought she knew the answer, but didn't like it. *Probably because you're better looking. Of course, because you get up and get going quickly after an accident. A good farm hand, now aren't we?*

Realizing her face was turning into a look of disgust, Hannah caught herself in time, lest someone think she was looking disgusted over the singing. It was not the singing, it was Sam. *What an impossible boy.*

After the singing, the chatting began, cut short at times as a girl had to leave to catch either her brother's or her boyfriend's buggy. Hannah got up to leave when Silvia did and followed her out.

Hannah could not help wondering what it would be like to be going out to Peter's buggy, but he wasn't there. If he were, it would be a car, not a buggy. *Sam's probably wondering what it would be like to have me coming out to his buggy,* she thought ruefully in the middle of her thoughts about Peter. *What a strange world, and so mixed up.*

James had news for them on the way home: "Ernest Byler just took Betsy home tonight."

"I don't believe it," Silvia told him. "He's going on thirty already."

"Well, it's true. I saw it with my own eyes. Betsy walked

right by her brother's buggy and climbed into Ernest's. They must have had it planned like that to try and sneak it by everyone."

"She's got to be close to thirty, too," Silvia announced. "Who would have thought it? I didn't think either of them would ever get married."

"I guess the leftovers take the leftovers," James proposed as an answer. "Everyone needs someone."

Hannah did not say anything and just let the two of them talk.

"You're not saying anything," Silvia commented on Hannah's silence.

"Just listening," she said, to say something, since she preferred not to say where her thoughts were.

"You shouldn't have any problem," James told Hannah.

"Don't torment her," Silvia told him.

"Just commenting," he said.

"Well, it's hard," she told him. "Seems like you either get no one or you get too many."

"Ya, that's my problem," he said.

"Which one?" Hannah ventured.

"No one," he said, keeping his gaze out the storm window of the buggy.

"Don't pay any attention to him," Silvia told Hannah. "He just wants you to feel sorry for him. He's got all the chances a decent boy should have. Just can't make up his mind, I think."

James simply grunted, and Hannah was glad they did not ask her what her problem was.

❧

57

A few evenings later, Hannah stood before her open window and knew winter must be fast approaching. Although the air, stirring in gentle ripples around her, was still warm in the days of Indian summer, she realized those days were numbered. Along a spot on the flat northern Indiana horizon, the full moon cast its first glow into the sky. It would be another fifteen minutes before the moon grew visible, but Hannah could see low hanging clouds accented against the branches of the old tree. *Is Peter really coming?* She wondered. *What am I going to do if he does?* The question scared her.

Having had enough of such musings, she shut the window. It slid downwards softly in that way new windows do. Her father had finished the house two years ago. As Amish homes go, it was rectangular in shape, had two stories, and although plain, it looked new with its nondescript white siding.

Turning the latch on the window, Hannah paused as an object struck the wall, rattled down the siding, and was followed by a ping on the window glass. Slowly she opened the window again. The moon was just peeping over the horizon and soon the night would be flooded with light. However, at present, she could see little in the darkness. No form stood by the tree or anywhere else in the open. Glancing down the fencerow towards the road, she saw nothing. Out by the barn, their dog, Shep, barked sharply. She felt like telling him to be quiet, but that might attract attention. His barking was bad enough. *Surely Peter's not coming.* Then followed the next unbidden thought. *But if he does, does he know about the dog?* That a problem might come from that corner of the universe had not occurred to her. Shep barked louder, his bark urgent and aggressive.

*Oh, I can't believe I'm thinking this. I don't want him to come. I don't want him to come.* She chanted the thought to herself, but she couldn't move herself away from the window.

Hannah stood listening and the barking moved from the back of the barn to the front and then stopped. There was silence and then a few short yaps. Nothing more happened. On the horizon the moon visibly slipped upwards until it cleared the tree line. From there it settled into a warm glow of light without revealing any further signs of movement. Even with more light, she could see nothing unusual. Soon tiring of listening, she closed the window.

But she couldn't stop thinking. *What was that? Would Shep just bark over nothing? What if it was Peter and he got chased away? Now he's never coming back. What if he did come to the window?* Hannah shivered again. *Oh, I can't be thinking like this! It's so wrong. Stop it. Stop it* she told herself.

At breakfast the next morning Kathy commented, "I wonder what Shep was barking about last night."

"I heard it, too. Probably one of the cows running around," her father said. "The barking came from the barn."

"Was one of them out?" Kathy asked.

"I saw nothing while doing the chores," Roy said. "They are all accounted for."

"That's strange," Kathy responded. "Did you hear anything Hannah? You are often up later than the others."

"I heard Shep barking," Hannah said, keeping any emotion out of her voice. She was not sure she liked the direction this conversation was taking.

Kathy looked at her. "Did you hear anything else?"

"Some noises on the side of the house," she said in the same tone of voice. "A bong and a ping."

"Well, that could be anything," Kathy said.

"Probably the tree limb on the house from that old tree," Roy added. "I need to cut that limb off before it falls on the house."

Hannah almost said, "No, don't cut it down," but caught herself in time. However, she did not keep a slight flash of emotion out of her face. Kathy saw it but assumed it was because the children used the limb in their play.

"You had better not, at least not right away," she said to Roy. "The children like to climb around on the thing."

Hannah sighed in relief, but managed to show enthusiasm instead. "It's real good to climb up on the roof with," she said. Her younger brother nodded his head from his place at the table.

"I don't know," Roy responded to their looks. "You shouldn't be climbing around on the roof anyway, and the limb could be a danger to the house in one of the wind storms we get here in northern Indiana. I think it needs to go."

"Whatever you think," Kathy acquiesced quickly.

Hannah said nothing, figuring there was no use, and besides her dad would not get to the project right away. *Maybe Peter would come before that.* Then she quickly reversed her thinking, *I don't want him to come. I don't want him to come.*

The next night the moon rose a little later, lighting up the yard with its glow. *He's not coming.* Hannah stood by the window looking out, unable to stay away. *It's much too light. What if he did come and Shep chased him? Dad might catch him. I wonder if he liked me enough to come anyway.* The thought caught her fancy. *What if he wants to see me so bad he comes charging across the yard even if the moon is shining? What if he chased Shep away? Does he like me that much? Wouldn't that be something?* Warm circles played with each other around her heart as she stood there in the moonlight, her slim figure outlined by its otherworldly light.

Finally, moving away from the window, Hannah closed it and pulled down the spring-loaded shade. She got ready for bed, and then put the shade back up without raising the window. The moon hung like a warm globe in the sky. *What if he came now?* She shivered standing there in the moonlight. She had stopped trying to reverse her thinking.

❧

On a night a week later the moon did not rise as soon. Hannah was no longer spending as much time pondering by the window as she had recently. She was tired from helping her mother can peaches all day. The heat of the wood oven, carrying the jars around, and pealing peach after peach made for a long day. There was little time for thinking of other things.

She did not forget Peter completely, though, and she paused for a moment by the window. Her body and mind equally weary, she did think for a moment about the situation. *He's not coming. He's scared, that's what he is. It's too good to be true, anyway. Maybe Dad is right about him, and this is not love at all.*

As Hannah dropped off to sleep, a mile away a blue MGC with its 6-cylinder engine barely purring traveled slowly along the dirt road.

"Why don't you go faster?" the passenger asked the driver.

"I'm not ready to get there, yet," Peter told his cousin, Lester, who was about his same age and also into *rummshpringa*.

"Scared, aren't you?"

"I am not."

"Then what am I along for?"

"I already told you. You need to feed the dog while I see the girl."

"So what keeps the dog from feeding on me?"

"Look, I have been feeding this dog every other night for almost a week now, ever since I got chased off by him. Please, he's not a vicious dog, just noisy."

"So you are trying to see this girl, right?"

"Yes."

"What is so important about her? I mean, there are plenty of English girls in town to see, like a certain girl I know of." Lester looked at Peter slyly. "Not everything is a secret you know.

"This one is Amish."

"Well, there are plenty of Amish ones in town, too. *Rummshpringa* doesn't leave them behind, you know."

Peter paused for effect. "This one is different, okay?"

Lester looked skeptically in Peter's direction. The lights of the car cast too little light for Lester to catch a good glimpse of Peter's face. "How old is this girl?"

"About sixteen, seventeen, I think. Around our age, certainly not older."

"Have I seen her before?"

"Don't think so. I never did either, till we met in the hospital. They live several districts away from our usual stomping grounds."

"Was that when you had your appendix out?"

"Yes."

"So what is this girl like?"

"Would you quit being so nosy?"

"What are you going to do when you get up to her window?"

"That's my business. Now just be quiet. We're getting close to their place."

Lester was not done yet. "I hope she knows what she's doing. I certainly wouldn't trust you."

"That's what's so cute about her. She doesn't know what she's doing. Got all kinds of stars in her eyes. Look, I'm just going to take her out for a ride. You'll wait while we go for a spin."

"I don't trust you."

"Come on, would you be quiet now? And get that bag ready to feed the dog with."

Lester grunted, "You'd better not get into trouble, or I'll tell on you."

"I won't. Besides, I'm not doing anything wrong. Sure, she's only sixteen, but that's not too serious. What's her dad going to do if he catches us? Give me a lecture on how it's a little early for a girl to *rummshpringa*, but that's about it."

"I wouldn't put much of anything past you. What is a certain other English girl going to say? The one I saw you with on Saturday night?"

"How is she going to find out? Besides, she doesn't have to know."

"I didn't say she did."

"Your voice said so. Look, just keep your mouth shut and feed the dog once we get there, okay?"

Lester grunted, tired of the harassment, then asked, "Why we are coming here in the middle of the week? Throw the regular crowd off the scent?"

"Now you're catching on," Peter grinned, the headlights of the MGC piercing the darkness along the edge of the dirt road. "Now, here go the lights," he said softly. "It's darkness from here on in." Peter switched off the lights as the car bumped along, its tires crunching on the gravel.

"You'd better not go too far without lights," Lester told him.

"I'm not. It's just around that bend."

The MGC slowly pulled to a halt by the fence line. Here the Miller property was separated from the land of Roy's cousin, a spread of more than 150 acres, farmed completely with horses. Opening the car door, the boys cautiously got out.

"Bring that bag of food," Peter whispered to Lester.

"Why don't you carry it?" Lester hissed back.

"Because you are feeding the dog and I am seeing the girl."

Lester said nothing and calmly pulled the bag out of the back seat. With Peter in the lead they crept up the opposite side of fence line using the trees and bushes to hide their approach.

"Where's this dog at?"

"I've always found him around the barn."

Passing the silhouette of the house in the darkness, they could see no lights through the bushes.

"Everyone's in bed," Lester whispered.

"Good," Peter responded.

"What if she's in bed, too?"

"That's even better," Peter whispered back. "Would you be quiet now?"

Lester didn't respond as a root caught his foot and he went crashing to the ground.

"You'll wake everybody up," Peter shot in his direction.

"I couldn't help it. Something tripped me."

Their breath came in short gasps from the tension as the boys waited in silence for any reaction from the house. When no lights came on or noise seemed apparent, they continued towards the barn.

The driveway circled around in the back of the house and in front of the barn with the fencerow about fifty feet away. On the opposite side of them the main driveway was located. Everything seemed quiet as the boys paused again to listen.

"Okay," Peter said. "Ready, and we slowly approach the barn. When the dog comes out, I will do the talking. Whatever you do, don't run."

"What if he doesn't come out? Maybe he's at the house."

"Stop worrying. Just be quiet," Peter said, starting across the open space towards the barn. Lester followed him without much space between them. The night was pitch black without a breeze stirring. Off to the left and across the open, plowed field, a dog howled. What sounded like a bat squeaked by them in pursuit of an illusive insect. Apparently missing its prey, it swooped in closer over the boys' heads. The red side of the barn loomed up before them. Peter put out his hand to steady himself. The horizontal barn siding squeaked under his hand.

"Quit making noise," Lester's voice was tense.

"Where's that dog?" was Peter's only response, ignoring Lester's warning to be silent. A kerosene light flickered momentarily in the house and then went out.

# CHAPTER SEVEN

IT WAS ALREADY close to midnight, and Sam was tossing in bed, unable to sleep. His eighteen years of life seemed like a long time to him. He already felt old. *It must be the hard fieldwork and the early hours of doing chores,* Sam finally concluded.

Stretching out even longer were the years ahead of him. Amish life was what he was used to, and the way he planned on keeping it. His dad had promised him that, as the youngest boy, the farm would be turned over to him some day. *That part was taken care of, which was the biggest part,* he supposed. *Yet was it?*

Sam needed a wife. First of all, he needed a wife from his heart, but also from a practical perspective. She must be strong and able to bear children, because he needed children, particularly boys to help on the farm, both with him and after him. She must also be able to help with the farm work, especially when the children were young. Getting up at five each morning to do the milking required stamina, regardless of whether the weather was cold or hot, and whether one felt like doing it or not.

Many women, even Amish women, could not take it, or worse in Sam's mind, did not want to. That was why

Hannah was on his mind so much lately. Sure, she was still young, but he could wait a little while.

Running into her that evening at her parents' place was not a good way to start out a relationship. He frowned in the darkness, then comforted himself that he had already noticed her in school. This might just be God's way of bringing them together.

*That was it*, he decided. *Things would get better as time went on. That was how love worked*, he was sure. *A little rough in spots, but you worked things out.*

In his mind, conditioned by an absolute rule against divorce among the Amish, there was only one difficulty to be overcome. That was to arrive at the point where the bishop married them. There would be no turning back from there. Nor could there be any turning back. The battle was won and over with. *Was it not?* There could be no other answer, because he was marrying an Amish girl, and she would never divorce or leave him.

Hannah was the one, of this Sam was sure. Seeing how quickly she had bounced back from the accident fully convinced him of that. She had spunk and was also beautiful. That helped, he thought, as he dwelled for a moment on the vision of her. Then he pushed the thought away. Be that as it may, there were more important things than physical beauty.

Beauty faded away fast — he was sure the minister had said that in his sermon just this past Sunday. Sam would take the lesson on beauty to heart and not let it play a big part in his decision. That it played some part could not be helped, he supposed. Hannah was a pretty girl, and God was responsible for that, too.

With their backs against the barn wall in the darkness, Peter and Lester flattened their bodies into the contour of the building. In the house, to the left of their line of sight, the kerosene light kept flickering on and off. Thunder, which they had not heard before, now sounded in the distance. The wind stirred and whipped the leaves at their feet.

"Let's get out of here," Lester whispered to Peter.

"Be quiet, the dog will hear you," Peter hissed back.

"I thought that was what we wanted? That's what my bag of meat is for. Where is the dog?"

"Just be quiet. I've got to see this girl."

Along the fencerow, the wind moaned in the trees as it picked up speed. The weathervane on the barn roof rattled as it spun around to the southwest. The back door of the house abruptly creaked open, revealing Roy in the back glow of the kerosene lamp. He lit a flashlight, cast its beam first on the ground and then towards the barn. The bright beam raked the side of the barn.

"He's seen us. Let's run," Lester whispered shakily.

"No, the dog will catch us easily."

"Where is the stupid dog?"

"He's around here somewhere," Peter assured Lester.

The flashlight bobbed up and down as Roy walked towards the barn with the gravel crunching under his feet. Peter was the first to notice: "He's not coming our way. Maybe he hasn't seen us."

Lester said nothing, trying to keep air moving into his lungs without causing too much noise. Roy opened the side barn door on the side away from them. They could tell by the creak of the hinges in the night air. For the first time, lightning lit the sky to the south.

"He's come out to check on the animals," Peter said quietly.

"Maybe he's come for us with his gun," Lester managed to get the words through his lips.

"He doesn't keep his gun in the house. Besides, he wouldn't shoot anyway. He's Amish."

"What if he wasn't?"

"Then I wouldn't be here. Now don't be silly. I want to see his girl."

"I just want to get out of here."

"We will, as soon as this man gets done checking his animals and I can get up to that window."

"He's not making any noise," Lester managed to say.

"What do you mean?"

"In the barn. There's no noise. There should be."

Peter thought about that as he listened. The wind was picking up, its moans increasing in the treetops down by the fencerow. The weathervane spun around and creaked on the barn roof. A roll of thunder followed the dim flashes in the distance, but inside the barn it was quiet. "That is strange," Peter ventured.

"He's up to something. If he catches us my dad will tan my hide to a crisp."

"You're too old for that."

"This is really bad," Lester's whisper trembled.

"Would you just be quiet," Peter said in exasperation. "There's no one going to catch us. He's going back into the barn in a minute."

Peter's last words were interrupted by a quiet insistent voice right beside them: "Shep, come here. Shep!" A shadowy figure came around the barn to the right of them. A flash of lightning revealed the distinct shape of a man. "Come here, Shep," he said. "Come get him."

Lester and Peter ceased breathing, their bodies taunt against the barn's wooden siding. The flashlight beam in Roy's hand swept up and down the fencerow.

"Shep, Shep," he repeated. There was no response. *Where is that dog when you need him?*

Slowly Roy walked past the boys, his back turned towards them, his flashlight scanning up and down his property. Finding neither his dog nor anything else, he returned to the back door. As the door opened, the light from the kerosene lamp flickered into the dark yard. Lightning flashed closer, followed by a sharp roll of thunder.

"That was a close call," gasped Lester. "Let's get out of here."

"No, it wasn't," Peter told him. "He was looking for his dog. He has no idea we are out here."

"Let's keep it that way then."

"We will, but I have to see this girl."

"You can see her by yourself."

"I will, but you are staying around to watch out for the dog. Otherwise, I could be up that tree when her dad shows up."

"What am I going to do?"

"You are standing by the tree while I climb up, of course."

"I am not."

"Yes, you are. Now be quiet and follow me."

"I'm going home."

"How are you going home? I have the keys."

Lester grunted in the darkness, knowing he was hemmed in with no way out. "I'm waiting by the fencerow," he said in protest. "If there is any trouble, I'm leaving and you are on your own. I would rather be caught out by the car than here near the house. It'll look better. I'll say it was your idea and I didn't go along."

"Just be quiet and wait," Peter instructed him as he headed out to the fencerow and down towards the tree.

"Wait here," he said when he got to the tree. Reaching for the first low hanging branch, he turned back to Lester. "It looks like an easy climb."

Lester said nothing as he backed up near the fence row. Peter continued upwards. Lightning now flashed clearly on the horizon, splashing bright light in all directions. Only the shadow of the barn kept full illumination from flooding the tree.

"Someone will see," Lester hissed from the fencerow.

Peter ignored him, or maybe it was the thunder that drowned out the words. Then suddenly, there was old Shep, who immediately saw this something in the tree. Perhaps the dog was returning from a dalliance of his own and needed to absolve his conscience, because he went right to work barking beneath the tree.

"Shut the dog up," Peter hissed from the tree, a little too loudly even in his own judgment, but he was desperate.

Lester, shaking badly, dug around in the bag. At least he thought it was a bag. It turned out his hand was clutching nothing, the fingernails biting into his palm. *Where is the bag?*

"Shut the *bloomen* dog up!" Peter demanded from the

72

tree limb. Lester was trying as he cast around for where the bag might be. Finally seeing it lying by the foot of the tree during the next lightning flash, he crept out of the fencerow towards it. This only assured that he was noticed by Shep. With a deep growl in his throat, the dog came towards him. He was still three feet shy of the tree and the crumpled up gunny bag.

"He's going to eat me," Lester whispered into the night air.

"No, he's not," Peter said from up in the tree. "Shut him up with some food. Now. Quick!"

Lester, desperately wishing he had stayed home instead of coming on this mad adventure, debated whether to run, to advance, or to wait this out. Shep took a step towards him, the hair on his neck straight up. The lightning cast crazy shadows on the lawn, making the dog look five times his real size.

"Good doggie. Good doggie," he managed to get the words past his dry lips, the bag now between him and the dog.

Shep seemed unimpressed as he advanced another step and then paused. His head was right above the bag of tidbits, its raw smells wafting into his hungry nose. Lester, in spite of his own precarious status, noticed the subtle shift in the winds of fortune. Changing his mind about outrunning the dog to the car, he held his ground instead. "It's good stuff," he croaked out of his parched throat.

Shep lifted his head and growled. "I'll get it out for you," Lester whispered, taking a step forward. Apparently understanding the gesture, the dog backed off slightly and waited. Walking up to the bag, Lester pulled some of the things out

Peter had brought along. *Ugh, what is this stuff?* It was too late to worry about that. Shep was looking expectantly at him. Lifting his hand, Lester tossed the tidbits towards the dog. Shep lowered his head, loudly chopping his jaws.

"What's going on down there?" Peter's voice whispered into the night.

"I'm feeding the dog," Lester whispered back, a sound from the house following the end of his words. It was the sound of a window opening. Shep lifted his head towards the upper story and ceased chewing the food. Lester dug into the bag and threw everything he had towards the dog.

～

Hannah awoke from her sleep, after tossing about in her dreams. The world had been a confusion of noise, thunder and flashes of light, the sound of Shep barking, and the sense of an unseen presence. She felt fear forcing its way into her, but found comfort and hope in the thought that Shep was outside. *He'll bark if someone is around. He was barking.*

Now Hannah sat bolt upright in her bed. As her room came into focus, there was nothing unusual to be seen in the darkness. Everything was in place. Outside, she could see lightning playing behind the barn. Distant echoes of thunder bounced off the walls of the house. She walked over and opened the window. Its new vinyl sides opened with a mere whisper.

Her eyes searched the horizon for any signs of the rising moon. There was no sign of anything. *It can't be too late. I wonder what is going on.* She looked at the roof of the house and then towards the barn. Nothing was apparent.

It sounded like Shep was smacking his jaws on something, but he did that all the time. *Probably found a stinky groundhog to chew on.* Sleepily, she turned and closed the window.

❦

Outside Peter pressed his body tightly against the tree limb and Lester blended into the trunk. They froze until the window closed again.

"Let's get the fuss out of here," Lester hissed sharply.

This time Peter obeyed as he moved down the trunk of the tree as fast as he could. This took old Shep, who had just finished the last scraps from the bag, by surprise. He barked sharply.

"Shut up, old dog!" Peter commanded, now almost on the ground. His voice must have sounded familiar, because Shep was quiet. Then Shep looked back and forth at the two of them and changed his mind as his barks became urgent.

"Let's go," Peter said as he led the way rapidly down the fencerow to the car. Pushing the MGC a hundred feet before starting it, the boys drove off into the night.

"That was the craziest thing," Lester snapped when he felt free to breathe again. "I'm never doing that again."

"We'll see," Peter told him calmly. "I still want to see that girl."

There are plenty of other girls," Lester insisted sharply.

"Well, yes," Peter concurred. "But not quite like this one."

"So why didn't you say something to her when that window opened? I'm sure it was the one you were heading for."

"I don't know," said Peter thoughtfully. "I wasn't sure it was that window. I couldn't see too well in the dark. My first instinct was to freeze. What if it hadn't been her? I just can't mess this up. This may be my only chance, you know."

"There are all those English girls in town."

"Ya, but it's not the same. I want to get this Amish girl out for a ride in my car. Now wouldn't that be something?"

"You are a skunk," Lester told him. "I'm sure you have other things on your mind."

Peter only smiled in the darkness.

❦

Hannah was just dropping off to sleep when Shep barked again. Sure that it was not a dream this time, she rolled over and lifted her head. Then everything became quiet again. *He probably got tired of chewing on that groundhog.* She rolled over, pulled the covers up tight, and drifted off to sleep again.

## Chapter Eight

IN THE MORNING, Roy was none too happy. "There sure was an awful lot of fuss going on around here last night," he announced at the breakfast table.

"I heard you go outside once," Kathy said quietly. "Did you see anything?"

"Shep was gone," Roy told them. "There was not a sign of him, but I was sure I heard something. I just don't like the feel of things around here right now."

"You sure you're not imagining things?" Kathy asked him.

"I could be," he acknowledged, "but Shep did bark a little later then. I thought it sounded serious. Then it didn't last for very long. Just awfully strange, I would say."

"I heard Shep, too," Hannah volunteered. "It sounded to me like he was chewing on a groundhog he dug up."

"There you go," Kathy jumped on the explanation. "It's probably just the dog doing these things all along."

Roy only grunted, not at all convinced, "I just don't like it, that's all I can say."

Hannah kept her eyes on her bowl of oatmeal, not because she was trying to hide anything, but because she had given up hope. *He's not coming. He's just a big liar. If this is what love is like, I don't like it.*

Kathy looked at her in concern. "Is there something wrong?"

Hannah shook her head, "No." She figured dashed hopes did not quite qualify as something being wrong.

"You weren't expecting someone, were you?" Kathy asked in a surprising stab in the right direction.

"Not really," Hannah said quite forthrightly because she really had nothing to go on. Then she decided to say what she did know in case her mother figured out she was hiding something. "Just hoping," she said, keeping her eyes on her cereal bowl.

Kathy laughed out loud. "You silly girl. I guess you're old enough for thoughts like that, but there's really nothing to worry about. There's still plenty of time. Someone is out there for you."

"What are you talking about?" Roy demanded to know.

Kathy smiled. "I think she was hoping it was a boy coming to see her, even if she didn't have a light on, I suppose."

"Who would do something like that?" Roy wondered out loud. "It's not even Friday night. Besides, she's not dating like that. I wouldn't let the boy in the house. She will do it the proper way, not with lights in the windows and boys seeing her in her bedroom."

Hannah, already close to tears, could not keep them back. A few tears slid down her cheeks and splashed into her cereal bowl. Putting down her spoon, she lifted her hand to wipe them away.

"Now, look what you've done," Kathy said. "You've broken her heart."

"It needs to be broken from ideas like that."

"That's not what I meant," Kathy told him. "It's not that anyone would actually come. I'm sure Hannah would not allow it. It's the idea that they might care so much as to come, that's what's bothering her."

Roy's look told them he was not convinced.

"I wouldn't want it to actually happen," Kathy assured him. "It's just the thought, I guess."

"Did you want me to come around to your window when I was dating you?" Roy asked.

"Well, you never thought of doing something like that," she told him, preparing to clear the table of dishes now that breakfast was over.

"That's not what I asked," he replied, then waited.

Knowing she needed to say something, Kathy told him, "You did just fine."

Roy shook his head. "I still don't think it's proper or in order."

"I know it isn't," she told him, heading for the kitchen with a stack of dirty dishes. "Girls just have dreams sometimes."

Hannah stood up to follow her mother's example while fighting back the tears.

Roy said nothing more as he got ready to go outside to his routine in the fields, as he was working home on the farm that day.

❧

It was a week or so later that the tap came on the window pane in the night, a soft ping of knuckles on the glass by someone who did not want to make any great racket. Hannah had just come into her room after another late evening of fall housework. Slipping off her shoes, she stretched out on the bed, weary to the bone. It felt so absolutely divine to rest.

The taps were repeated on the windowpane, this time more insistently. She sat upright, swinging her feet onto the floor. Her eyes went to the window, and her hand went over her mouth. A shadowy figure crouched in front of the pane as a hand rose to knock again.

She felt a scream coming from deep within her, but no sound came out. The shadow moved and waved a hand. Hannah's conscious thoughts registered nothing, just a gripping fear that shook her hands. Again she made an effort to bring sound out of her vocal chords, but it was useless. All she could do was stare, unable to tear her eyes away from the window.

The figure reached into a pocket and produced a long silver item. Using the other hand to cover the end, a small flash of light appeared directed at the person's face. To her astonishment she saw it dimly lit the face of Peter. That was when it made sense. He had come to her window.

Walking over quickly, Hannah raised the window, as Peter moved away from the window to wait. Embarrassed and red-faced, she waited. No moon was shining; there was only the light of the twinkling stars above their heads.

"Hi," he said.

"You came?" she finally asked him.

"Of course," he responded. "It just took a little while."

"I told you not to come," Hannah told him, finding that with Peter in front of her, she was no longer sure what she should feel.

He ignored the comment. "I worked hard on this, now don't go spoiling it."

"How was that?" she wanted to know.

"That dog of yours has been a great nuisance. I spent all the last few evenings becoming friends with him."

"You went to all that trouble?" She found herself impressed.

"I wanted to see you," he whispered in the darkness.

The feelings were coming back now. "You did? Really?" she managed to ask.

"Ya," he acknowledged, "Can I come in?"

"No," she said instinctively, feelings or no feelings.

In all her thoughts about Peter coming, and the anticipation that he would come, she never quite knew how she would react. Now she knew this much: "We can talk here," she told him.

"It's pretty uncomfortable on this roof. It would be nicer inside."

She felt it deep inside. She didn't like it. What it was, she was not sure, but he was not coming in.

"Come on," he coaxed, "I won't stay long."

Hannah made no movement away from the window, and Peter was not about to push her aside. He knew he could not do that. If she wouldn't let him in, she wouldn't, but he was not happy about it.

"I went to all this work to see you, at least let me inside," he told her.

She couldn't see his face in the darkness, just the outline

of his form. "No," she shook her head this time. "We can talk right here."

Shep took it upon himself at that moment to bark. "Oh, no," he said, "the dog."

"It's not serious," she told him. "I can tell by his bark. It sounds friendly."

"Are you sure?"

"Yes."

"Can I come inside then?"

"No," she repeated.

"Will you go for a ride then in my car?"

"Where?" she asked him, wishing she could see his face.

"I'll take you downtown for a drive. We can just climb down the tree and follow the fencerow down to the road. We won't see anybody, and I'll have you back in no time."

There was a pause as Hannah thought about it. The darkness made things look so much different than in the daytime. Why she wouldn't want to go baffled her at the moment. While trying to decide, she was very conscious that Peter was there, in the dark, looking at her.

*What harm could it do? Your father doesn't want you to.* That thought seemed to bear weight, but she overrode it. Searching for feelings to match not going she found none, but found plenty to give her reasons to go. "I'll go," Hannah told him.

Shep barked again, sharper this time. "I have to be going," Peter whispered. Maybe you can get the dog quiet?"

"Yes," she whispered back in the darkness.

Peter made a motion to go, reaching out for her hand to

help her out the window. Hannah refused to take it, having climbed down the tree often enough as a child to do it even in the dark.

Following him across the roof, she noticed Peter's clumsy efforts while he was on the roof and when climbing the tree. Hannah compared her own skill and ease to his and assumed these resulted from her years of practice. When Shep saw her, he quieted down.

Telling Shep to stay, Hannah followed Peter out along the fencerow to his car. The blue color of the MGC was even darker than in the daytime. She opened the door on the passenger's side herself, while Peter rushed around to the other side. She was already in when he slid into the driver's seat.

"She's a beauty," he whispered, turning the key.

The motor started and purred in the darkness. "Don't drive too fast," she told him.

"You scared?" he asked, and although she could not see his face in the darkness, she was sure he must be grinning.

"Maybe, but just don't do it, okay? You said a nice drive."

"That it will be," he said. "Let's go, then."

Slowly, so as not to make noise, he glided off, and then picked up speed when they were away from the house. "Not too fast," she repeated, their speed making it feel even worse in the darkness.

"I'm not," he assured her, but he slowed down a little.

They crossed two blacktop roads, barely slowing down for the stop signs. "You can see the headlights in the dark," he offered as explanation, then turned left onto a gravel road. Ahead of them the road dipped into a low spot, the night giving the lay of the ground an effect of a miniature canyon. Just on the edge, Peter bounced to a stop off the side of the road, stopping the car beneath some overhanging trees, their branches casting a dark pall on the ground even in the darkness.

"Why are we stopping?" Hannah asked. "You said you were going downtown."

"Just a minute," he said, as he slid over close to her. She could not see much of him, but his presence overwhelmed her, his hands reaching out for her face and finding it in the darkness. Brushing lightly against her cheeks with his fingers, she knew he was coming closer until his lips touched hers.

In the great silence of the heavens full of pulsating beacons of starlight, Hannah felt what all mankind feels at the first moment when they discover the power of this unbidden emotion. Great feelings ran through her. Delight and guilt all mixed together.

The difference startled her. On the one hand, there had been her dream in all its purity and rightness. On the other, now having a boy kiss her, Hannah realized she was not so sure. *Was it right?* She swallowed hard as Peter made no attempt to move back to his side of the car.

Her dream had been like eating tomatoes out of the garden, with their luscious richness and flavor. Now this was like running one's fingers through the earth from which they grew. Only this was the opposite, and yet was it? Her dream had come first, and now she had touched her lips to the ground. She trembled as this knowledge filled her, for, with it, came the realization that while she could never make or change the tomato, she could shape and mold the earth with her hands.

The decision came to her with force and certainty.

"Take me home," Hannah told Peter in the darkness. "I don't want this."

"Why not?" The question did not want to be asked. "There's nothing wrong with this."

"Yes, there is," she told him. "Take me home."

"You're just like your father," Peter told her, disdain in his voice. "What a waste! To just throw your youth away, pining around in the house."

Hannah said nothing, and although Peter could not see them, the tears now threatened to come. Sensing her distress, he slowly complied and turned the car around. Its headlights cut a clear path into the night air.

Then hearing her sniffle, Peter exclaimed, "Don't go crybaby on me! We didn't do anything. I just kissed you."

"Just take me home," she repeated, the full impact of where she was and what she was doing descending upon her like a ton of bricks. It would not take much now for the dam of tears to break.

## Chapter Nine

Roy awoke out of his dreams with a start. What it was, he could not tell. Sitting upright in the bed he listened. The house was silent. Shep was not barking, and yet the uneasy feeling he had was firmly with him.

The feeling was serious enough that he dressed and walked out to the living room. Carefully he avoided the furniture lest he stub his toe or create noise. Walking up to the living room window he looked out. Outside the night was moonless and dark. Stars twinkled brightly in the sky, and when he opened the front door and glanced around, nothing looked amiss. It did not feel so, though, as his instincts were now fully aroused. Something felt very amiss.

He went back to the bedroom and woke Kathy. "Something's going on," he told her.

"Like what?" she asked sleepily. "Is Shep barking again?"

"No," he told her, "something else. It feels serious. Would you get up and check the children's rooms?"

"That serious?" she asked him.

"I would feel better," Roy told her.

"Okay, then," Kathy muttered as she reached for her housecoat and put it on over her nightclothes.

When Kathy left to go upstairs, Roy went out to the front

porch again, stood there and listened to the low hum of the night sounds as he wondered what was wrong. The headlights of a car cut into the night from a distance. It came, driving fast with bouncing waves of light on their uneven gravel road. Yet, there was nothing exactly unusual in that.

It was when he heard the car abruptly begin to slow down that his attention became focused. The tires slid on the gravel of their driveway as the car came to a stop, still mostly on the road.

The passenger door opened, and a girl got out. Because of the distance, Roy could not make out any voices, if there were any. However, there was no mistaking the sound of squealing tires on stone as the car sped off. The girl was left standing in the middle of the road.

Roy, startled out of his surprise, moved with his first instinct, which was to get Kathy. Opening the front door, he called to her, "Kathy!"

She was just coming down the stairs, her eyes wide. "She's not here."

"Who is not here?" he asked.

"Hannah."

"Look there," Roy said, pointing towards the road and holding the front door open.

Kathy joined him, as they stood together and looked at the form standing by the road.

"Where did she come from?" Kathy finally asked him.

"A car just dropped her off."

"It can't be Hannah. She wouldn't be out without telling us."

"Maybe we ought to go and see," Roy ventured. "You had better go with me."

"But she wouldn't do something like this."

Taking Kathy by the hand, Roy led her down the steps and out the driveway. They approached the still figure standing by the road with her back turned towards them. As they came nearer, the unmistakable sounds of sobbing became evident.

"Hannah," Kathy said, when she was close enough to speak, "is that you?"

The only answer was yet louder crying.

Approaching the girl, Kathy reached for her hand and then her shoulder until she had pulled her tightly to herself. "What are you doing out here?"

"He just dropped me off."

"Who is he?"

"Peter."

"Why were you with him?"

"He came to my window and offered me a ride."

"To your window?" Kathy was horrified.

Hannah's only reply was sobbing regret: "I'm so sorry."

"So, then what happened?" Kathy wanted to know after Hannah calmed down.

"Peter said he wanted to take me for a ride."

"And you went with him?"

Hannah nodded in the darkness, obviously miserable.

"Don't you know that's wrong?" Kathy asked.

"Yes, but I couldn't resist. It seemed like a harmless thing to do, just take a nice ride, he said, and then he would bring me right back. I thought it would be easy. We climb up and down the tree onto the roof all the time. It doesn't hurt us then."

"Have you done this before?" Kathy wanted to know.

Hannah shook her head, the motion visible in the starlight.

"What happened then?"

"We drove a little and he parked."

"He parked?" Kathy's voice echoed in the night.

"He said we would drive through downtown."

"What happened then, after you parked?"

Hannah's voice was weak. "He leaned over and kissed me. Just once, Mom, really. It was then that I told him to take me home."

"Did he bring you home then?"

"Yes, but he was really mad. He just dropped me off at the end of the lane, making a big fuss. I knew then I could never climb back into my room without you and Dad finding out."

"Is that why you are crying?"

"No," Hannah broke into fresh tears. "Oh, Mom, how can something like this turn out so terrible? I feel just awful inside. He was not nice at all."

Kathy pulled Hannah to her again, saying nothing. What was there to say? Especially when it's dark outside, and they had just found their daughter at the end of the driveway after being dropped off by a boy she was not supposed to be out with.

"We had better go inside," Roy made his presence known. "We'll deal with this more in the morning."

As Roy turned to lead them in, his eyes caught a brilliant flare of light in the distance. Red and yellow lights rose in a cloud of color that looked close, and then died down, replaced with a low hue that also soon faded.

Neither Hannah nor Kathy saw the lights, since they

had already turned and begun to walk towards the house together.

*I wonder what that was?* Roy thought, although his instincts were telling him that he knew what it was, but he was hoping they were wrong. *That's the way I go to work. I'll check then, it's surely not what I think.* Then he changed his mind and decided he would go check it out tonight.

"Get Hannah to bed," he told Kathy when they got in the house. "We will talk some more about this tomorrow. I need to go check out something."

Kathy nodded and headed for the stairs with Hannah in front of her. Kathy then stopped and asked him, "Where are you going?"

"I'm taking the buggy, don't worry."

"Do be careful," she said, not moving, standing by the stairs as she looked at him.

"It's not what you think," he told her. "I will talk to you when I get back."

           ≋

Officer Coons, from the Indiana State Police, also saw the fireball as he pulled his cruiser off of 331 and headed east. It did not take him long to find the source and report in. "We have a one-car vehicle accident, two miles west of 331, on the County Line Road. Have fire and rescue respond."

"Causality report?" the response came back.

"Unknown at this time," he said. "Exiting cruiser to examine the scene now. Does not look good."

The flashing lights momentarily blinded Officer Coons when his head came up to the level of his vehicle. He turned his head to get the lights out of his eyes. Half a mile in either direction, the blue and red sequences pulsed up and down the road.

Using his flashlight, Coons jumped the ditch and approached the vehicle. Small fires were still burning from the mangled frame of the car wrapped around the tree. There was no sign of life.

The approaching clip-clop of horse's hooves interrupted his concentration. Although he was in Amish country, he had been expecting the sound of sirens coming, not horses at this time of the night.

When the buggy stopped, Coons had to jump back across the ditch to deal with it. "Can I do something for you?" he asked.

"My name's Roy," the man said, leaning out of his buggy. "My daughter was just dropped off by a young boy. I was wondering if this is the same one."

"What time was that?" Officer Coons asked.

"About twenty minutes ago."

"You have any information about him?"

"Just that his name is Peter."

"Well, this one will be hard to identify by his name, I'm sorry to say. Hit that tree pretty hard." Officer Coons turned his flashlight in the direction Roy had just come from. Long black skid marks were clearly visible. "Looks like whoever it was, was going too fast. You know what kind of car he was driving?"

Roy shook his head. "I'm not sure. I never saw it myself. I think my wife mentioned a blue MGC once."

"One of those deals." The officer was sympathetic. "The color of the paint won't be much help either, I'm sorry to say, but we can look at the make of the car."

Coons' flashlight beam shone across the ditch towards the wrecked car frame, partially reaching it before fading away. Shaking his flashlight to get more light, the officer succeeded, then brought the beam to bear on the rear of the car. Even from that distance, they both could read the distinct MGC letters.

"Sorry to hear it," the officer said. "Someone close to the girl?"

"No, they were just out for the first time."

"Some kind of fight or something, for him to be driving this fast?"

"Yes," Roy said reluctantly, "there was a fight. I only found out about it when he dropped her off at the end of the lane."

"He still shouldn't be driving like that," Office Coons was quick to say. "Bad hormones, I guess. Cost him big this time."

The wail of sirens came from the distance, as the emergency vehicle lights mingled with those of the trooper's cruiser. "I should be going," Roy said, as he slapped the reins and made a swing on the road to turn around. He passed the first rescue vehicle 200 yards from the accident.

❧

When Roy returned home, Kathy was in the kitchen waiting for him. She had a kerosene lamp burning on the table. "What was that all about?" she wanted to know, sitting there in the glow of its low light.

Seeing Roy's white face framed in the kitchen door, she sucked in her breath. "Oh, no, what happened?"

Roy sat down, numb and hurting all over, weakness where strength should have been. "I saw something when we were walking towards the house. You and Hannah did not see it because you had your backs turned. It looked like a bad accident. That was what I went to see."

"And?" she asked as her question hung in the air.

"It was him," Roy said quietly.

"Peter?" Her hand went to her face.

"Yes," he said, "I'm afraid so. How are we going to tell Hannah?"

"What happened?" Kathy wanted to know.

"There was an officer there already. From the skid marks, he thinks he was driving too fast. When I asked questions, he started asking me questions. Now that I think about it, I probably should have kept my mouth shut."

"You didn't tell him that Peter was out with Hannah?" Kathy tried to keep her composure.

"I'm afraid I did. I wasn't planning to, but the officer started asking direct questions, and it just came out."

"Oh, my." Kathy made as if to rise from the chair, but sat down again. "What if this comes out? They weren't even dating."

Roy numbly nodded his head.

Roy and Kathy sat there for a long time, saying nothing. Finally the fatigue of the day took over and they stumbled off to bed. When the alarm went off, it was all both of them could do to get up, but duty called.

Unbeknownst to either of them the *South Bend Tribune* already was telling the world the news. The morning edition carried the headline, *Amish Boy Killed After Dropping off His Girlfriend*, and went on to give what details were known.

Any alleged acrimony between the boy and girl was not mentioned, nor was her name.

Since starting his full-time factory job, Roy had to leave for work early. The farm work was now limited to evenings and weekends. His ride always came by at six-thirty. "I'm sorry not to be here," he told Kathy, as he sat at the kitchen table eating his breakfast. "We can wait 'til this evening to tell her."

"I'd rather not wait," Kathy told him. "I'll tell her. If it doesn't work out, you can help this evening."

Roy nodded and dashed out the door, his lunch pail in his hand, as the sound of his ride came up the gravel road.

Kathy let Hannah sleep in an extra hour before waking her. Still sleepy-eyed, Hannah came downstairs fully dressed in short order.

"Sit down," Kathy told her, motioning towards a chair at the kitchen table.

Knowing she deserved a scolding and then some, Hannah was ready for whatever punishment was coming her way. Sitting calmly, she steeled herself for what was coming.

"I have something I need to tell you," Kathy told her, sitting down beside her.

Hannah looked up, confused by the gesture and the statement that information was coming. "I'm sorry," she said looking at the floor. "I know I deserve to be punished for what I did."

"It's not that, dear." Kathy put her arms around her,

tears coming to her eyes. "Something really bad happened after Peter left here last night."

Hannah looked blankly at her.

"He was killed in a car accident." Kathy's lip trembled.

Hannah's face went white. "He's dead."

"Yes."

"Just like that?"

"I'm sorry."

"But," Hannah's voice struggled, "you don't just die like that. I was with him last night. He kissed me. He can't be dead."

Kathy simply moved over closer to Hannah and pulled her close.

"How did it happen?" Hannah finally asked when she had composed herself slightly.

"The officer thinks he was driving too fast. He hit a tree with his car. It was pretty bad. Your dad went down there last night already."

"Why didn't you wake me then?" Hannah wanted to know.

"Dear, he was not your boyfriend. It just didn't seem appropriate."

"So it was all my fault," Hannah stated numbly.

"It was not," Kathy assured her. "We don't know why these things happen."

"I sent him away. If I had been his girlfriend and not made him angry, it wouldn't have happened. It was my fault."

Kathy refused to take Hannah's statements seriously and brushed them off. Hannah continued to insist on her guilt until the tears finally broke through again and came in great gushes.

Trying the best she knew how, Kathy comforted Hannah, but they got little work done that day. When Roy came home that evening he found an exhausted wife and a grieving and guilt-stricken daughter. He tried, but there seemed to be nothing he could do to comfort Hannah either.

## CHAPTER TEN

TOWARDS ELEVEN O'CLOCK that evening, Hannah had finally settled down enough for Kathy to leave her alone in her room. She stood listening until there seemed to be no more crying from inside, then went downstairs and sat down wearily beside Roy on the couch.

"When is the funeral?" she asked him.

"Day after tomorrow. Do you think we should go?"

"Most certainly," she told him.

"What about Hannah?"

Pausing to think, Kathy took a deep breath. "I'm not sure, but it may be the best thing for her. She's taking it really hard. I don't think staying away will help matters much. Sometimes facing the problem is the best route to take."

Roy nodded. "I think that's the best. Why is she taking it so hard?"

Kathy gave that some thought. "You know, I'm not sure I have it figured out yet. If he was her steady, it would make sense, but he was not."

"Do you think she loved the boy that much?"

Kathy shrugged her shoulders. "It's hard to imagine that. She hardly knew him. She saw him maybe two or three times."

"You don't think they've been seeing each other secretly, do you?"

Kathy's brow was puckered. "The thought has crossed my mind, but she is not one to lie. Hannah never did and I see no signs that she has started now. No, it must be something else. I don't think she has been seeing him."

Roy accepted Kathy's assessment. "We need to keep an eye on her, though."

Kathy agreed, then said wearily, "Don't you think we should get some rest? There are some tough days ahead of us."

"The papers carried the accident in the headlines," Roy told her before she had a chance to get up off the couch.

"What did they say," she asked him.

*"Amish Boy Killed After Dropping off His Girlfriend,"* he said, keeping his eyes straight ahead. "Just thought you should know what else might be coming."

"Did it give Hannah's name?"

"No, I mentioned no names to the officer, other than my name, Roy. They can hardly trace it with that."

Kathy sighed deeply. "This could be bad for her, if that still comes out."

"Maybe God will help us?" he asked more than stated.

"Let's ask Him," Kathy said, turning to Roy, who responded by going onto his knees as she followed. Roy prayed as Kathy sobbed into the upholstered cushion. Roy asked that God would have mercy on them and give them help in this time of great need.

The day of the funeral was a cloudy, overcast day. Roy and Kathy got up early. It would be nearly an hour's drive, since Peter's family lived two districts away. Hannah, who had said little in the past two days, also said nothing when told that she would attend the funeral with the rest of the family. Roy and Kathy had been to the first of the two viewings, but none of the rest of the family had gone.

They were on the road by a quarter to eight, wanting to get there early. Long before they arrived the road was lined with long lines of buggies. Vans slowly passed them, clearly not the regular people usually on the road.

"It's going to be a huge funeral," Kathy observed.

"Quite large, since it's a tragedy," Roy agreed.

When they finally turned onto the final road, the buggies had slowed down to a slow walk. Before they had gone a hundred yards, it was stop and start, and then stop again.

"Drop us off at the house," Kathy decided.

"You think you'll get into the house service?" Roy wondered.

"Since we're not relatives, I doubt it, but they have a large pole barn out back. I'll wait for you at the house, and we can head out there after you put the horse up."

Roy nodded his agreement. Amish funerals were often conducted in two locations if the main building could not accommodate everyone. On such occasions, there were separate preachers and preaching, with the secondary meeting kept informed of the progress by someone going between the two meetings. In this way, equal schedules could be maintained.

Roy slowed the buggy to a halt and let Kathy out with

the girls. The boys would go with him. As Kathy got out with Hannah and her younger sisters, the usual sight greeted them: there were two rows of white-shirted men and boys attired in black suits on each side of the driveway.

While the lining up was usually done, the effect this time was quite unusual. Normally the lines were out by the barn and away from where the women walked in. This morning there was simply no other place to stand.

Hannah tried to catch her breath as she followed Kathy up the driveway towards the house. The weight of so many somber and black-clad males was palpably in the air.

*I am guilty*, Hannah cried on the inside as she fought back the tears. *You're condemned*, the weight pressed in on her. *Peter is dead and it's your fault.* She felt like screaming, but no Amish woman or girl ever screamed in this situation. She kept walking, keeping her eyes on her mother's back.

Hannah felt like telling her mother, but that was also inappropriate. Besides she knew what Kathy would say. *It's just your mind. No one thinks it's your fault.* She knew this because Kathy had said it often during the past two days.

Putting one foot in front of the other, Hannah kept going, fighting with her thoughts and her guilt. Neither Kathy nor Roy had told her about the newspaper article, and they sincerely hoped no one else would either.

Stopping outside the house, Kathy greeted some of the women there. Most of them were unfamiliar and there were simply too many to move around much. Some talking would come later, but, for now, everyone stood silently waiting for the ushers to let them know when it would be time to go inside.

When Roy appeared, he motioned for Kathy to follow. His plans were to lead them over to the pole barn and the secondary service. However, an usher stopped them and indicated they were to get in line for the primary service in the house.

"We're not relatives," Roy explained to him.

"It was one of your cousin's friends, was it not?" the usher asked him.

"Yes," Roy replied.

"That's good enough, then," the usher motioned with his hand. Elaborating, the usher then said, "Most of the immediate relatives are already seated."

Roy shrugged his shoulders and got in line with Kathy and the rest of the family trailing behind him.

There was no singing, as there never is at Amish funerals. There was just the abrupt start of preaching as if to accent the suddenness with which death often comes.

Hannah sat numbly beside her mother, not moving. She had not cried since the day of the news. Since Hannah was not close family or known to be connected by friendship in any way to the deceased, an outpouring of tears would raise eyebrows anyway.

Hannah listened to the preaching, hoping something would be said that would help. They were now on the third speaker, all of whom spoke, as Amish ministers do, without notes or a Bible. The love and mercy of God was mentioned in passing, but the main point all three were making was the evilness of sin, and how God calls us before the judgment seat at unexpected times and in unexpected ways.

"The judgment day comes quickly," Minister Alvin was saying. "Like the turning of a page or the opening of a door, we do not know what lies beyond that door." He clasped his hands in front of him, holding them at chest level. His black beard, not yet showing any signs of gray, came down far enough to lightly touch his clasped hands.

"A holy God demands an answer for sin." His voice was gathering in strength. "We cannot live as we want and then die expecting that He does not care. Our lives are all as a vapor that today is rising, and then tomorrow suddenly it may be gone. Then comes the judgment. Today we have been given a warning in the life of one of our young people. We do not know what he found on the other side of that door. Maybe he cried out to God and found mercy. How will we know until we ourselves arrive over there?

"What we do know is that time is still with each of us." Alvin was thundering now, his face intense, his eyes raised to the ceiling, focused as if on eternity itself. "Time to repent, time to turn away from the world, time to come back to our families and the church, time to find God and good. The question is only, will we? Will we take the warning? Will we heed the call of God? Will we listen to what He is saying?"

Hannah listened with her whole body numb, feeling only a deep terror, quite sure that she was worthy of being burned to a crisp on the spot. *It's my fault that Peter's dead. If I hadn't made him mad he wouldn't have driven so fast. Now nothing, for all eternity, can bring him back.*

Hannah could not have cried if she had wanted to. She was too cold. Even in this warm room full of more than 600 bodies, she shivered. Kathy glanced at her, concerned.

Alvin was coming to the end of the sermon. "It is only by the mercy of God that any of us can ever stand before the

Almighty God. If He had not sent His only Son, the beloved and Holy Jesus, then all of us would be without hope. It is by the blood of Jesus, shed on that cruel cross, that our sins can be washed away. But we must all turn from our sins to Him. May God have mercy on us all."

With that Alvin took his seat, while Kathy pulled the shivering Hannah close to her. The ushers rose and began escorting the lines of people past the closed casket. One by one they filed by until only the family was left. Those seated inside the house returned to their seats, while those from the barn meeting stood outside waiting.

Peter's immediate family — his father, mother, two brothers and three sisters — rose from their front row seats and gathered around for their last goodbyes. More than a thousand people waited patiently inside and outside the home for whatever time was needed by the family.

The bowed shoulders and tears of Peter's family around the coffin were not what startled Hannah. This was a common sight among the Amish. It was the English girl that rose with them to stand around Peter's casket. Hannah, seated to the right of her mother, had not noticed her before, seated.

There was only one explanation for why a non-family member would accompany the family at these last moments. He or she would have to be either engaged or a longtime steady of the departed. It was Alice who stood with the family.

Kathy felt Hannah jerk upright and saw her face fill with horror. All morning no tears had gotten past the numbing coldness of Hannah's body. Now the dam broke. She sobbed silently until her shoulders shook.

Kathy was on the verge of taking Hannah's hand to lead her outside, lest she distract from the family's moment. Already several heads were turning. Wanting to put her arm around her, but thinking this would only attract more attention, Kathy squeezed Hannah's hand instead. This seemed to bring a diminishing of the flow, so Kathy squeezed tighter.

Somehow they got through the moment until the family was again finding their seats. As the ushers got the lines moving out in preparation for the trip to the graveside service, Hannah was still sobbing quietly.

Roy must have noticed Kathy's predicament from across the room on the men's side of the seating, because he headed immediately out for the horse and buggy. Getting in line, they were soon on their way home, with the weeping Hannah in the back seat. Once they were away from the house, Roy drove down a side road towards home. Roy felt his first responsibility was to his daughter, and today was the day to put that principle into action.

# CHAPTER ELEVEN

SURROUNDED BY THE majestic mountain ranges of north-western Montana, the Greyhound bus pulled hard in the curves as black smoke poured out of its tail pipe. He sat almost in the back, as he had during the entire trip, now going on three days. At the last stop, seated in the restaurant, he had taken off his straw hat and turned it slowly over and over in his hands.

Memories flooded through his thoughts, memories he wished to forget. Summers in the hay field; autumns set-ting the oat shocks until his arms burned; mornings getting up at five to milk — and of her. The latter memory caused the most violent reaction and pain, yet he could not keep it away.

Unbidden it came as he laid his head back on the Grey-hound headrest. The whine of the motor as it tackled another steep incline barely registered with him; he could only see her face. In summer her face was tanned from her work out-side on the farm. In winters her face appeared softer, but never less lovely, he had always thought. He had noticed her soon after their eighth grade school graduation, even before either of them ever went with the young folks.

He had never looked at another girl after that. There

was simply no need to. She was too perfect. Her smile, when she looked at him at the youth gatherings or as she stood outside her brother's buggy, had left him with a feeling of dizziness — sometimes for days afterwards. Now he violently forced his thoughts to cease, made himself look at the mountains outside the little window. The mountains were simply awesome, were they not?

Finding the sight and the thought soothing, he decided then and there. This was it. This was as far as he was going. His ticket was for fifteen days of travel on the Greyhound, for wherever he wanted to go, but this was it. He would get off at the next town. Perhaps there he could find the answer to his pain and relief for the sorrow of his soul.

A town seemed to be coming up. Glancing out the window he saw the smattering of houses was thickening. Sputtering from its valiant effort at ascending the mountain, the Greyhound bus pulled into what was obviously the station. He climbed out, leaving his straw hat lying on the seat. Already on the bottom step, he remembered and returned for it.

This might be a new life for him, a new start, but he was not leaving his old life entirely behind him — hopefully only the memory of her.

He stood there and looked around for the name of the town. Finding it, he spoke the word out loud: "Libby." What a strange name for a town, but it would have to do. His mind was made up.

Resolutely he picked up his luggage and headed for the depot.

Kathy got Hannah up the next morning at the usual time. She figured it was better that way. The girl's tears were still evident, but they did not appear to be fresh. Kathy was not sure whether this was good or not.

Hannah seemed to anticipate the question from her mother and answered it without being asked. "I can do breakfast, Mother, just like always," she said without any emotion in her voice.

"Are you sure? I can manage without you for a few mornings."

Hannah shook her head. "I want to help." She got her apron out of the closet in the hall and fell into the regular routine of fixing oatmeal, eggs, and slices of bacon.

Again, Kathy was not sure about this, but let it go. Kathy had never been here before and did not know how to deal with a daughter whose heart must be broken, to say nothing of the guilt she seemed to feel. How was one to handle that? There was nothing in the *ordnungs brief* (church rules) on how to proceed in such a situation.

Pushing her doubts aside, Kathy proceeded with the day's work. That was the Amish way. Do your duty and God would find you.

Hannah seemed to be accepting of her mother's decision, even expecting it. Yet she was obviously numb, and she performed her tasks all day as if she felt nothing.

Kathy kept watching for hidden moments when the tears might be falling in secret, but detected none. If they were happening, she was sure the signs would be there. She looked in vain for them all day.

❧

At the ticket counter in Libby, Montana, the attendant was very helpful. "The Sand Man Motel," he said, "is the best place to stay, I think. Are you staying long?"

He nodded his head. "Any jobs available in the area?"

"Well now," the attendant paused, "about the best place to start would be the Forest Service. The Kootenai National Forest is close by and they are always looking for adventurous people. You look like you might be up for an adventure."

He grinned weakly. "I don't know about that, but I will need a job. Where is this Forest Service office?"

"Right down on Highway 2, going south out of town. You'll come to the motel first, and then the Forest Service's Supervisor's Office Building."

"Can I walk there?" he asked.

"Sure. That would be cheaper, too."

"Suits me," he said, "and thanks for the help."

"No problem."

He walked outside and set out south as directed. To his right, across the plain where the town was situated, rose majestic mountains that soared skyward. Having grown up on the flat farmlands of Iowa, he simply stopped and stared. How long he stood there, he was not sure afterwards; he was simply sure that he had arrived at the right place. Somehow he must reach those mountains.

He arrived at the Sand Man Motel where the bright letters on the sign gaudily announced the name. The West was definitely different, he decided.

Going inside he inquired at the front desk beneath the giant grizzly bear head mounted on the wall: "How much per night?"

The manager quoted him the rate.

"What are your weekly rates?" he asked.

Again the price was given.

"I'll take a room for one night, and then we will see from there."

"Sign here," the manager told him, after he had filled out the paperwork. "Put your license plate number here."

"No car," he commented. "I came in on the Greyhound."

"No problem," the manager told him.

Glancing back down, he signed his name slowly on the indicated line. The letters under the pen formed into the name "Jake Byler."

By evening, Hannah's numbness began to really bother Kathy. Tears were one thing, but the silence that hung over her daughter, like the ice from a glacier, was even more troubling.

After the children were in bed, she brought up the subject with Roy. "Hannah is not doing well."

"I thought so," he said, laying his Bible aside from where he was sitting on the recliner. In the evenings Roy liked to get in some study time when everything was quiet, but this matter took precedence at the moment.

Kathy sighed, "I might try talking with her, but I'm afraid I won't get anywhere."

"At least try," Roy said, pondering the situation. "It's really strange that she is taking it so hard. I know she shouldn't have snuck out with him, but it was only once. That is, if that was the truth."

"You're not doubting her, are you?" Kathy asked, alarmed.

Roy sighed long and hard. "Let's just say I have no reason to, absolutely no reason. I haven't heard anything, you know, talk and such. If she had gone out with him, someone would surely have seen them."

"They could have stayed away from people," Kathy said, then gasped at what she had just implied. "Surely she's not lying?"

"The only thing that makes me wonder is the ruckus the few weeks before. Shep did a lot of barking. Maybe something was going on, but longer than that, I doubt. Even then, that's hardly enough to get so deeply attached to a boy."

"Maybe she just fell hard for him," Kathy ventured, now feeling herself drawn into this alternative scenario.

"There is, of course, the possibility of her guilt driving much of this. But why is she feeling so guilty? Again, it does not tie into anything that we know. She barely knew the boy. She talked to him at the hospital and once in town. Then she sneaks out with him, once that we know of, maybe a few times more. How can that cause such intense guilt when he has a fatal automobile accident?"

"I have no idea what to say, Roy. It's just beyond me. I just know the girl is troubled and we really need to give her some help."

"Let's pray about it," Roy finally ventured, as he reached for his Bible again. Opening it, he found the passage he wanted and read it out loud: "Call unto me, and I will answer thee, and shew thee great and mighty things, which thou knowest not."

"You think that has an answer for us?" Kathy wondered out loud.

"I think we ought to believe that God will do what he says He will do."

"Well, let's call on Him then," Kathy said.

Roy nodded, "Yes, we can do it now in prayer, but let's do it during the day whenever we feel the burden to do so. God is not restricted to set times of prayer."

Kathy nodded in agreement as she knelt by the couch and Roy knelt down by his recliner.

⟨≈⟩

The conversation was going well for him. "Most certainly, young man," the smiling, uniformed Forest Service representative was telling him. "We have immediate job openings, if you are willing to do lonely work."

"What would that be?" he asked, already liking the sound of it. "Will it be on the mountain?" he pointed west towards the range of peaks topped with snow.

"Oh, the Cabinet Mountains?" the uniformed man grinned. "You do want loneliness, don't you? Let's see, there is at present a position open on our eastern ridge fire lookout post. Almost to the top of the mountain, nice cabin there, too. As long as you work there, it is yours. We also rent them out in the off fire season."

"Sounds good," he nodded. "How do I apply for the job?"

"No questions about pay?" the representative lifted his eyebrows.

"No, I'll take the job," he said.

"Not so fast," the representative chuckled. "All applicants still have to fill out an application. Fill this out" — he handed a clipboard over with official forms attached — "and we will go from there."

He took the clipboard with him, pulled the pen out from the top and found a seat over by the front door. Carefully he wrote his name on the top of the application. When it came to former occupation, he wrote in *farmer*. When the line asked for the closest living relative, he wrote in the number of the Sand Man Motel and a name from home. He hoped no one would notice.

Handing in the completed form, the representative took it with a smile. "Well, this looks great. Let's take your measurements for a uniform. Let me process this, then come back tomorrow and you should be all set. We will give you some basic training and in a few days you should be on your post. Where are you staying?"

"The Sand Man Motel."

"Write that number down, please."

He copied it on the paper thrust towards him, carefully keeping his eyes from straying over to the completed form. If the Forest Service representative noticed the same numbers on each form, he chose not to mention it.

## CHAPTER TWELVE

B Y THE END of the week, Kathy finally decided it was time for the talk. The younger children were playing outside that morning so the house was quiet. The wash was on the line, flapping slightly in the mid-morning breezes. Hannah had been her numbed self all morning, helping as much with the household chores as she usually did but showing no real emotions about anything.

"We need to talk," Kathy told Hannah as she pulled a chair up to the kitchen table and sat down. She pulled out another chair for Hannah.

"I don't want to, Mom," Hannah said without much feeling. "It won't do any good."

Kathy ignored her. "Can you tell me how you are feeling?"

"Just dead inside," she said. "It was my fault that Peter died."

"But you weren't," Kathy protested. "It was wrong for you to sneak out like that, but that was not enough to be the fault of his driving too fast. He did that on his own."

Hannah hung her head, but even that effort seemed to tire her.

"You weren't out with him more than you told us, were you?" Kathy asked quietly, her voice trembling.

Hannah shook her head.

"You are sure?"

Hannah nodded this time.

"Then why are you taking this so hard?" Kathy asked as she looked at Hannah. Kathy's countenance showed her puzzlement and that she was not really expecting an answer.

"It was my dream," Hannah said in a monotone, without looking up.

Deep in her own thoughts at that moment, Kathy almost missed this explanation, but she jerked back when she realized what Hannah had just said.

"Your dream? You dreamed that he would die?"

Hannah shook her head. "My dream of what love would be like. If I hadn't had it, I wouldn't have gone out with him, and Peter would still be alive."

"But," Kathy paused, "a lot of people have dreams of what love is like."

"Do their dreams get people killed?" Hannah asked.

"No," Kathy said, "of course not."

"Then why did mine?"

"Are you sure it did?"

"Yes," Hannah nodded emphatically.

"So tell me about this dream," Kathy told her.

Hannah did not seem certain how to begin as her eyes, already clouded over, became even darker.

Kathy waited.

In the silence that followed, Hannah finally spoke: "I read this poem about love."

Kathy raised her hand to stop her. "Hold it right there.

Can you get me the poem, so I know what you are talking about?"

"Yes," Hannah said, rising to run upstairs to her room. She was back quickly and gave the piece of paper to her mother.

Kathy read it slowly, taking her time. "Well," she ventured when she was finished, "there's really nothing wrong with it. Kind of harmless, I would say. Idealistic, yes, but we all want someone to love us like this. What happened after the poem?"

Hannah looked relieved that her poem had survived her mother's reading. "I then started thinking of who could fit this love that I wanted."

"You mean, who could give it to you?"

Hannah shrugged her shoulders. "Something like that. Mostly who it could be."

"And you came up with Peter?"

Hannah stared, unmoving, at the wall. "Not that I just picked him. I had the feelings around him that seemed to be what the poem was talking about. So I was certain he was the one."

"So you think that if you hadn't had the dream you wouldn't have snuck out with him?"

Hannah nodded. "I would have listened to Dad, but I thought the dream must have been right and Dad was wrong."

"Love between a man and a woman is wonderful." Kathy decided she had better say that, considering the direction the conversation was taking. "We just have to put right and wrong first before our feelings on love. You must always remember that."

"I don't want to dream anymore," Hannah stated simply, still without any emotion.

"You must let God bring you the right person," Kathy told her.

"I suppose so," Hannah said, indifferently. "Following the dream did me no good at all. I don't want to feel any of that again."

"I don't think that's the right attitude either," Kathy protested. "Love between a married man and woman has many wonderful feelings."

"It's more trouble than good," Hannah said, a little emotion creeping into her voice.

Kathy decided the conversation had gone far enough in this direction. "What about your relationship with God. Are you bitter?"

"No," Hannah said, "just sick of myself."

"Maybe this is an opportunity to renew your dedication to Him," Kathy suggested. "I know you gave your heart to Him when you were younger. Now might be the time for a fresh commitment."

Hannah agreed with a nod, but made no comment beyond that.

"Maybe even baptism," Kathy ventured. "What about a new, perhaps more mature, start with God, and then with the church?"

"I suppose it would be a good idea. Do you think God wants me?"

"Of course," Kathy told Hannah. "He loves all of us."

"Maybe if I told Him I would stop dreaming He might forgive me," Hannah said, the emotion completely lacking in her voice.

"You poor thing," Kathy said, her heart breaking and her eyes full of tears. "You shouldn't be thinking things like that at all."

"I am an awful person," Hannah said. "I wanted what I wanted, and now Peter is dead." Her eyes stared at the wall, blank and open.

Kathy got up in alarm to put her arm around her daughter's shoulder, but there was no reciprocal movement towards her by Hannah.

"I will tell God I am so sorry," Hannah said, without looking towards her mother. "That way He might not blame it all on Peter."

Kathy stroked her face gently. "Hannah, you shouldn't be thinking such things. Peter is in the hands of God. He will judge righteously according to what is right. You must not think that He won't."

Hannah hung her head. "I am so sorry."

Kathy held her, expecting the weeping to start any moment, but it didn't. That seemed even worse to her. What to do was the question? At the moment, the day was slipping away and duty was calling. "God will take care of you," Kathy finally said, lifting her arms from around Hannah.

Hannah nodded. "We had better get the work done." She rose from her chair, her eyes dry.

That alarmed Kathy again. She pondered it all day as they worked side by side.

❧

Bumping along on the rough forest road, they climbed the mountain. "It is beautiful up here," his escort said enthusiastically. "We would all love it more if it weren't so lonely."

Jake nodded his head, agreeing for agreement's sake. The basic training supplied him was over now, and he was in the forest green uniform. His hair, though, was still in an Amish haircut. That could not go. Yet even with it, no one would have recognized him as from Iowa. Loneliness was what he wanted, but it might not be wise to mention it, he thought.

Shifting into first gear, the jeep lurched forward again. *That's something I wish were possible, a driver's license.* For now, he doubted whether he would go that far, and so he would have to depend on others to drive him around.

"Beautiful," he said out loud to make conversation. Below them was the full expanse of the valley in which Libby, Montana, was located. The view cheered him, like little had in weeks. Again he felt this was where he was supposed to be. He was sure of it.

"Ever been to the mountains before?" his escort asked.

"Nope," he said shaking his head.

"Where're you from?"

"Iowa."

"Kind of flat, right?"

He grinned. "Mostly cows and farmland."

"You'll like this then."

To this he vigorously nodded his head, the jeep bouncing violently on the edge of a sheer drop off. "We're fine," yelled his escort, jerking the wheel towards the side of the mountain.

He only smiled. At the moment he was fine whichever way he looked at it, except going down the edge of the mountain. However, he trusted these Englishmen more than that.

"I had a long talk with Hannah today," Kathy told Roy as they settled in for the evening, the stillness of the house all around them. There was no phone threatening to ring, no clicking of appliances, and no sounds of either a television or radio.

Roy looked up from what he was reading. "Yes?"

Kathy felt the tears coming at the memory of Hannah's blank stare. Roy noticed them from across the room and laid his paper aside. "It's that serious?"

"Yes," Kathy said, "the girl is really troubled. She needs something more than what we are giving her."

"We are praying," Roy reminded her.

"It may require doing something also," Kathy suggested, wiping the tears away that had escaped down her cheeks.

"Was she out with him more than once?" Roy wanted to know.

"I really don't think so."

"Did you find out what is causing her sense of guilt? It still seems much too great for the circumstances."

Kathy nodded. "Poor girl, she is really disillusioned with it all."

"That could happen, considering her crush on Peter," Roy allowed.

"It's more than that, though," Kathy told him. "She really thought it was the real thing. She's a serious girl, in a way. I know it's hard to tell with the flighty things she does sometimes."

"Like crawl out of a window at night to ride with a strange boy?"

"Like that," Kathy said, "but underneath I really think she had her hopes set in the right direction. Why it went wrong, I guess God knows, but it's hard to understand. She really wanted to love someone in the right way."

"Did you tell her that the right way involves a decent boy, and not just someone who can talk sweet talk?"

"I tried," Kathy told him, "but her heart is what concerns me at the moment. It's not just broken — that would be one thing — but she has lost hope. That is what seems so serious to me."

"She can find an Amish boy anywhere," Roy ventured. "It shouldn't be that hard. She's good looking and capable. I don't think she has anything to worry about."

"That's not what I mean," Kathy said. "Plenty of boys will want her. It's her own feelings that are a problem. She thinks God is angry with her."

"That's not all that bad a thing, depending, of course."

"In this case," Kathy said, looking at him from across the room, "I think we should be concerned. It's not something that will just go away by itself. The girl is truly hurting, so much that she can't face the pain."

Roy acknowledged that with a turn of his head. "Did you ask her about joining the church? Maybe this would be a good time to get that taken care of. It might help in the healing process."

"I did, and she agreed."

"Well, then let's try that. She can join in the next instruction class."

"I think she needs something more," Kathy said gently.

Roy stopped, his hand halfway to the paper, waiting.

"You know my sister Betty, in Troy, Montana?"

"Yes," Roy nodded his head, "that small Amish community they helped start awhile back. They're still not that stable, are they?"

"They have a minister and bishop now," Kathy told him. "Anyway, Betty keeps writing all the time about how beautiful the country is out there."

"Poor, too," Roy added.

"Yes, but they also can't get much hired help. It's just too expensive. Betty also just mentioned in her last letter how surprised they have been with the demand there is for the riding horses they have. They just started it as a sideline, but so many tourists stop in there over the summer, it could almost keep someone busy full-time."

"And you're thinking Hannah could help?"

"Yes, free of charge of course, unless Betty thinks they can pay her something, but like you said, they are poor. I would be happy if Hannah could just work for her room and board. Then, if she gets help, we would be more than paid back."

"What kind of help would she get that we could not give her here?"

Kathy was not sure how to explain it, but tried. "A change of scenery, a change of place, of the church maybe. Meeting different people. I don't know. It just might be the thing to do."

"When would she leave?"

"There's a van load going up from here in two weeks. Some ministers plan to visit, I think, and several other couples who are just curious are going along. Mr. Bowen is taking them."

"You have it all planned out?" Roy said, laying his paper down to reach for his Bible.

"Not really," Kathy assured him. "Just thinking out loud. What do you think?"

"I think we should see if she wants to go. If Hannah wants to go, then see if there is still room in the van. It shouldn't cost too much for another seat on the ride. How expensive are the motels on the way out?"

"I think Betty said they can space the drives each day to hit Amish or Hutterite communities in the evenings. It's about a three-day drive, two nights, I think."

"Maybe this is the answer for us. Ask her in the morning."

"I will," Kathy said, rising to finish some last-minute things in the kitchen before bedtime.

# CHAPTER THIRTEEN

THIS HAD BEEN Jake's first full day of fire watching. Standing on the fire deck in his forest-green uniform, the insignia of the State of Montana attached firmly above his left shirt pocket, he breathed in deeply the brisk morning air.

The absolute stunning mountain range took his breath away. He was supposed to watch for smoke, and he did so diligently, sweeping the slopes and the valley with the powerful binoculars they had supplied him. When Jake saw the slim column of smoke by mid-morning he thought perhaps his intense mind was playing tricks on him.

Yet bringing the binoculars to bear on the base of the forest floor, as he had been trained, there was no mistaking the licking of the red flames. This was no contained campfire. Jake clicked the microphone on his radio. "Fire Station 075 to base, 075 to base."

"075 come in," came the response.

"I have a small fire, two o'clock to my station. Looks about two miles out, but I'm new at this."

"Roger that, will be right on it," the voice on the radio responded.

Jake stood watching through his binoculars as the flames licked the base of a tree, and then he saw the lower branches catch fire. From there it spread quickly until the whole tree was engulfed in flames.

Sweeping the binoculars sideways to each side, Jake caught sight of a dust cloud coming from the north. It materialized into a pickup truck with obvious fire-fighting equipment. Arriving on the scene, two men scrambled out, quickly cut a perimeter around the area, and started back-fires, which burst out with their own streaks of flame.

An hour later, only a small section of burnt woods was visible in his lens as the truck drove back towards town. Jake kept on sweeping the slopes the rest of the day but found nothing more.

≋

When her mother approached Hannah the next morn-ing with the plan, Hannah herself was surprised that she found it agreeable. They discussed it as they washed the later breakfast dishes and put them away. Roy ate early in order to catch his ride to the factory.

"Maybe it would help me forget," Hannah ventured.

"You need to heal," Kathy told her. "I don't think forget-ting is as much of a problem."

"I just never want to dream again," Hannah said as she carefully lifted the breakfast plates into the cupboard.

"We all have to love," Kathy told her.

"Not in the way I did," Hannah replied. "I never want to do that again. Do you think God will forgive me in Mon-tana? Do you think He's closer to us in the mountains?"

"He's close to us right here," Kathy assured her. "That's why we want you to go. It might do you some good, and Betty can use some help, I'm sure."

"Do they clean houses out there, too?"

"I suppose they do," Kathy chuckled, "but it's their horse-riding business that you would be helping with."

Hannah's eyes brightened for the first time in weeks. Kathy could have wept right then and there with relief, but held back her tears. They were on the right track, Kathy was sure now. "I'll write to Betty today. She'll get the letter in time to write back if she doesn't want you to come. But I'm sure she will want you to come." Kathy wanted to add, but only thought it: *This could be the answer to our prayer.*

"What if Betty doesn't want my help?" Hannah asked with concern.

"You'll be working for room and board, so there should not be any problem. In the summers they are really busy giving rides on the farm with the two horses they have. If you go out, they might even get another horse. With you there to help, that should not be a problem. Then the increased business would more than pay for the horse." Again Kathy wanted to say it out loud, but decided against it: *We would be helping them while they help us.*

"When will we know for sure?"

"I'll go ask Mr. Bowen this morning. He should know if there is still room in the van."

Kathy left around ten to talk with Mr. Bowen. She returned with the news that two spots were still available, one of which Hannah could have.

So it was that Hannah boarded the van early on a Wednesday morning, heading for the far distant land of Montana. A letter from Betty had arrived the day before the departure expressing great delight in the plan.

Kathy had read the letter aloud to her family. "Christian

greetings from the mountain lands of Montana," she read. "We received your welcome news of Hannah's coming. Of course, she can come. With her skill with horses, she can take care of the riders all summer. We might even get another horse." Kathy paused in her reading as if to say, "See, I told you so." "The extra income would be welcome. As you know, money is tight around here. Thanks again for your offer of her help. We will put her up to the best of our ability. With love from your sister, Betty. "

"See, it's good news," Kathy had told Hannah after finishing the letter.

Again the slight smile on her face convinced Kathy that they were doing the right thing.

Now the van was loaded with Hannah's suitcase, and she was settled on the back seat. Beside her were Lois and Elmer Zook with Lois's sister, Ruth, all of whom Hannah knew well as they were from her church district.

Ruth had never married although she must have been in her thirties by now. Elmer and Lois, it was rumored, were interested in moving to Montana. In discussing who was going along the night before, Roy had commented that poor people shouldn't be thinking of moving out West. He went on to say he expected that was precisely what poor people did — make poor choices — and that was why they were poor.

Kathy had protested that they themselves were not exactly rich, and certainly used to be much poorer, which Roy conceded was true.

Minister Alvin, the one who preached at Peter's funeral, sat in the passenger seat beside Mr. Bowen. His wife was in the next row with her sister and husband. Both of them

were almost old in Hannah's book, since they were somewhere around fifty, she figured.

Occupying the second row was an older couple whose
son and his wife had moved to Troy from the area. They
were lonesome to see their grandchildren, as well as the
West. With them was the wife's sister, whose husband had
passed away some years before. Her name was Naomi, a
kind, gentle soul who gave Hannah a ready smile when she
climbed into the van.

There followed two days of hard driving, as much as
Mr. Bowen could take. Up they went through Chicago and
west onto Interstate 90.

The second night Mr. Bowen almost could not make
the designated stopping point at one of the Hutterite communities north of Billings. He persevered, but by the time
they finally arrived he was exhausted. He requested that
he be allowed to retire early, and he even turned down a
supper the Hutterites had quickly prepared for them at the
common eating hall.

"I need sleep more than food," Mr. Bowen explained to
them. The hosts willingly acquiesced and showed him to a
room they had reserved for visitors. They put the married
couples up in their own homes, while Hannah stayed with
one of the young girls.

"You're staying with me, is that okay?" the girl asked her.

Hannah was too tired to really care, but nodded "Yes."

"You're from Indiana?" the girl asked.

Hannah said "Yes" this time, then added further information since the question was coming anyway, she figured.
"We live just outside of Nappanee. I'm going to spend the
summer with my Aunt Betty in Troy, Montana."

"Is she Amish?" the girl asked.

"Yes," Hannah told her. "It's just a small community in the mountains, I think."

"Not a lot of mountains around here," the girl said wryly, "except way off in the distance."

"It is pretty flat." Hannah had not seen many hills during the trip. "Big sky country, right? Have you lived here all your life?"

"I was born here," the girl said. "Where else is there to go? You have to have a good reason to travel since the colony pays for it."

Hannah's eye was caught by a piece of embroidery on the dresser. Under the bottom the name Jane was stitched in fine, exquisite lettering. So that was the girl's name.

"Are you Jane?" she asked.

Jane nodded. "I'm named after my grandmother and her grandmother before her."

"That's nice," Hannah commented. "Do you have horses in the colony that you ride?"

"Lots of them," Jane said. "The boys ride them mostly for work."

"Can you girls ride them, too?"

"Yes, when there is a chance. Some of us like it and some of us don't."

"Do you?" Hannah wanted to know. "Looks like you could ride here for days and never stop."

"Sometimes. We girls are kept pretty busy with the housework. We all have chores that need to be done each day. There's not much time for things like horseback riding."

"Well," Jane smiled, "maybe we should get to bed. You have to be tired."

Hannah agreed as the lights out in their room was followed a few minutes later with what was obviously a communal deadline when the whole community went dark.

That morning the sun had risen in its full glory, its light streaming against the Cabinet Mountains. Jake was up early and at his post, although signs of fire at this hour were still unlikely. Only later, when the mist rose from the ground, could he spot the haze of smoke from any burning fires. There was always the occasional campfire still smoldering from the night before. Those differences he was now trained to pick out.

She came up the trail later in the day — an English girl accompanied by what he assumed was her family. He gave tours often to hikers who stopped by his station. This was an effort in public relations that was well worth its weight in gold, his supervisor had told him.

Jake was down at ground level at the moment the group appeared. Maybe that was why the full impact of her face was not lost on him. They were already close when he saw her. The similarities were startling. She could have been her sister, but that was not possible. This was an English girl.

Unable to take his eyes off her, he blushed with feelings of shame and anger. Memories he had been trying to keep buried came rushing back full strength, undiminished now by time or distance.

With great effort Jake remembered his present status and managed to croak out a "good morning" to the tall, clean-shaven man in the lead.

"Good morning," the man replied as he extended a muscular hand to Jake. "Are you open for tours?"

"Certainly," Jake said, wishing with great intensity that this guy's daughter were not with him. "Do you want to climb the tower?"

"I do," the man announced. "Anyone else up to climbing the tower?"

Jake stepped aside awaiting the outcome of this decision, hoping they all would go. However, his wish was not to be granted. She decided to stay on the ground, along with what must have been her sister and mother.

Awkwardly Jake stood there, but they ignored him while they conversed among themselves. This closeness to her and their indifference to him only added to his feelings of anger. From his station on the side rails of the lookout post he could see the side of her face. It had the same curve to it, the same outline of the lips, the same long dark eyelashes; only slight differences kept him from jumping to the obviously impossible conclusion that someone else had also left the Amish.

Only Jake had not left the Amish, at least he had not in his own mind. He was just trying to get away from the pain, not the life he once knew. In fact, the old life was what he wanted, yet its present form had all come to a halt that Sunday evening.

If something had prepared him for it, perhaps it would have been easier, but there had been no preparation. His ignorance of the obvious made the hurt even worse. Why had he not been aware of what was going on? That was the question that haunted him.

In her father's house that night where they had sat on

the couch so many times over the years, she had told him. Soon after he had brought her home, with the gasoline lantern hissing on the ceiling, she had simply and without any expression of emotion said that it was over.

"But the wedding is in three months," he had managed to get out of his completely parched throat.

"I know," she had told him calmly. "That is why I am quitting while there is still time."

"But I thought we cared for each other," he had said and knew the hurt was in his eyes, and felt the shame of it even more.

"We do," she had said, still without showing any emotion, her eyes avoiding his now tear-filled ones, "just not in this way. I am sure you will find someone else better suited to you."

Later he was thankful he had had enough sense to leave when he did. He had found his horse in the dark and driven his buggy out of her driveway without any lights on. It was not until he was halfway home that he even noticed he had forgotten the lights. Two weeks later she was dating his first cousin.

The tramping of feet interrupted Jake's thoughts as the men descended the wooden stairs from the tower. "It's a nice view," the man announced to the women.

"We can see it from here," his wife responded.

As the group left, one of the young men whom he had assumed was a brother took her hand in his in a clearly un-brotherly gesture. They smiled deeply into each other's eyes.

Glancing away from the sight, the hurt in his heart cut even deeper. Jake's anger smoldered against the unfairness of it all. *I'll never trust a girl like that again,* he told himself.

## CHAPTER FOURTEEN

THE NEXT MORNING, Mr. Bowen insisted on an early start. That translated into the travelers being able to eat breakfast at the eating-house with the first round served for the men. The sun was just coming up when the van of Amish pulled out of the colony. Billings was an hour away, and two hours beyond that the mountains started.

Hannah, riding in the back, could not tear her eyes away from the windows of the van. The scenery was impressive and so different from what she knew. Mountain after mountain came into view, faded away, and then more appeared even taller than before.

During early afternoon, Mr. Bowen took the Thompson Falls exit off of the Interstate and up 200. From there they drove the west side of the Cabinet Mountains on 56 and arrived in Troy by 4:30.

"Do you have your directions to your aunt's place?" he asked Hannah from the driver's seat, after pulling to a stop in front of the town hall. Its gray stone front was offset by the colors of the U.S. and Montana flags flapping in the breeze on a tall flagpole.

"Yes," Hannah said as she pulled them from her carry-on bag.

Mr. Bowen studied them before proceeding north out of town. A mile or so later he turned into a driveway, its mailbox a mini log home with *Mast* printed plainly on the top.

Hannah thought the house looked rustic with its unpainted, rough-sawn logs as siding. The barn had the same kind of siding and two horses stood looking over the rail fence leading from it.

Hannah was not sure this was her aunt's home, so she hesitated and stayed on the back seat. Mr. Bowen echoed her uncertainty: "Do you think it's the right place?"

From the front seat, Alvin observed, "There are no electric or phone lines around, so it could be the right place unless the English live like that around here, too."

"I doubt it," Mr. Bowen ventured. "Why don't you go to the door and find out?"

Hannah felt unsure of herself and climbed slowly out of the van. Once she was out, the full smell and feel of this land hit her. A rush of water was running heavily in the distance. Trees were everywhere. Through the branches were the outlines of mountains, which seemed to her to be almost on all sides. Timidly she walked towards the house, trying to absorb what she was seeing.

To Hannah's great relief, Betty opened the door before she got to it, her white apron dusted with flour. "Oh, it's you. I thought I heard a van drive up, but with all the sounds around here, you can't be sure. Where are your bags?"

"In the van. We weren't sure this was the right place."

"Oh, I can see that," Betty agreed. "We don't look like the Amish places back east. This is the west, and it took a little getting used to for me, too, I must say, but we just love it now."

Approaching the van, Betty shook hands with all of the others in turn. "I'm so glad to see all of you. It seems like it has been years, although I'm sure it has not. If you had the time, I would start with the questions now, but I guess it can wait 'til Sunday."

"Yes," Mr. Bowen ventured, "I should get these people dropped off. It has been a long trip."

"I suppose you are exhausted yourself, having to drive so far," Betty told him. "The others can just ride along."

"I am," Mr. Bowen acknowledged, "although it wasn't quite as long a drive today as yesterday."

Naomi smiled from her seat on the second row. "He did real well. I haven't had a better driving in a long time."

Mr. Bowen nodded his thanks from the driver's seat.

"Well, like I said," Betty told all of them, starting to close the van door, "you can tell me the news on Sunday."

Turning to Hannah as the van pulled out, she asked her, "So what do you think of the west?"

"I haven't had much time to think of anything yet, but it sure is different."

"Do you think you'll like it?" Betty asked without much apprehension in her voice.

"Es iss so grohs" (it is so big), Hannah told her, motioning all around with her hand.

"That it is," Betty agreed. "God must have really used his imagination when He made this country."

"You think so?" Hannah asked, stirred by the thought.

"Yes," Betty said confidently. "Like I have said to Steve, the East is made for the practical people — you know, the ones who make the money and, I guess, keep the country running — but the West is made for people who dream."

Hannah gasped, "But I didn't come out here to dream. I came to help you."

"I'm sure you will," Betty assured her. "Now let's show you your room and then we can look at the horses. Supper is waiting to be made after that. Dreaming will be on your own time."

Hannah was going to tell her that there would be no dreaming on her part, but decided it might not be respectful, having just arrived and all. She simply picked up her suitcase and followed Betty inside.

That morning, sitting in his cabin, Jake finally decided that it was time to update his folks on where he was. They had all been down to the Greyhound bus station to see him off, but he had been clear from the beginning that he did not know when he would be coming back.

"Just stay in the Amish communities," he recalled his mother's last words to him.

She would want to know what Bishop he had reported to. The fact that he had not done so yet was not the best news, but there was still time to do something about it. Since coming here he had learned of a small community of Amish in Troy, just west of Libby. He had not yet made any attempt to join a church service. This was partly because of his job, but mostly because he did not want to be reminded of anything to do with her.

The gathering of his kind on a Sunday morning could bring it all back. Jake was not sure, but he felt the possibility was there. He was afraid he would remember how they had spent the times in passing glances when they could see each other in church or in the schoolhouse where he had first noticed her. Then there were the times during the summer weeks when he had gone past her place, and she had been out helping in the fields. Her suntanned face would light up when she waved at him.

All of these were things he wished to avoid, but he was also determined that he must stay Amish. How to make it all work together Jake was not sure. He had kept his Amish clothing, but did not wear it on his job. He imagined that could be explained satisfactorily, although, as a member of the Church, it might take a *word confession* to repair.

That was all he ever would be willing to risk, he had decided. Not that he was sure whether he had crossed the line now, but that would be bad enough. He would have to confess his error and to beg forgiveness of God and the Church, and a church vote would be taken. That was much better than a *knee confession* required for serious offenses, which also required much greater research by the Bishop and his fellow ministers. On the way back into the fold, a lengthy time of instruction was stipulated, followed by a weighty vote that was harder to get passed, and then the confession made on one's knees before them all. Yes, he wanted to stay out of the *knee confession* area.

Jake had been baptized in preparation of the wedding and the thought of that now sent bitter feelings through him. Yet it was time to let his parents hear from him.

Getting out his paper and pen he wrote, "Dear Mom and Dad, I arrived in Montana and have been working for the forestry service since then. The work is wonderful with beautiful scenery all around here."

His pen faltered. Did he have enough courage to tell them what they really wanted to know? Gripping the pen tightly, Jake tried, "There is an Amish community close to here, but I have not been there yet. I have no plans to become English. Please understand that I need some time alone. If Deacon Henry asks about me, you can tell him that."

Again he paused, wondering if enough had been said. He decided it had not. "If I decided to come home today I would look exactly the same." Those were code words for his haircut and they would know what he meant. Few identifying features are as guarded by Amish males as much as are the haircuts. Clothing can be changed in a few minutes, but cut hair takes months to grow out. "Thanks for your understanding on this matter. I will try to be at church at the Amish fellowship in Troy this Sunday." Then Jake signed his name, addressed the envelope, and dropped it into the outside box where it would be taken into Libby later for mailing.

Hannah awoke the first morning of her stay in the west feeling more rested than she had felt in a long time. It was still dark as Betty's voice came from the bottom of the stairs, "Time to get up, Hannah."

She answered in a muffled voice, which seemed to suffice because the calling stopped.

Hannah got dressed and started downstairs. There was a kerosene lamp on the dresser in her room but no light in the hall. She managed to find her way down without tripping on the sawn-log stairs and opened the door into the living room. It was dark there except for the light from a gas lantern hissing in the kitchen.

"We get up early around here in the summer time," Betty informed her from the kitchen. "Winter's a little different. Now it's breakfast at five thirty. Steve has to be up on the mountain by dawn since his ride comes at six."

Hannah rubbed her eyes, washed her hands at the sink, and got busy without having to be told. Cracking the eggs into the pan, she flipped them at exactly the right time, bringing a look of admiration from Betty. "Your mother did teach you well. She always was the best cook around the house."

"She tried," Hannah acknowledged.

"Well, looks like you are learning," Betty told her, lifting the bacon out of the pan. "As soon as it's daylight, I will show you how we do the horseback riding. I know you saw the horses yesterday, but with the English riders it's a little different. You have to follow a set of rules with them, in case of injury and such, Steve says. We just have to be careful."

Hannah nodded as she lifted the last of the eggs out of the frying pan.

Steve came through the kitchen door and took a chair. "Breakfast smells good," he smiled.

"The other children eat later," Betty informed her. "Kendra is old enough to start getting up earlier, but I just haven't started yet."

"How old is she?" Hannah asked, searching her memory from the evening before. "Ten?"

"Eleven actually," Betty said. "Just turned eleven this month."

Steve glanced at Hannah from across the table. "You are about seventeen, aren't you? Any boyfriends yet?"

"Steve," Betty scolded him, "don't start that with her."

Neither of them noticed that Hannah was pale instead of the expected blush of red at the remark. They took her silence as a negative response. There was no boyfriend, and they assumed Kathy would have written if there had been a serious one.

Steve just chuckled. "We have several boys around here who are still single. There are not as many choices as there are back East, but still a bunch of decent boys. What we don't have is much selection in girls. Always a serious problem for the boys, of course."

Betty finally looked at Hannah and noticed the paleness. "Now, look what you've done," she told Steve. "The girl is scared."

"I'm sorry," he said. "Just trying to give her some warning. You don't have to be scared, Hannah — they don't bite."

Hannah was unable to find words, so she said nothing. In one sense it was a relief to know that Mom and Dad had told no one. But in another sense, which surprised her, a great sense of loneliness rushed over her. She was alone in more ways than one. No one here knew about Peter. Intending to keep it that way, Hannah turned her attention to the bacon and eggs on her plate.

## CHAPTER FIFTEEN

B Y NINE, TWO cars were already in the driveway. "Looks like it will be on-the-job training," Betty told Hannah. "I had hoped to give you some instructions first, but you'll just have to follow along now."

"I'm scared," Hannah told her. "I've never given rides to others."

"It's not really giving rides," Betty told her. "You read them the rules, saddle up the horses, give them a map of the land, see that they mount safely, and they're off."

"I'll watch you," Hannah said quickly.

"We would have had to do that anyway," Betty assured her. "I'll stick with you for a few mornings, and then I'm sure you'll be fine on your own."

With Hannah in tow, Betty headed for the barn. "Good morning," she said cheerfully. "Ready for horseback riding?"

The occupants of both cars were young couples. One couple was in a red jeep, the other in a blue Mazda. Everyone nodded.

"Well, it's first-come, first-serve around here. You get to decide how many horses you want and for how long."

"They were here first," the couple in the jeep admitted

graciously. "We'll see how long they take and then come back. There are things in town we can do."

"What are the rates?" the couple in the blue Mazda wanted to know.

Betty told them.

"We'll take an hour then," they said. "Both horses."

"Sorry we have only two horses," Betty informed the other couple. "It takes fifteen minutes to saddle up and go over the basics. Then an hour out for them."

"We'll be back," they said cheerfully as they started the car and headed back towards Troy.

"Okay, now for you," Betty told the other couple. "Let's see, here are the rules." She rattled them off and asked about prior riding experience. Both claimed to have had some.

With Hannah's help, the couple was soon heading up the trail towards the mountain. "One hour," Betty reminded them as they set off. "I would let you have some leeway, but the others are coming back."

They nodded their heads as they hung onto the reins of their horses and rode up the trail.

"We could use another set of horses," Betty told Hannah as they watched them go around the bend.

Just at that moment, another vehicle pulled into the driveway as if to underscore what Betty had just said.

It was another young couple, this time with two children. When they rolled down the window, Betty asked them, "Are you looking for horse rides?"

"Yes," the man said, "my wife and I were hoping to go riding. We also need a place for the children to stay for the time we are out. An Amish riding stable seemed like just the place." He smiled, then offered further explanation:

"We used to do a lot of riding before we were married. It brings back some good memories for us both."

"We would be glad to do both," Betty assured him, "but we have only two horses, and they are both out at the moment."

"When is the next available time?" the man's wife asked as she leaned down so she could see Betty's face. Her eyes sparkled with anticipation.

"I don't know for sure," Betty told them hesitating. "See, we let them go on a first-come basis, and they are already spoken for in an hour. From there, I don't know how long they will be out."

Their faces fell. "That's too bad," the man said. "Maybe we'll check back in a few hours. Maybe after lunch."

"That would be fine," Betty told them. "I'm so sorry."

As the car pulled out, Hannah asked, "Why don't you get more horses?"

"That's what I was saying all last summer, but I just can't take care of more and the housework, too. Not with five children, I can't. Kendra is of some help, but not enough yet."

"Well, I'm here now," Hannah told her, "for all of the summer."

"Let's see how the rest of the day goes first, then I'll talk about it with Steve tonight."

The rest of the day went as it had started, without sufficient horses to meet the need. Hannah caught onto the routine quickly. By late afternoon, Betty let her take care of the last riders of the day.

The last ride was the couple with the two small children who needed babysitting while the parents rode. Hannah kept the children in the barn and played little Amish games with them she had learned as a child. When the parents returned in an hour, the eyes of the children were shining, as were those of their parents.

"This has been a perfect ending to the day," the man told Hannah. "We are so grateful to you for babysitting the children."

"I want to play wolf at home too," the boy said. "We learned it real fast."

"Sounds like it was a hit," his wife chuckled. "Thanks for your time."

They paid Hannah the requested fee as well as a generous amount for the time she had spent with the children. Holding the money tightly against her side, she waved as they drove off.

Showing the money to Betty was a pleasure. Her face lit up with delight. "You did real well for the first day, and they paid you for babysitting."

"It was a lot more fun than cleaning house," Hannah assured her.

"I will have to talk to Steve," Betty said, "as soon as I get a chance."

After supper Betty talked with Steve. He was told the figures for the day's work. He scratched around on a notepad for a few minutes and quickly made up his mind. "I'm buying two more horses. Even if they aren't busy all the time, it will still pay off."

"When?" Betty wanted to know.

"Saturday," he told her. "That's the first chance I have. I shouldn't take off from my regular job for this. That would be expensive."

Betty agreed, and Saturday it was. Steve left early

with his horse and cart for Troy and some phone calls. He returned to report success before lunch. By two o'clock that afternoon a horse trailer had pulled into the driveway with two horses.

"These are perfect riding horses," the driver assured Steve. "I picked them out myself this morning. They are gentle and safe for anyone."

"What are the names?" Steve wanted to know.

"Mandy," the driver said, stroking the neck of the smaller mare, "and this gelding is Prince."

Prince jerked his head at the sound of his name, as if he knew he was being talked about. Hannah approached him cautiously, her hand stretched out to his neck. He lowered his head as if to oblige her. She gently touched him, her eyes searching his.

He neighed a soft, friendly sound.

"I think he likes you," the driver said.

Feeling her heart was simply too full, Hannah could say nothing. Prince was like her pony, Honey, only bigger and stronger. Prince's face was the same as Honey's.

"Looks like love at first sight," Steve chuckled. "I hope it works out."

The driver made a sound in his throat. "It doesn't always work out well for people, huh?"

Hannah heard nothing they said; her hand was stroking Prince's mane. She knew without seeing any more of him than this that this was a special horse.

"His name fits him," she finally managed to say.

"Well, take care," the driver told them. "It looks like everything's in order. You shouldn't have any trouble with these horses, Mr. Mast."

"Thanks for bringing them," Steve told him, as the driver got ready to leave.

~

That afternoon Jake Byler arrived at the home of Bishop Nisley. After a few inquiries, it had been an easy matter to find the bishop's residence. The Amish were enough of a novelty in the area that the locals seemed to know where they were located.

After the preliminary introductions had been made, Jake and the Bishop talked. With supper out of the way, they had settled into the living room. Nisley was just a young bishop, in age as well as in experience

"So you are from Iowa?" Nisley was ready to probe, Jake could tell. He was prepared for it, knowing that a strange Amish boy, even in full Amish dress, does not walk into an Amish community without questions. It was even more important that those questions were answered satisfactorily. If he had arrived on the Greyhound, straight from home, that would be one thing, but since he had walked in, this was another matter.

Jake nodded. "Kalona."

"Is that an old church community?"

"Quite old," Jake allowed. "I was born there."

"Your grandfather's name was Simon Byler, Bishop Simon?"

Jake nodded.

"I've heard of him. He was made bishop in his late twenties, wasn't he?"

Jake nodded again.

"He was living until a few years ago, wasn't he?"

"Yes, he died in the fall of year," Jake replied as he searched his memory, gauging the passing of the years, "now five years ago, I think."

With his lineage established to Nisley's satisfaction, the bishop moved on. "How long have you been in the area?"

"About two months now."

"This is the first that you have tried to contact us?"

"Yes." Jake decided not to explain further.

The bishop was not letting him get away with it. He might be new to his job, but he was also curious. "Why not?"

Jake took a deep breath. "First, I didn't know where any Amish churches were, but I promised my parents I would look the nearest one up."

Nisley was not done. "We are not that hard to find. Kind of new in the area, and I would say most everyone in town knows where we are."

"I know," Jake told him. "I found that out when I started asking, but see, I really didn't want to start asking any sooner."

Nisley liked that — it sounded better to him than excuses. Amish boys were not expected to lie, so he gave Jake no credit for telling the truth, but it was still good. "Are you a member at Kalona?"

"Yes."

"Your bishop will be wanting to know where you are. Was there a good reason for not showing up here sooner?"

Jake blushed, but he was not about to tell the bishop about her. Yet some explanation needed to be given. "You see," Jake tried to start, his neck red in shame, "I told my parents I needed some time away, visiting other places. They know and understand. I am not trying to get away from the Amish. It just took a little while before I could contact you. Of course, I didn't know it was you, but the Amish in the area."

Jake's red neck was all the evidence Bishop Nisley needed. There was some personal issue involved. A wild Amish boy, doing things against the church rules, usually did not feel much shame about it. This one looked okay. Nisley nodded his encouragement. "Well, I am glad that you have come. Hopefully we will see more of you while you are in the area."

Jake, greatly relieved, totally agreed. "I will try to come down every other week for services, at least."

"Where do you work?" Nisley wanted to know.

"On Cabinet Mountain for the forest service."

Nisley gave Jake another good look, although he had already looked Jake over pretty thoroughly. *The hair looks good.* Then he said out loud, "They have to wear uniforms, don't they?"

Jake nodded, hanging his head.

Nisley let it go. That was a matter for his home bishop to take care of.

## Chapter Sixteen

SINCE THE NEXT morning was Sunday, the need to get up early was not as urgent. Betty did not call Hannah until six-thirty. Already wide awake and wondering how the day would turn out, Hannah came downstairs.

Betty already had breakfast going, and Hannah joined in by setting the table.

"So, are you worried about your first Sunday?" Betty asked cheerfully.

"A little. I hardly know anyone but your family."

"Oh, you'll get to know the others fast. We're just a little group and real friendly. We don't get visitors from the East that much. In the summers, there are more visitors, of course, but we always look forward to them."

"At least there will be a whole van load of other visitors, so I guess no one will notice me."

"I suppose so," Betty allowed, "although a lot of the locals will be looking. You are the only young girl from what I saw the other day."

"I'm not out here for that," Hannah informed her emphatically, emotion in her voice.

"Never say never," Betty chirped. "You might see something you like."

"I'm not into that right now," Hannah told her. "No boys for me."

"Whatever you say. Just let me know if you need further information on any of them after the service."

Hannah was not smiling.

"Do you hate boys or something?" Betty inquired, a quizzical look on her face. "Or maybe you have someone at home?"

Hannah shook her head, "No."

"Okay." Betty dropped the subject as Steve walked into the kitchen.

Around eight-thirty they pulled into the home where the service was being held. Its log-siding look was the same as Betty and Steve's place. Hannah wondered if everyone built with logs.

Otherwise the service appeared normal. There were the usual lines of black hats and white shirts as the men and boys stood in front of the barn. The women got out at the house and headed up the wooden walk board that served as the entryway from the lane.

Hannah stepped carefully, lest she trip on the rough edges and fall in her Sunday clothing. That would serve to announce her arrival in a way she least wanted. Then she might always be remembered as the girl who arrived from Indiana and fell flat on her face.

The singing started in the usual manner, the song leader announcing the number forcefully and then leading with the first bar. Hannah fell quickly into the feeling of being home as the sound of their voices rose and fell together.

Hannah kept her eyes on the floor and made no attempt to look around. That lasted only as long as she felt she could and until she began to feel conspicuous. In the moments between the first and second songs she could feel every muscle and noticed every movement. She froze in place until a strong bass voice led out.

Relaxing, she allowed herself to look. That much she must do, lest everyone think she was a true *dumm kopp* (dumb person) from Indiana who was afraid to get her eyes off the floor. Then, remembering there were others from home sitting around the room, Hannah breathed easier. She would not be noticed.

Lifting her eyes cautiously, she instantly knew that she was being observed. The bench two rows back from the men's front line had at least six boys sitting on it. They were not young boys, like her younger brothers. Those were on the front row. These boys were Hannah's age.

Her heart wanted to jump in terror, but it subsided with what she saw. Letting her eyes start cautiously down the row, none so far looked dangerous. They were not staring at her but had their faces in various directions, just aware. And now she was seeing them. The first one looked rugged — a logger, no doubt, she thought. His arms had scars on them. The one to his right was thinner, his face pinched as if he had not seen too much good food in his life. The one to his left looked like the logger's brother without the scars.

So far, so good. Hannah felt she could relax. If this were all there was to get over in the West she would not have to fear any dreams being reawakened. A feeling of thankfulness swept over her, as her eyes took in the next two boys. God was being good to her, she thought. He was making the road easy, and the commitment to do the right thing possible. But which one of them was leading the singing.

She had yet to find him, and a certainty now settled on her that it was one of the young boys.

As if to answer her thoughts, the singer led out again, his voice full and powerful. The voice was that of a boy beside the last one she could see. It was then the first wave of horror swept over her. Such a sound could not come from the throat of the local specimens she was seeing. There was too much vigor, emotion, and feeling to it. Hardly ever had she heard the *Praise Song* being sung this way. This singer was the maker of dreams, his voice wrapping around the room, powerful and rich until the last notes of his lead blended into the others as they joined their voices to his. She felt a chill run through her body, her heart skipping a beat. Who was this boy?

A hefty man sitting directly in front of the singer blocked Hannah's view of him. The man's shoulders were strong and broad, those of an outdoorsman, healthy from both good eating and hard work. When he moved his head, his beard seemed to spread even wider than it already was, reaching almost to the outside of his stomach. The singer must be behind him.

Did she want to see? *No*, she told herself, but she must. Or must she? *Yes*, it could not be avoided. It was better to face the problem now than be surprised later. Surely, she thought, after coming all this way, God would not ask her to face a trial beyond her strength to bear? Because right now it seemed like there was not much that she could bear.

The hefty, broad-shouldered fellow, his mouth forming the words of the song, paused, as the little boy seated next to him thumped him on his knee, trying to say something. All in one motion the man bent sideways and the singer behind him became visible. Only one thought, potent in its energy and terror, penetrated her brain, searing past her eyes. *It's Peter,* her mind screamed as fear gripped her.

Hannah froze, unable to even drop her eyes in her sheer panic, yet she knew she must control herself. This was church. Everyone was watching, and a strange girl in a strange church could not be causing a scene.

This couldn't be Peter. She forced her eyes to the floor with sheer will power. Who then is it, her mind screamed? Could it be his brother? She must know, and to know she must look again. Raising her eyes slowly, her heart beating wildly, she found his face again in the sea of boys and men, visible now between the hefty man and his little boy.

He was in the middle of a new stanza, his face intent and focused. Slowly, sitting there on the hard bench, trying to make her face look like nothing was wrong, she knew. It was not Peter, nor his brother. Her mind had played tricks on her.

Older by a year at least, he looked more somber, like he had already suffered in his life. Peter's face never looked like that. The hair was much the same color, the outline of the face similar, yet the tilt of the head was different and his jaw line more pronounced. Other differences became evident as she now openly stared.

Moments later, as if coming to her senses from a daze, Hannah tore her eyes away lest he look up and see her watching him. What a *dumm kopp* he would think she was. He was not Peter. There would never be another Peter.

She must remember who she was and what she had learned. She must not dream about anyone again. Lowering her eyes to the floor, she did not raise them again until the ministers filed down from upstairs and the preaching began.

≈

Jake had the distinct impression that someone was watching him while he was leading the Praise Song. Being asked to lead the song as a visitor was not that unusual. No doubt people assumed by his clothing and bearing that he was a member from some Amish church and thus qualified. Arriving in Bishop Nisley's buggy probably also helped. In any event, the request had been made to him, and he was singing without any problem, just as he had done at home many times.

She had always told Jake that his singing was something he was good at. That was the only thing that bothered him now, but he pushed the feeling aside and proceeded. She was not here, and he was determined that he would not be haunted by his memories of her. So what if she thought he could sing? That did not change whether he could or not.

Starting another line, Jake was hit hard with the sensation that he was indeed being watched. Yet looking around during the song might break his concentration, so he avoided it. Instead, he kept his mind on the page in front of him and kept the rhythm and timing of the song in his head. The last line of the song was soon coming up, and then he could look.

He gave his all into the effort. With its haunting, stirring cry the last line of the last stanza pulled at one's soul. It was as if the agony of a martyr's impending death and final victory were calling out for all to hear.

After the sound died away, Jake allowed his eyes to

lift and his concentration to break from the melody, yet he saw nothing that could have caused the feeling of being watched. The big broad back and suspenders of one of the locals was directly in front of him. To the left and right of this fellow were the young girls, but none of them were old enough to be doing what he had felt.

That was when the man shifted his position again, this time rising to take his son outside to tend to him. The boy was crying as if in pain. He would be brought back in when his crying had been seen to so it would not disturb the service.

When the man stood up, Jake saw what could have definitely caused the feeling he had experienced. Her hair was black, her skin delicate, her appearance looked cultured. What struck him the most was that this girl was not anything like *her*. This girl's face was much more somber, serious, and her eyes were directed to the floor at that moment.

He half wished she would look up, although he really wasn't that interested. The thought that he still wanted her, and that he was making comparisons with this girl, struck him as wrong. If this were someone who reminded him of her, he would be angry and hurt. Now that it was someone different, why was he not happy? The thought found no resolution in his mind. He was puzzled with himself.

Finally, deciding that he did not wish to know, he turned his attention to the next song that was just starting. Girls were not on his list of things to be concerned with right now. There was a summer of work in front of him, and that was just that. He had better things to do than to try to trust any girl again.

*Besides, I don't want to,* he told himself. *Now think about*

64000

*something else. Just be glad you did not see anything that hurt too much — for example, someone who looked like her. If I had known this, I could have come sooner.*

⌇

The Mast family wanted to leave early. Betty found Hannah right after the noon meal of peanut butter sandwiches, jam, pickles, and coffee. *(That would not be peanut butter from a jar, but instead a delectable mixture, made by adding marshmallow cream with pancake or corn syrup to the peanut butter. About a third marshmallow cream is added to the peanut butter with syrup whipped in until the mixture can be spread but is not runny.)*

"I forgot to tell you we leave early," Betty told Hannah.

"Sure," Hannah replied, moving to find her bonnet and shawl.

They were both waiting out by the end of board sidewalk when Steve pulled up with the surrey buggy.

"The buggies look the same as at home," Hannah commented.

"Oh, I suppose that you are probably a little homesick!" Betty exclaimed.

"Yes, but not too much." There were actually worse things going on than homesickness, but she was trying hard to hide them.

In the back seat of the buggy with Kendra and two of the children chatting merrily away about the day, Hannah almost could forget. Betty was not about to forget, even if she did not know precisely what was on Hannah's mind at the moment. "Did you see anyone?" she asked cheerfully as she turned around from the front seat with Steve and the other two children.

Steve chuckled, "Don't you women think about anything else?"

"Well," Betty told him, "it's important."

Hannah was saying nothing.

Betty raised her eyebrows at Hannah again, but then got a puzzled look on her face. *There was something wrong with the girl. She was all white.* "Hannah, are you feeling okay?" she asked, now concerned.

"I think so," Hannah said quietly.

"She's tired, Mommy," Kendra offered as explanation.

"Are we working you too hard?" Betty was worried now.

"No," Hannah told her emphatically, "it's just, you know, church. It was my first time in a new place."

Betty turned back around in her seat. It was more than that she was sure, but this was not the time to deal with it. "So, did you get to talk to all the men, Steve?" she asked him.

"Mostly," he told her. "It was just good to have a visiting minister here. Ours are good, but having others brings a fresh perspective, especially if they are from one of the established communities."

"I like our young church," Betty informed him.

"I do, too," he said. "I guess we don't have the problems some of them do, either."

Hannah, riding in the back listening to them, was hoping they were correct. She desperately wanted a new start, but having to look at someone who looked like her past was not going to help. They might not act the same, but looking similar made things more difficult.

It was then that she got the courage to ask, "Who was the boy who led the *Praise Song*?"

"I don't know," Betty said without turning around. "That's the first time I saw him. Do you know him, Steve?"

"No," he said. "He came with the bishop, so he must have some stability. His name's Jake, Jake Byler, I think. Beyond that, no one seemed to know anything about him."

In the back seat, Hannah felt great relief flow over her. She would not have to see the boy every Sunday while she was here.

They were already pulling in the driveway when it occurred to Betty to wonder why Hannah had asked about the strange boy. *What is going on in that girl's mind anyway?* Betty was determined to find out soon.

## CHAPTER SEVENTEEN

IT WAS ALREADY ten o'clock and Betty was walking to the mailbox. The morning was well on its way, promising clear skies and warmth. Things were progressing well at the barn, and Hannah had the first two horses out on the trail with what looked like competent riders. At least this was what Betty hoped was the case, and she would check on them when she went back to the barn.

It was amazing how fast Hannah was catching on. She already knew how to saddle a horse, of course. Beyond that, her comments and suggestions were well accepted by the riders. Betty was sure it was going to be a good summer for all of them, and she was certain they could put the extra money to good use.

It was then that the thought, for the first time, really crossed her mind. *Why did Kathy send Hannah out here in the first place?* That train of thought had been there before, yet had not really been well processed up to this point. She paused on the way to the mailbox before resuming her steps. *I know my sister, and she usually does things with a reason. It would take a good one to send her daughter almost across the country. I know what she told me, but could there be more?*

Reaching the mailbox, she turned her concentration to

removing the mail, suspending the need for a conclusion for now. *Letters.* Her delight, which started at the first sign of one letter, now grew when it became obvious there were more. *There's one for me from Kathy, one for Hannah from her mother, and one for Hannah from — that's strange, it does not say.*

Puzzled, she turned the letter over. There was nothing on the back except their address — *in care of* — and Hannah's name on top. The writing was distinctly male, with clumsy scrawls as if the writer was trying hard, but the hand just wasn't working right.

*So there is more to this than I was told.* The conclusion came with blinding speed, cementing itself in her mind. *That's why Hannah is out here. She's running away from a boy.* Betty's mouth hung open at the implications. *Maybe Kathy and Roy don't want her seeing him and are hoping she will forget him with a summer out West. That must be it. That's why Hannah refused to show any interest in the boys yesterday. She's being true to her love.* Betty thrilled all the way to her toes. *My, and I'm in the middle of it. Oh, I have to be true to Kathy and Roy's wishes, but this is going to be hard.*

She held the letters tenderly. *Oh, what mighty things might be in a little letter like this? The years of love, the yearning to see each other.* She shivered. *Stop it, you goose,* she told herself. *You have to be on the right side of things. Hannah must not see this letter.*

Walking back to the house, Betty could not decide. Should she throw it away? Should she hide it for the time being until Hannah's feelings had begun to weaken? *Oh, it's too much for a poor soul like me. I'm just a simple goose. What am I to do?*

Hannah solved the problem by appearing suddenly

in front of her. In her fixation on the letters Betty had not been looking ahead of her. Now there was no time to hide anything. If she slipped the suspicious envelope behind her back or into her pocket, Hannah would see. How was she to do that anyway, since she had all of the mail in one hand, and didn't know, at the moment, which letter was which?

"Mail!" Hannah exclaimed cheerfully. "Anything from Mom?"

Betty made one last desperate attempt. "Have you got the other two horses off yet?"

"Yes, they just mounted and left." Hannah stood waiting expectantly.

"Well, there is one from your mother, and one for me from your mother, too."

Hannah held out her hand, a big smile on her face.

Betty wished with all her heart she knew which was which, but she did not. The result was that she had to look, and in looking Hannah also saw. "Oh," she said, "I have two of them? Who is the other one from?"

Betty looked at her sorrowfully. "You shouldn't be a bad girl like this."

Hannah could not have been more puzzled. "What do you mean?"

"You are seeing someone secretly, and your mother doesn't like it."

Hannah paled. *How does Betty know what happened? Did Mom just write her?* "Did Mom tell you?" she managed to get out.

"No," Betty told her, "I guessed it."

Hannah was puzzled again. How could Betty guess about Peter? "You guessed?" she asked.

"Yes. I did. Look at that letter. Isn't that the handwriting of a boy? A clumsy one, I must admit, but most boys are, especially when in love. Now I may be a dumb goose, but I can figure that out. I can also figure out that this is why you are really out here. Your mom wants to get you away from someone whom she does not like. Now isn't that right? That's why you were not interested in any boys at church yesterday, wasn't it? But then why you were asking about that strange boy? That's the only thing that doesn't make sense."

Hannah was at a complete loss for words. Where was she supposed to start? Most importantly, what did she want to say? Her mom was staying mum. Was that not the best way to keep it?

"I'm right? Am I not?" Betty asked triumphantly. "Now the question is how can I help your mother out? I thought of hiding the letter, but you didn't give me a chance."

"Ah," Hannah cleared her throat, "I can't really tell you why I am out here. There is a reason, but it's best kept quiet. If my mother ever tells you, then that's okay. But until then, I can't say. And as far as this letter being from a boy, I have no idea. Well, yes, I do have an idea that it's from Sam." Hannah looked closer at the letter. "Yes, that's who it's from."

"From Sam." Now Betty was confused. "He likes you?"

"I think so," Hannah said numbly.

"So that's why you are out here," Betty asserted, now changing gears. "It's your doing to get away from Sam, and your mother wants you to take him."

"I don't think so," Hannah said.

Betty was sure not going to be wrong twice in a row.

The other time had been way too much trouble. My, her heart still was pumping from the scare it gave her. This time she could be on Kathy's side without any problems, and she was not giving that up.

An inspiration came to her. "Look at your letter, and see if I'm not right."

"Which one, Sam's?" Hannah's face puckered up. "What will that prove?"

"No, your mother's."

"What will that show?"

"Just open it." Betty was putting all her eggs into this basket, her lips firmly pressed together. She had to be right.

Hannah slowly opened the letter and read out loud, "Dear Hannah, we are all missing you. Our weather is nice and sunny."

Betty interrupted, "Keep reading, on down, something about Sam."

Hannah scanned the page, then turned it over and read, "Who do you think I saw the day after you left?" Betty's face had a big smile on it. Hannah kept reading, "It was Sam. He looked so sorrowful when he asked for your address that I gave it to him. If he writes at least send him one letter back. Well, I must be going, love Mom."

"See." Betty was giddy. "There it is. Your mother wants you to see him. I knew it."

"I don't think it means what you think it does," Hannah protested.

"So what does it mean then?" Betty challenged her.

"He's got a crush on me, that's all. I don't like him at all."

"But you're trying to get away from him, right?"

"No," Hannah said, "that is not why I'm out here."

Betty smiled and held up her hand. "Look, I know how it is. You don't have to tell me. It's okay. But I think you really should consider this young man. If your mother likes him enough to give him your address, than I am all for it."

Hannah felt her mouth drop open. *Confound it.* She promptly shut it. *Am I never to get away from this boy?*

Betty was greatly encouraged by Hannah's actions and her silence. "You liked him in school," she proclaimed in another stroke of genius, something of a faint memory niggling at her brain.

"Yes," Hannah said angrily, "but that was when I was stupid."

"My, my," Betty said, "such an outburst! You do have it bad. I really think you ought to consider what your mother wants. Parents often know quite a bit about what's best for their children."

"Look, it's not what you think," Hannah said, trying to calm herself.

"Just remember," Betty said in a motherly way, "consider your mother's wishes. Now, I have to run, and you have the first riders coming back, I see."

With that Betty left Hannah standing in the middle of the yard while she bustled on towards the house.

Hannah walked toward the riders and took their horses from them as they dismounted. She then puzzled all day about whether to tell Betty about Peter, and what happened. She kept deciding against it. Things were best left alone, she determined. *But if mother wishes to share it with Betty, then it would be okay.*

In the meantime there was the letter from Sam to deal

with. She still had not opened it. The last riders left a little early at 3:30. Watching Prince and Mandy coming down the trail with them, Hannah had the overpowering urge to ride herself.

With that in mind she had left both of them tied up outside. Stroking Prince's neck, her hand hardly made an indentation in his muscles even when she pressed them firmly. Her love for this horse filled her again.

Running into the house she found Betty. "Will you come riding with me? I haven't had a chance yet, and the horses still have energy left."

"Ah, I can't do that," Betty told her. "I never was much of a rider."

"You don't know what you're missing. It's never too late to start."

Betty chuckled. "That's easy for you to say. Just don't stay out too late, and stay on the trail."

Hannah puckered up her face but took off running back out to the horses. Leading Mandy inside, she unsaddled her and led her through the gate to the pasture. Prince neighed to join her. "Now, now," Hannah told him, when she got back out, "you and I are going for a ride. Now isn't that going to be fun?"

He jerked his head up and down as if he were agreeing with her.

Glancing around to see that no cars were coming in the driveway, she went into the unused milking parlor to pull on, under her dress, an old pair of pants Betty had given her earlier. "In case you want to ride," Betty had told Hannah.

This was the proper attire of Amish girls on horseback. Yet Hannah was still slightly embarrassed, afraid that a car might still pull in while she was in the unused parlor. Hannah resolved in the future to wear the pants whenever she managed the rides. Betty would understand. That way, when she wanted to ride, she would be ready.

Now, properly attired, she swung on and took Prince up the trail. All around her the beauty of the country called to her. Once away from the buildings, the land rose to reveal the town in the distance and behind that the Cabinet mountains. To the North were more mountains, seeming to surround her with their vast ruggedness.

Now, well into late spring, they were no longer snow-capped as Betty had told her they were earlier. Summer was coming along, even here in the northwest corner of Montana.

Coming upon a wide river — Hannah assumed it was the Kootenai — she pulled Prince to a stop. This was where the sound of running water came from that occasionally reached her ears.

This was a huge river by eastern standards and Hannah drank in the sight of it. The hardy pines that grew everywhere descended the riverbank, in some places right up to the edge of the water. Rippling in its vigor, the water seemed in a great hurry to get where it was going.

Hannah knew the headwater was in Canada because Betty had told her that. She pondered how all that was possible. Water flowing in front of her had begun perhaps as a small trickle in the mountains of Canada. All of this from a mysterious place where she had never been.

Now it was here, going to unknown places, propelled by a power beyond itself. It was destined for the ocean, unless man, beast, or land diverted it first.

She patted Prince on the neck and leaned into his mane. The smell of horse soothed her mind. "What do you think, old boy?" she asked him out loud.

He lifted his head towards the river, neighing sharply. "Do you have friends around here?" she asked him again.

Jerking his head back and forth, he arched his neck. "Do you see something?" she asked again.

Glancing up and down each bank of the river, she could see nothing. *Maybe he smells something.* Hannah decided it was nothing to worry about as she headed along the river, going north away from town.

Before long the trail opened up to reveal a flat plateau along the bank. Rocks were jumbled on the riverside with a steep bank down to the water, but up to where the foothill started again it was flat. The land was level for a long stretch into the distance. "Ah," she exclaimed, "let's go, Prince!"

He seemed to understand as she gave him his head. Bending low on his neck to avoid the wind, she rose in the stirrups and rode with complete abandonment. His hooves pounded on the trail, his stride smooth as he galloped in great bounds.

She shouted aloud in sheer joy, her heart opening itself wide. It seemed as if there was no evil anywhere that could touch this. For one glorious moment, she could forget that anything else existed besides her and Prince and this wonderful world.

Pulling on the reins, she drew him in, laughing, until the sound of her voice made her remember. There were problems that needed to be faced, and this might be the exact place to start.

"Well," she told Prince, her voice still ringing with happiness, "that was very good. Now let's just stand here and let me look at some of my troubles."

Pulling the letter from Sam out of her pocket, she looked at it. It didn't look quite as threatening as it had before. Shaking the envelope so that the contents slid to one end, she pondered the situation. *Why not just throw the thing away without opening it? Why do I want to see his letter? Why spoil this joy?*

Prince stretched his neck out towards the ground and blew his nose. "See," she told him, "that's what you would do, wouldn't you? Right?"

But what would her mother want her to do? She had given Sam her address. Did she also think it was a good idea that he wrote her? Betty was sure she did, but was it really true?

Hannah could ask, she supposed, but that did not help now. On second thought, she decided not to ask. That would be foolish, she figured. Her mother might not want to tell, lest it influence her own decision. That would be like her mother. Probably Betty was right.

*Is this not too early to be thinking of boys anyway?* She wished she could forget about the whole thing, but boys somehow just didn't seem to go away.

*Do you want them to go away?* Hannah asked herself.

She pondered the question. *Maybe not.* It would be wonderful to be loved, but in the right way this time. That was it. She had done it wrong. Now it must be done right, and would it not feel a lot better to be seeing someone her parents approved of?

Maybe Sam should be examined closer, open mouth and all, especially if her mother thought so. She laughed out loud at the thought. Out here, sitting on Prince, with the mountains all around her, Sam's open mouth did not seem so serious at the moment. She supposed he kept it shut sometimes.

*Maybe he can learn to keep it closed,* her thoughts suggested.

"Maybe," she muttered to Prince. He twitched his ear as if a fly had landed on it, but she didn't notice a fly.

Sighing, Hannah tore open one end of the envelope and put the piece of paper she tore off into her pocket.

## Chapter Eighteen

THE SUN HAD set behind the Cabinet Mountains. At this hour there were still traces of its presence in the evening sky. Jake sat in his cabin having just finished his meager supper of bean soup out of a can. He found himself longing for his mother's cooking. She would never fix soup out of a can, at least not for supper.

The day had seen its share of visitors come past his outpost. Most of them were younger or middle-aged people who were into the hiking thing. Occasionally a vehicle made the climb to his cabin with an older couple who wanted to see but not hike that high. He took time out for all of them and let them climb the tower if they wished. Those were the instructions he was under.

"We are the employees of the public, so show them every courtesy," he had been told in training. "Only in times of a crisis, when the tower is needed, is it to be off limits to the public."

Today there had been no fires to report, but Jake was still tired. Not sure whether it was all the people who had come past, or just tired of thinking, he stretched his legs out on the kitchen chair. Not able to stop himself, he pondered some more.

Before him was the notepad on which he intended to write his parents. It was high time he did, plus there was good news to report. He had found and visited an Amish church.

Pushing his fatigue and negative thoughts aside, he started:

Dear Mom and Dad,

Greetings in the name of Christ our Savior. I am happy to report that I have found an Amish church and I attended it on Sunday. I spent the night at the bishop's house. His name is Nisley. He knew my grandfather, and took me in very well.

On Sunday morning, they even asked me to lead the Praise Song. They are just a small group, but very friendly. I have plans to attend there at least every other Sunday. Hopefully this will be okay.

The peanut butter tasted strange. Not that it was bad or anything. Maybe they don't use the same syrup as back home. They have a bunch of boys in the young folks, but not much of any youth activities.

Your Son,

Jake Byler

Twiddling his pen Jake contemplated his letter. A great desire came over him to ask about her. Did he dare? It would just be embarrassing, he decided. If anything had changed they would no doubt have let him know, hoping it would bring him home. That would be important enough to write about immediately.

*She's probably already planning her wedding.* Anger mixed with pain as the thought surged through him. He rose from the table and paced the floor. *How could she do something like that? Did she not care anything for me? What of all the times she said she loved me? Was that just made up?*

Not only did his heart hurt from thinking about it, his head did also. *It's no use,* he told himself. *You have to forget it.*

He rose from the table and walked over to look out the window at the valley. His thoughts were not on its beauty. *But it will be a long time before I trust anyone else. They'd sure better not even look or act like her.*

This he resolved firmly, and then he sealed the letter and dropped it in the box for pickup the next time someone went down to Libby.

❧

Sitting there in the saddle on Prince, Hannah slid her fingers into the envelope and extracted the letter. Holding it gingerly, as if it might bite her, she opened it. Prince shifted his weight beneath her and lifted his head high into the air.

"Easy, boy," she told him. "Let's see what this says."

Dear Hannah,

I suppose you will be surprised at a letter from me. It is just that I could not help myself from writing to you.

I wondered how it would be with you gone. I miss you a lot already. I saw your mother in town and asked for your address. I hope you are doing well. Montana is a big state, I think. Don't get lost in it.

I would very much like to write some more

to you while you are gone. Would this be okay? It might make the time go faster for me, and if you would write what you are doing that would be interesting as well.

So long,

Sam Knepp


"There it is," she pronounced loudly, although no one could hear her. "The monster himself. Now what shall we do with him? Mommy's love and Aunt's perfection, yet shall he be mine?"

She threw her head back and laughed at her poetry. Out here things like this letter did not look that serious. But life was not all like it was out here, was it? She sighed.

Prince looked back at her, turning his head as if mildly interested.

"You have no idea what is going on, Mr. Prince," she told him. "Your little horse life is not complicated at all. Just ride when you're told, and eat when you're hungry. Hmmm, what a life! Is that not right, Prince?"

Since Prince gave no answer, she turned back to her thoughts. *Oh, to dream, or not to dream? That is the question, now is it not? Yet no more dreaming for you, Hannah. No more wonder boys who charm you. Now it's time to do what's right. Try the other path, the one mother wants.*

"Well, Mr. Prince," she asked, "are you going to write the letter? Of course not," she answered herself. "That falls on me, the one who needs to do penance for her sins. Oh, if I had never strayed from the path, then this would not have awaited me." She sighed again. "But I must bear my burden, take my cross and follow the best I can."

Now the emotions turned in her, and a tear trickled down her face, as Prince neighed in sympathy.

"You understand," she told him, looking down to pat him on the neck. "Of course not. Don't be silly," she said to herself. "He's just a horse."

Now it dawned on her that the sun was setting and it was time to go back. Not in any mood to gallop, she still urged Prince into a run to save time. It was suddenly later than she had realized. When the riverbed narrowed out of its wide plain, she had to slow down, taking the rest of the way at a trot.

"Where were you?" a worried Betty called out of the kitchen door when she came in from putting Prince up.

"Time got away from me, I guess," she told her. "I was thinking some things through."

"Any decisions?" Betty asked, her curiosity bubbling to the surface.

"I'm going to write him back," she half muttered.

Betty was not to be deterred. "Would that be to Sam?"

Hannah nodded, "Yes."

Betty gushed, "Oh, that's such a wonderful name, so full of meaning and purpose. Does he have a lot of money? Your mother will be so happy."

"He's going to inherit the farm," Hannah said scornfully.

"Oh my, that's nothing to sneeze at," Betty proclaimed. "You don't have to look down on that."

"I'm just writing a letter," Hannah told her.

"You never know," Betty said with a broad smile. "Little things lead to big things. Remember your mother likes him."

"I will try," Hannah said half-heartedly, as she headed for her room.

~

Hannah began her letter, "Dear Sam ... ."

Then she went on to give the general news of her trip and what was going on around her. Coming to the end, she told him what he really wanted to hear.

"I guess writing would be okay, for now. I don't know how often I can, but I will try."

Then signed it simply, "Hannah."

After that, she could not resist it. It was too tempting. Carefully she drew a little smiley face after her name. *That would do it,* she told herself, the mirth from earlier in the evening returning.

In her mind, Hannah saw Sam's mouth drop open as plain as day. *My, oh my, we will have to do something about that, though. Maybe he can be trained.*

*Stop it, stop it,* she almost shouted to herself. *You are just writing a letter. Just a letter,* she repeated, and she sealed and addressed it to go out with tomorrow's post.

~

That night for the first time, Hannah dreamed of Peter. It was a moonless night again, but there was an awful roar in the air. She was out with him on the roof of her home in Indiana, leaves and branches flying all around them. In the distance great flashes of light came and went. She clung to the roof in terror, while he bravely walked around calling to her to come. She tried to find the courage, knowing she had done this many times before, but the strength was not in her to move.

From there she was suddenly in his car, without having climbed off the roof, speeding along a gravel road, the wind whistling through the open window. She was rigid with fear, clutching the handle bar above the window. "Stop, stop," she screamed to him, but he only told her to be brave. Now blue and yellow light was everywhere as they raced along in the night.

Her father's face appeared above her, through the car windshield, telling her to come home, but she could not get Peter to stop the car. His voice hovered, calling her name.

Hannah finally got herself awake, sure that her moaning was being heard somewhere by someone in the house. Trembling under the covers in fright, she knew she needed to do something.

Finally, getting the courage to slide out onto the floor, she got onto her knees. There, with the night air from her open windows blowing around her, she begged God to forgive her and to never let her dream about this again.

"I will listen to Mom and Dad from now on, I promise," she said very quietly, supposing that saying it out loud was better than just thinking it.

"Just give me the strength to walk away from my own ways of doing things. Help me, please."

She stayed there until peace came over her, and she was able to return to bed and fall asleep.

❦

Sam got Hannah's letter three days later. Controlling himself, he gingerly pulled it out of the pile of mail his mother had left on the kitchen table. If this was truly who he thought it was, he was a man now and must act accordingly.

"Is somebody writing to you?" his mother, Laura, called from the living room where she was ironing.

Sam did not respond, wanting to see the letter first. All was quiet as he cut open the end of the envelope and slid out the piece of paper. It was all a little too much for him, but he took in the contents calmly with a sweep of his eyes. At least he did on the outside.

It was from her. The gentle feminine sweep of the words on the paper told him so. Her name at the end confirmed it. He rubbed his forehead. That Hannah was writing him should not come as a surprise, he told himself. He had asked her to write, but he knew deep, deep down at the bottom of his heart that it nevertheless was a surprise.

He had gone on sacred ground, holding out his hand to a beautiful blossom. Straining, he now had touched it. *Was that too much to suppose?* He pondered the question, not coming to any conclusion. Then Sam read the letter in total.

"Is somebody writing to you?" his mother repeated her question from the kitchen door. "I guess someone did," she answered the question herself when she noticed Sam with his head down, pouring over the words.

Sam read quietly all the news Hannah was writing about to him, including her trip out there and Prince, the new horse, and how much she loved him. At the end came the news he really wanted to know, and the conclusion to what he thought was the purpose of this one letter. She was, indeed, going to write more and he could write to her.

The smiley face Hannah had drawn struck him to his

heart, sending emotions all the way through. His face, though, was sober and his mouth was closed. He was thinking hard. A girl was writing to him. Not just any girl, but Hannah Miller — the one from school who used to smile at him, but after that would have nothing to do with him. The world almost changed colors in front of him, the living room window glass doing strange things to his eyes, as his mind processed the information. He could barely grasp the fact that it was true. She was writing to him. Hannah Miller was writing to him.

Sam shook his head and walked out to where his mother was still ironing. Her ironing board stood on the living room floor and it creaked as she ran the iron across it. On one side, she had the stack of ironed clothing, and, on the other, the basket still to be ironed. "Hannah wrote me," he told her.

"Hannah Miller?" she asked, raising her eyebrows.

"Yes," he said.

"How did that happen?" she wanted to know.

"I wrote to her," he said simply.

"It is just one letter, though?"

"No," he said, "we are writing."

"Really?" she asked, many questions obviously in her voice. "Are you sure you are up to a girl like that?"

"By God's help," he said, "and Dad is giving me the farm someday."

"Well, yes," she agreed, "but I'm kind of surprised."

"I was hoping," he said, and, with that, Sam firmly squared his shoulders. "I want to be a good man for her."

"Aren't you moving a little fast?" she asked him.

"No," he shook his head, "she's writing me."

## CHAPTER NINETEEN

On Sunday morning, Hannah sat with Betty and the other women for the services. This was simply a whim of hers for this one Sunday. It would hardly be looked at well for a girl her age to be sitting with the married women. Once firmly an old maid, perhaps, but that time was not anywhere near.

For now, however, Hannah was enjoying the company of the older women. It took some of the awkwardness out of having to sit with girls much younger than she. The real reason, though, was that it removed her farther from the boys on the second row. Not that they were a threat, but she felt like she stuck out sitting there with the younger girls. Having another Sunday to get used to being the only girl her age was a welcome relief.

Hannah thought of the one boy to herself as *Mr. Scarred Logger.* His real name was Ben Stoll. He came from a good family, she supposed. It was just that she felt no interest in him at all. That he had an interest in her was the foregone conclusion, she thought. Hannah had already decided that his options were probably not that many, or that his knowledge base of what he really wanted that wide. That this thinking might be snobbish or condescending on her part did not cross her mind. It was simply the way things were.

No, this boy was not a problem to her. No dreams were threatening on the horizon to torment her conscience. Yet would he ask to drive her home? Yes, she figured he would. The impression was so strong that she made a note to tell Betty that it was "No" before he even asked. That would be if he approached either Steve or Betty to serve as an intermediary. But then he might just ask her instead of going through either of them.

Well then, Hannah would simply have to deal with it. She was writing to someone. That would serve as a good enough excuse and prevent too many hurt feelings, she supposed. That course of action appealed to her. Why not do it before anyone asked? Have the word passed around by a select mentioning of the fact by Betty.

It was a good plan, and she would run it by Betty when they were at home this afternoon. Now, though, it was time to look like she was singing along instead of thinking on other things. So she joined in.

*At least I don't have to deal with someone who reminds me of Peter. Well, he doesn't really look like Peter. That was just my imagination. There was just enough resemblance to bring back the memory of Peter. That's what it was,* she told herself.

Since Sunday school was being held today instead of a main church service, the ministers were not upstairs in conference. Bishop Nisley had gotten up right after the singing ended to read a scripture and had then dismissed them for classes.

Hannah followed the youth filing upstairs to the open foyer area that served as their temporary classroom. All of the bedrooms had been designated for use by classes for the younger children.

Bishop Nisley was the youth teacher. This suited Hannah, especially since she was the only girl. Although some bishops did not have a comforting presence to her, she thought that Bishop Nisley did.

The whole church, except the children's classes, followed the same text, and today the selection was the tenth chapter of Proverbs. It was read in High German, not in their common language of Pennsylvania Dutch. The first verse caught Hannah's attention: "Ein kluger Sohn macht ein froher Vater; aber ein dummer Sohn ist die Last seiner Mutter." (A wise son maketh a glad father; but a foolish son is the burden of his mother.)

Bishop Nisley went on to explain that this verse applied not just to sons but to daughters as well. Obedience to one's parents was a staple requirement of the Christian life. One should always honor one's mother and father.

Hannah drank it all in and resolved to apply this to her life. She would do what her mother wished. Betty would help her, and she would get it done. Wisdom was what she wanted very badly, and here was a chance to get it.

Just before the class was dismissed, Bishop Nisley took the time to announce that a youth gathering was planned at his place for the next Saturday. "We don't have many youth," he explained, "and only one hymn singing a month. Now we have Hannah with us for the summer, and Jake will be down every other Sunday," he said. "Since next Sunday is the planned hymn singing, we can have an extended youth weekend."

The boys were smiling and nodding their heads. Hannah was sure she looked pale. Was not Jake the name of the boy she did not want to see? She was sure that was what Betty had said. So he was coming in every two weeks? Focusing hard, she hoped no one noticed the confusion on her face.

The class dismissed, everyone gathered together again, with the whole group going over the text one more time. Here, only the men spoke. In a mixed congregation during a church service, it was considered inappropriate for a woman to speak.

No lunch is served after such a Sunday-school Sunday, so after some talking, people were getting ready to leave. Betty seemed ready to go, so Hannah went to gather her shawl and bonnet in the front entrance. It was then that *Mr. Logger* came in from the main part of the house. Since she was caught alone in a crowded house, she figured either he had timed his appearance well, or the women were giving him room. Hannah suspected it was the latter. *Probably they were helping one of their own find a girl.*

Aloud Hannah said, "Hi."

He stood there, towering over her by nearly a foot, 200 pounds of muscle and scars turned into blushing redness, his hat literally in his hands. "Do you need a ride to the youth gathering on Saturday night?" he asked.

Hannah was not going to make it easy for him. A part of her thought he needed toughening up for later encounters with his true love. "Not really," she told him. "Betty and Steve can take me."

He cleared his throat; obviously this tree was not going to fall without the direct application of the saw. "I would like to take you."

"That's nice of you," she told him, looking straight at his face, "but I'm already writing somebody."

"Oh." He was rapidly gathering his wits about him. "I'm sorry. I didn't know."

"That's okay," she told him. "You wouldn't have known."

"Well, okay," he nodded in conclusion. Then he put his hat on and reached for the doorknob. He opened the door and was gone.

The women seated in the living room turned to catch a glimpse of him leaving. "Do you think Ben had any success?" Bishop Nisley's wife, Elizabeth, asked those assembled.

"Not from the look on his face," Barbara Yoder, the wife of one of the younger men, said quickly.

"I could have told you," Betty spoke up sagely. "Hannah's already writing to someone, but I didn't want to make up her mind for her."

"Oh, she is?" The disappointment was audible in the chorus of voices. "Who is he?"

"I've not seen him," Betty told them, enjoying the attention on such an important matter as this. "His name is Sam. She got a letter from him this week already."

"They must be really serious then," Elizabeth said. "That's kind of soon."

"It sounds like it," Betty told them. "Her mother, Kathy, is all for it."

On the buggy ride home, Betty spoke to Hannah from the front seat. "That was a good girl today, Hannah."

"I didn't want him," Hannah retorted.

"I know," Betty smiled. "It is just good practice. Keep saying 'no' to everything else. You're writing, remember?"

"Would you stop talking in riddles?" Steve demanded. "What are you two talking about?"

"Oh, nothing," Betty told him. "I just couldn't wait to get home to tell her that."

"Really?" Steve raised his eyebrows, slapping the reins of the horse. There was no use digging deeper right now. She would not tell him in front of everyone anyway. If he felt like it, he would inquire later. That was not likely though, he supposed. It was no doubt just women's talk which would not interest him.

❧

Jake had no way of knowing about the planned youth gathering when he arrived at Bishop Nisley's on Saturday around three.

"It's at six o'clock," Elizabeth told him, "after supper, of course. We're having popcorn and cider, and, of course, volleyball."

"Are there enough youth to make a team?" Jake wanted to know.

"Probably not," she told him, "but some of the married folk come, too. We have to come, you know. There aren't enough young people."

"You play, too?" Jake asked, a dubious look on his face.

"Now, now," she said, "don't be down on us old folks. We used to grow up playing volleyball."

"I guess you're not too old," he ventured. "Just the bishop thing makes you think old."

"Well," Elizabeth said, "church does weigh down on John sometimes, but we haven't had it too bad. The people around here are real nice. Of course, being a young church helps, I think. People try harder to get along when there's only a few of us."

Jake nodded.

"There's also the Sunday night *singing* this weekend. Do you think you can stay for that?"

That caused Jake to ponder hard. It was important that he stay, he was sure, but how was he to get back to work by Monday morning early? "I'm not sure," he finally said. "I need to be back at the cabin for work by five the next morning."

"Maybe something can be worked out," Elizabeth suggested. "We rarely have visiting young people for the singings. It would be a real treat."

Jake was still not sure how he would be able to stay, but this definitely needed to be worked on. Other than his desire to attend there was the matter of how it would look if he did not stay. That was a big concern. Things were already being pushed to the limit by his job so that he did not need any disgruntled feelings on the part of the church people who lived here. "I will ask John about it," he told her.

A few minutes later John appeared and asked whether Jake would help him set up the volleyball net.

"Certainly," Jake told him, getting up to follow John outside.

Together they pushed John's two buggies outside to use as end posts. Laying the net out on the ground to judge the distance, they parked the buggies, one on either side of the net. Then they lifted the net to tie the strings around the middle of the buggies. Once that was done, they used pieces of logs under one side of the buggy wheels to give added height.

John's single buggy was not much of a problem to lift, but the surrey required both of them on each wheel, while they pushed the log blocks in place with their feet. Once this had been done they retightened the strings on the net and pulled the top of the net level with the top of the buggies. The result was Amish to the core, two tilted buggies on wood blocks, holding a volleyball net taut. The fact that this worked was the main thing since how it looked was not important.

As they stood there examining their handiwork, Jake brought up the subject of Sunday night. "Elizabeth says you are having a hymn singing this weekend."

"Yes," John told him, "we really would like to have you stay. There are so few youth the way it is. We might as well make the most out of your summer with us."

"How do I get back in time for work on Monday?" Jake asked him. "I usually use Sunday afternoons to get back up the mountain."

"We'll think of something," John assured him. "There are a few of the Mennonite people who come to our hymn sings. I will personally see that I ask one of them. If that doesn't work, there are English drivers we can hire to take you back."

"That would be kind of expensive, wouldn't it?" Jake asked.

"Yes," John agreed, "it would be. Let's just hope one of the Mennonites can do it."

Jake agreed, as this was simply a risk he would have to take. It was that important. Missing the Sunday night *hymn sing* as a visiting young fellow was apparently not an option around here.

Elisabeth opened the kitchen door behind them to call out that supper was ready.

"Well, we'd better go eat before the crowd gets here," John chuckled, heading for the house with Jake following.

## CHAPTER TWENTY

BACK IN INDIANA on a sunny Saturday afternoon, Sam was upstairs preparing to write his next letter. There in his sparse room — a bed, a chair by the window, and an old oak cabinet handed down from past generations — he pondered things long and hard. He felt that his next letter or two could be a watershed of sorts, and so they needed to be just right. Pen poised, he took his time to compose it.

Downstairs the door to the outside kept swinging open and slamming shut. The only thing he heard was the slamming with no running feet back and forth on the living room floor. It must be his younger brother, he decided, standing on the front porch amusing himself. The sound was a sore distraction to this concentration, but he doubted if it would do much good to try to stop it.

His mother would side with his younger brother and not with him. Plus, going downstairs might reveal his letter writing work. She still seemed uncertain about his venture with Hannah, even when he had repeatedly reassured her that he felt it was the right thing to do.

It was time to write the next letter, distractions or no distractions. Confidently he began.

Dear Hannah,

Christian Greetings in our Lord and Savior's name. I received your welcome letter. The news was very interesting. Things around here are about the same as always.

Sam filled in some more details about the youth gatherings and the general community news before getting to the important part.

I am so glad we are writing. I guess it is second best to seeing you. I look forward to that when you come back.

My feelings are really strong about this. I see it as the right thing, the way our lives have crossed so many times before. I am still sorry for hurting you that night of the game at your place. Yet, God works in mysterious ways, and I cannot but see his hand guiding us together.

My joy is great that you see it also. I will wait for your next welcome letter.

Yours truly,
Sam Knepp

Sam sealed the envelope and got it ready for Monday's mail. It would not do to place it downstairs with the regular mail. Something this important needed to be personally handled. Too many things could go wrong.

❧

Hannah stood in the yard with Prince that afternoon,

stroking his neck while he looked out towards the road as if expecting someone to come pulling in the driveway. The summer weather was an absolute delight — warm, with no sign of the humidity of the east. Over at the Nisleys, Jake was just arriving for the weekend.

Prince perked up his ears as a car passed on the road, but there was no sign that it was stopping. Hannah decided there must be a break in the stream of riders. Seeing the opportunity to ride with Prince, Hannah took the chance. "I'm going for a ride," she stuck her head in the kitchen door to tell Betty, before heading out.

"Be careful and be back in time for the youth gathering tonight."

"Yes," Hannah spoke through the screen door to the kitchen where Betty was preparing something to eat for Sunday. *It must be for supper,* Hannah thought, since this was the Sunday when the meal was served after church.

Stroking Prince's long neck again before mounting, Hannah told him what a wonderful horse he was. "You are a beauty," she said as she stepped into the stirrup.

He bounced his head as if eager to start out.

Letting him walk until they got to the river, Hannah was overcome again with the beauty and grandeur of this land. The water of the Kootenai seemed to be flowing faster than it had been the last time she was here, the ripples pronounced even out in the middle of the wide body of water.

"It looks wild," she told Prince. "Of course, all of this country is wild."

She breathed in deeply, exulting in the joy that filled her. Turning Prince north, Hannah reached the plateau along the river and let Prince have his head. They galloped, the wind whistling past her face, until she pulled back on his reins. As he slowed down, she threw her head back and laughed for the sheer joy of it. Prince snorted loudly as if to join in her exuberance.

"You're a good horse," she told him, turning him around. "Now, let's trot back. One run like that is enough for you, I think. You have worked hard all day already."

Going back Hannah noticed the sheer blue of the sky above her. It opened as if one giant expanse of the heavens, going on and on, into forever. A few fluffy clouds hung on the horizon, but the rest was just blue and more blue.

"God is really something," she told Prince. "How did He make all of this? Then He made you and me, and He makes it all work together. Well, unless we mess it up, of course." Hannah patted him on the neck, "I don't mean you, Prince. You are just a horse. People mess things up. Look at me, and what I have done already. A real mess, I would say. I really want to straighten it out, though, and be a good girl. Do you think I'll make a good wife for Sam, Prince?"

Prince simply trotted along and said nothing.

"Sam? I guess it is a nice name, like Betty said, but doesn't it take more than a nice name? Doesn't there have to be love? See, Prince, there I go again, dreaming on and on. Of course, Sam will love me. The best way really, I guess, in the way that a farmer loves his wife. We will grow old together working the land, with a dozen children probably. I'm sure Sam wants that many. To help on the farm, I would say. Little old me, I'll just be a farmer's wife for sure. Do you think God wants that, Prince? He wants me to obey my parents, don't you think?"

This time Prince jerked his neck.

"I thought so," Hannah told him, urging him on a little faster lest they arrive late back at the house.

Once back at the barn, she pulled the saddle off of Prince's back and turned him out into the pasture behind the barn. "That's it for the week," she told him. "Enjoy your break, because it's back at it on Monday morning, I'm sure."

"I need some help," Betty called to her from the house.

"Coming," Hannah hollered back as she hurried into the house.

"Carry this out to the buggy for me, would you?" Betty pointed towards a plastic bucket. "Popcorn," she offered, at Hannah's look. "Everyone brings something. If there's too much, we just bring it back home."

"Okay," Hannah nodded. That was not unusual, just all these married folks involved in the youth gatherings was. "Will there be a lot of the married people there?" she asked.

"No," Betty told her, "just a few. Not everyone can come, of course. It's kind of informal I suppose, but it suits our purposes at this time. Maybe someday when we have a lot of young people it will be different." Her face brightened at the idea. "Maybe you and Sam want to move out here. You like the country, don't you?"

"You forget that he's to inherit his father's farm. That kind of locks things in, I suppose."

"Yes, that would," Betty allowed. "It would be so nice, though, to have more young couples living here. We've never had a wedding out here yet."

"Don't look at me," Hannah told her. "I can't change the way things are."

"That's true," Betty agreed, "we each have to be where God wants us to be."

Hannah nodded as she headed for the door with the bucket of popcorn. "Who is bringing the cider?" she asked as the thought occurred to her.

"The Nisleys supply that, I think. We have to buy it in town, though. None of the Amish have an orchard. That is up to now. We really need to look into it. They make some of the best fresh cider around her."

"Better than in Indiana?" Hannah wanted to know.

"Without question, and that's spoken as one who is loyal to Indiana."

Hannah chuckled. "I believe you, but we'll see tonight, I guess."

The sound of horses being hitched outside reminded them of the time, and Hannah that she still was holding the bucket of popcorn. "I guess I can take this out now when we go," she told Betty.

"I'm coming," Betty told her, going to call the children as Hannah waited for her. Together they headed for the buggy and the ride to the Nisleys.

Jake was still lingering at the supper table with John, talking about his job with the forest service. The two small children of the household had left to go outside. John took the opportunity to ask what had been stirring his curiosity. "Are you dating?" he abruptly changed the subject from the forest service job.

"No," Jake told him without looking up from his plate.

Elizabeth, coming in from the kitchen to gather up the supper dishes, overheard the question. "Are you sure that's your business?" she asked her husband, chuckling.

"Not really," he said. "I'm just curious."

It was Jake who volunteered the information. Maybe it was the safe atmosphere of their home, or just that he was lonesome from all the hours alone on the mountain. "There was someone," Jake told them.

"Oh." Elisabeth stopped with a stack of dirty plates in her hands. "Was it serious?"

"Yes," Jake said, "very serious. Almost married, in fact — three months away." The pain in his voice was obvious.

"Oh," Elisabeth said again, "that does hurt. But you want to be sure it's the right one."

"I thought it was," Jake told her.

"We can be wrong sometimes," she said. "The ways of God are not our ways."

John nodded his head, "That's right."

"I don't trust girls now," Jake continued. "She gave me no warning at all. Granted that I was stupid, but it was because I trusted her. It was just over, like that. Now she's dating my cousin right there in front of me."

"You really loved her?" Elisabeth asked, sympathy in her voice.

Jake simply nodded.

"Still, it's better if you find out now. That's what dating is for, I guess," she offered.

"God has His ways," John offered. "We must learn to trust Him and not become bitter."

Jake numbly nodded his agreement. Not that his feelings agreed, but his head did.

The first of the buggies started arriving, and the volleyball game was quickly organized. Until enough players arrived it was a hit or miss knocking of the ball across the net, but it soon turned into a fierce competition of opposing teams.

Hannah was not sure how it would go with this strange boy around who reminded her of Peter. But he ended up on the opposite team from her, which helped a lot.

Two games later, they broke for popcorn and cider. The women, headed up by Elisabeth and Betty, brought out the heaping bowls of white fluffy stuff.

"Bring up the picnic table," Elisabeth told John, who was just winding down from playing. "If we set it up under the tree it should be okay since no wind is blowing."

John agreed and asked Steve to help him move the table. Together they carried it from the barn overhang to where Elisabeth wanted it.

Once the table was in place, she set the bowls of popcorn on it, with smaller bowls scattered around in which individual portions could be served. Betty went back into the house and returned with the cider which was also set up so it could be poured out as needed into glasses.

Seeing that the women were ready, John announced, "Let's have prayer." He then led out in thanks for the food that was before them and finished by asking for the grace and mercy of God to be with them for the rest of the evening.

The boys filled their bowls with popcorn first and then splashed cider into their glasses, spilling generous amounts onto the picnic table, although no one seemed to mind. Hannah went next, at Elisabeth's insistence. "You are our honored guest," she said. "It is not every day we have a girl your age visiting us for the summer."

"Is that good or bad?" Hannah asked with a chuckle.

"Good, of course, even if she's writing to someone already."

"How did you know that?" Hannah asked quickly and looked around to see who else had heard the comment. All the males seemed busy, and the boys were again knocking the ball back and forth across the net, their bowls of popcorn and glasses now abandoned in the grass.

"Oh, a little birdie told me," Elisabeth said, looking in Betty's direction.

"You did not!" Hannah exclaimed in mock horror, but partly serious, in spite of pretending not to be.

"I couldn't help it," Betty protested. "It just came out. It seemed like they should know. It's good news, is it not?"

Hannah smiled, not sure what to say. They took her hesitation as a sign of love's sweet work, and turned the conversation quickly to other women's subjects to spare her any further embarrassment.

Taking a deep swallow from her glass of apple cider, Hannah was amazed. It was better than Indiana cider!

## Chapter Twenty-One

Sam's dad, Enos, had wanted to talk with Sam ever since Laura had told him about Sam writing to Hannah. Tonight he got the chance when he and Sam were alone in the living room. Enos did not mind Laura overhearing the conversation, but he did not want the other children to hear what they were discussing. The opportunity now presented itself since they were playing outside at the moment.

"Mom said you are writing to Hannah Miller," Enos started the conversation.

Sam looked up from the *Farmer's Almanac* he was reading to nod his head.

"Do you think it's something serious?"

"Yes," Sam said this time. "It's pretty serious, I would say." Then he asked, "Do you not like her, Dad?"

"No, no, it's not that," Enos quickly told him. "She's a good girl as far as I know. She comes from a good family. I was just wondering if Hannah's right for you. It seems to me that a real nice farm girl would be the way to go."

"Hannah knows how to farm," Sam protested.

"Well, maybe she does," Enos said, "but her father's only a part-time farmer. He doesn't seem to make a good enough go of it to stay home full-time. He has that job at the factory now."

Sam was not happy with where this conversation was going. "What has that got to do with Hannah?"

"It might reflect on her since she is not being brought up on the farm. I'm just concerned about you. When we leave you the farm," he motioned towards Laura working out in the kitchen, "you will need a wife who was raised on a farm. You'll need a wife who knows what it's like to get up early, milk cows, and put up hay in the hot sun. Farm life is hard. You know that, Sam. Just make sure you choose wisely. That's all I'm saying."

Sam nodded soberly. "I will think about it, but I really feel that this is the right thing to do. Maybe when Hannah comes back from Montana she could come over to visit, of course." Sam waved his hand around as if to indicate the more than 200 acres of the farm. "We can make sure that she is comfortable with what life is like here."

"That would be wise," Enos allowed, "but you also need to keep your eyes open. Don't let feelings of love, or her beauty, blind your eyes. You will always regret it, even if she is a decent girl."

"I will consider it," Sam assured his father. "Maybe once you see more of her, you can tell me what you think."

"When is Hannah coming home?"

"I don't know for sure," Sam told him. "I think by the end of summer."

"There is another thing I wanted to talk with you about," Enos told him. "This would be whenever you get to the point of marriage, and I don't mean any specific girl, but just marriage in general. I'm not quite ready to retire, but I was thinking of building a smaller house down the road, on our acreage, of course. It would eventually serve as our *daudy haus*. Until I am ready to retire, you and your wife could use it."

"How soon were you thinking of building it?" Sam wanted to know.

"Are you in such a big hurry?" Enos chuckled.

"You never know how things work out," Sam acknowledged. "I haven't asked her yet, although I think it will come to that. We're just writing."

"It is serious then." Enos pondered the situation. "I don't think we can do anything for at least two years. If you should marry before that, I guess you could move in with us. There is a large upstairs bedroom. That might work for six months or so. Not much more than that. They say two women in the house, no matter how well they like each other, never works for long. I hold to that opinion also."

Sam nodded his head as if to say that this was fair enough, and went back to his *Farmer's Almanac*.

Enos got up and went to the kitchen. After making sure he was out of earshot, he approached Laura. "Sam's really serious about this girl."

"I'm afraid so," Laura told him.

"Do you think she's the right one for him?" he asked.

"Look," she told him. "We never made decisions for any of our other children, other than that they had to be in the church and all. Looks like they turned out all right. We'd better do the same for this one, don't you think?"

"I suppose so," he agreed. "I guess I'm just getting jumpy in my old age."

"Ah," she chuckled, "you're still young."

"I am?" he asked. "I wish I was, but we must trust and place this into God's hands."

"This is true," she said, and they left the matter at that.

As the sun set, another side had been picked for the volleyball game. Hannah could not help but notice that this time Jake was on the same side as she was.

Although darkness was threatening, they hoped it would be light enough for one more game. Bishop Nisley brought out two gas lanterns just in case. Lighting them, he placed one on top of each buggy. Their hiss added atmosphere to the game, but at this point, it was still light enough that they affected little else.

The boy who had picked the team on which Hannah found herself was also in charge of the playing line-up for the game. He instructed her to play between Bishop Nisley and Jake. Her heart sank at this, but there was nothing that could be done about it.

Self-consciously Hannah took her place. John was on her left and Jake on her right. Jake's nearness bothered her a lot. Although now that she was really close to him, she could tell that her early impression that he looked like Peter had indeed been mistaken. Jake was a unique person.

From what Hannah could tell from the corner of her eye, Jake appeared to be relaxed as he stood there. Taller than she was, yet he did not tower over her. He had an air of calm assurance about him, with what she thought appeared to be tender edges. Hannah's instincts told her plainly that Jake had suffered some kind of deep hurt somewhere along the line and she wondered what might have caused that.

Now convinced that her mind had been playing tricks on her, Hannah tried to relax, but it was difficult with him standing there so close to her.

"Test," the call was made, with the ball coming over the net from the other side.

It flew up in a clean arch to come down into the second row, then returned without any problem. Back it came, right towards where Hannah stood in the front row between John and Jake. She expected a waving of arms in her face as some male tried to reach for the ball, but was surprised.

Clearly the volleyball was coming in her direction, but both John and Jake were staying in their places. It was to be her play. She gathered herself together, took a deep breath and lifted both hands. A solid swat sent it back over the net.

"Hey, a setup next time!" Jake told her.

Hannah looked at him and was shocked out of her shyness. "Will you set up for me, too?"

"Of course not," he said. "You just set up for the tall people."

"That's not fair," she retorted. "Girls want to play, too."

"And I want to win," Jake told her. "Is that fair?"

It was then that Hannah realized that she was really speaking to him, and her good sense forsook her. "I guess so," she muttered, or thought that's what she said.

Seeing her flustered state, Jake assured her in a voice that made clear he thought nothing of talking to her. "I want girls to play, too, so don't pay any attention to me."

*My,* she collected herself. *We are talking, but so what? It means nothing. Just control yourself. He's not Peter, and you're not dreaming anymore. So calm down.*

"I'll setup for you when I'm in the front row," she conceded to show her contrition.

"Well, that's settled then," Jake said. "Now we can play."

*Well indeed,* she thought, the matter wasn't settled. Events had just taken a strange turn. She was talking to this boy. *Now what did all that mean? Stop dreaming things into situations,* she told herself firmly. *If he wants to talk to you, then talk to him. It means nothing.*

So Hannah and Jake talked to each other and played volleyball, too. She quickly lost her nervousness around his self-assured, non-invasive attitude. He was an excellent player, and she was excellent in setting up the ball for him.

John finally grumbled that he was not getting to play, so Hannah sent the next one to him. Hannah laughed when John fumbled it, sending the volleyball into the net instead of over it.

"See that's why she's sending them over to me," Jake announced loudly.

"You young people!" John protested. "You don't have to laugh."

"We're not," Jake told him. "We just want to win."

"Here it comes again," John announced. "Stop talking."

They stood at the ready in the front row. Hannah saw that the ball was coming her way again. She firmly lifted her hands and sent the volleyball sideways towards Jake in a beautiful high arch.

Effortlessly, Jake rose into the air and brought his arm around into a round sweep that sent the volleyball just over the net and at a forty-five degree angle into the ground on the other side.

Their actions were greeted with groans from the other side and smiles from Jake's side. "We get him next time," someone from across the net shouted.

"There will be no next time. It's too dark," John told them. "If we don't hurry, this game won't get done."

As much as such a game can be hurried, they hurried. Hannah was soon rotated into the back row and never made it back up front before the game point was called.

Apparently the interaction between Hannah and Jake had been so natural that no one thought anything of it. That was the way it played out anyway in the weeks to come.

That night, with such a beginning between them, no one bothered to tell Jake that Hannah was writing to someone. There seemed no need to since they were obviously not into the love thing.

From her place next to Steve on the front seat, Betty echoed the sentiment on the way home. "I saw you and Jake talking during the game. You seemed like old friends. Are you sure that you two don't know each other?"

"I never saw him until he was here the other Sunday," Hannah told her.

"Well, I'm glad there is nothing going on, you know. I would hate to see your mother disappointed." Betty smiled knowingly, although Hannah almost missed the look in the darkness.

"It does seem like we know each other," Hannah told Betty. She almost added, "I can't understand why." She caught herself in time, because she did kind of know why. Jake had reminded her of Peter, which was why she thought she knew him already and also why she did not want the relationship to go any further.

Jake got the same thing inside the Nisley house at the kitchen table. "You seem to know Hannah," Elizabeth commented.

"I never saw her until I was here the other Sunday."

"That's interesting," John added his opinion. "You both seemed quite comfortable around each other."

Jake also was going to say he didn't know why, but he stopped himself. Hannah was unlike her. That was why he knew her, as one of those girls he had never noticed before. The only reason he noticed now was because Hannah was not her. That, he decided, was not a fair reason to show interest in any girl, so that was as far as it would go.

"Hannah's a nice girl," he said aloud as if to grant them something.

"That she is," Elisabeth said, but since Jake did not seem sweet on her, she did not add that Hannah was writing to someone. Why should she say that? It might just insult him, since it would imply that he had shown an interest in her and needed to be called down.

"I'll head for bed," Jake told them. "Thanks for the wonderful evening."

"Are you staying for the singing tomorrow night?" John asked.

"I think so," he said. "Hopefully someone can give me a ride back on Sunday night."

John nodded, "I will see what we can do."

❧

Sunday went along without any hitches, Jake arriving with the Nisleys and Hannah with the Masts. Bishop Nisley had the main sermon, which Hannah thought was pretty good. He spoke on the life of Jesus and our need to accept Him as our Savior.

"It is a personal decision," the bishop explained. "Jesus does not look at us as numbers or as pages in a book. We are all individuals to Him. Each of us, as a person, has one's own needs and faults. Yet Jesus cares about all of us, and knows what our strengths and weaknesses are. We must not only let Him into our lives at some moment of decision, but on each day of our lives. Every day, we must take up our cross, deny ourselves and follow Him."

It made Hannah think about the baptism that needed to be done. Maybe she should ask for it here. That would be wonderful, and something special out here in the West. Practically speaking, however, Hannah wondered whether it could be done. From the looks of things, six months of instruction classes could hardly be worked into the time she had left of summer.

On the off chance that it could be done, however, Hannah asked Betty who suggested Steve ask Bishop Nisley. The long and short of it was that an instruction class was organized with two of the younger local boys also joining.

Bishop Nisley said they were more than glad to make special provisions, not just in starting the class late, but also in completing it by the end of summer.

Hannah found that she could not turn down such an offer.

❧

Jake, for his part, that Sunday found himself looking at Hannah more than he wanted to, especially in the evening when the singing started. *Maybe*, he thought, it was the setting and the reminder that Hannah was not her. *That must be it,* he decided, and also decided again that he was not being fair to Hannah.

Hannah attracted him in a way no girl had before. *Maybe*, he thought again, he just had never noticed this kind of girl. The infamous she had always been strong, and there for him, so that he had had to do little but follow. Hannah was not like that. She would draw on him to lead rather than follow, he decided.

*Stop it,* Jake told himself. *Now you're doing it because you are trying to get away from the memory of her.* Jake's thoughts seemed to accuse him and he believed them enough that his feelings were held in check.

Turning his attention back to the present situation, Jake joined in the songs, singing with the best of them, his voice rising and falling with the others. All sang together in unison. The voices of a few of the Mennonites in attendance tried to sing the parts. It was frowned upon where Jake came from and apparently here also, because he heard none of the Amish youth doing it.

Afterwards, Jake saw John speaking with one of the Mennonite men. The result was Jake got a ride back that night to his cabin in the mountains.

# CHAPTER TWENTY-TWO

S AM'S NEXT LETTER came on Wednesday along with the monthly paper, *The Young Companion*, from the Amish Publishing house, Pathway Publishers. This monthly magazine, along with two others, is a staple in many Amish homes.

Hannah knew the letter had arrived earlier in the day, but she did not read it until that evening when she was in her room. She could not find the emotional energy any earlier.

The day had gone well with riders coming in a steady stream. To see Prince doing his part, gracefully walking up the trail with whomever Hannah had decided should ride him, moved her deeply. This letter just did not seem to be a part of any of that.

Stopping to pick up the envelope on the living room table after supper, she saw that Betty had laid the copy of *The Young Companion* with her letter. Apparently there was something she was supposed to read in it, or Betty was just being helpful, supplying her with reading material. She would find out later.

Settling into her room, Hannah laid the magazine on the dresser table then opened the envelope. The shiny piece of paper, as she pulled it out, seemed almost to glow in the light of her kerosene lamp. Reading it, she could have cried. He was so certain. If only she was.

Yet this was what seemed right. Were there not to be bumps and struggles in the road? Yes, she decided there were.

Glancing up, Hannah caught sight of the magazine on the dresser table, its plain white paper softened by the light. The drawing of a buggy and horse on the front cover outlined the title story, *Struggling to Know.*

Maybe this was why Betty had placed the magazine with the letter. Hannah was supposed to read the story. Reaching out for the magazine, she brought it up to an angle where the light best reached it. Scanning the story, she found that it was about a young girl named Naomi who was struggling to find the will of God in her courtship.

Hannah was familiar enough with the work of the Amish Publishing House to know that almost all their stories were fictional. Naomi, no doubt, was also as well as her troubles.

As it turned out, Naomi was not a bad girl. She never was, Hannah discovered by reading the first part of the story. She was, in fact, a good girl who had already joined the church two years before. "Not like me," Hannah muttered.

Naomi had never done anything bad other than yell at a cow once when she was helping milk in the barn. The cow was almost done giving milk but was scared because of the yell and kicked over the bucket. Naomi had yelled because of being switched in the face by the cow's muddy tail. The story went on to relate how sorry Naomi felt about this. Even though it was not a huge amount of money lost from the spilt milk, Naomi's father told her the real loss was the damage done to Naomi's character by this loss of control.

"Well," Hannah said out loud, "I wish that were all I had done."

Naomi did have one big problem, though. She was just sure she was not in love with the boy she was dating. That was Johnny, Hannah learned as she read another two lines.

Johnny was also a very good boy, from what Hannah could tell. He had never done much wrong, driving his sisters to the singings even when it was out of the way and seeing that they had a ride home before he left for Naomi's house on Sunday nights.

Johnny's father was not rich. In fact, his family had to pinch and save for about anything that came its way. This did not come from any laziness on either Johnny's or his father's part. His father, Hannah found out, had been laid up for the past year with a bruising back injury he sustained from their biggest Belgium horse. The Belgium was actually a gentle horse, as most Belgiums are, but an unfortunate accident had occurred when the horse had stumbled while being led.

Johnny's father was expected to recover fully. It would just take some time and, during this time, Johnny had to take full responsibility for the family farm. He was doing this to the best of his ability, but it made for a lot of hard work and tight times with their income.

Naomi knew all of this and greatly admired Johnny for it. She just knew that there could not be a better husband for her anywhere than Johnny. Yet why did she feel the way she did? Or rather, why did she not feel what she felt she was supposed to feel?

According to the story, Naomi had gotten hold of some English romance books which led her to feel that there should be more feeling involved in this thing between her and Johnny. When it was not happening the way the story said it should, she was worried.

Naomi's mother told her to throw away the books. She said that those people did not live in the real world. People just wrote that stuff to make money off of other people's dreams. Well, Naomi tried that, but it did not help much because she still remembered the story and how she was supposed to feel.

Hannah was now fully into the story. How was Naomi going to figure this out? Was there really something wrong between her and Johnny?

Reading on, she found out that Naomi became so worried about her lack of feelings for this wonderful boy that she told him to no longer bring her home from the singings.

Johnny, of course, could not understand this and wanted to know what he had done wrong. She was unable to explain anything to him and this caused quite a lot of hurt feelings to a heart that was already burdened down with so much in life.

Johnny waited until he was outside of the house and in his buggy before he showed his true feelings. Then he cried most of the way home with great sorrow in his heart. Yet the next morning he got up at the same time at four o'clock to do the milking all by himself. He had so collected himself by that time that his mother did not even notice his tears when she served him breakfast at six.

All day and during the week that followed, Johnny carried his burden of sorrow alone, wondering if God had forsaken him. He did find peace before the next Sunday. He decided that God could take care of even the heart of Naomi, and that he, little Johnny, would leave the problem in the hands of a big God.

It was unclear how long these two young people so suited for each other might have been kept apart. Fortunately, the following week Naomi ran across her aunt who was visiting from a neighboring district. Naomi's aunt explained everything to Naomi. She explained to Naomi that we cannot rely solely on our feelings which come and go. Feelings are fleeting, here one day but gone the next. If it had not been for this talk, Naomi might never have gotten things straightened out.

Hannah sighed as she read through the conclusion. Naomi apologized to Johnny and really began seeing the value that he had as a person. It was then that her feelings for Johnny came rushing back, and Naomi resolved to keep her priorities straight from now on.

"Well," Hannah proclaimed as she put the magazine down, "now why can't I be like that?"

Picking up Sam's letter, she looked at it again. *I guess he does have a lot of good qualities. I'll try.*

Taking up a pen, Hannah found her writing tablet on top of her dresser and started writing. For half an hour she wrote Sam all about the weekend, the volleyball game, the delicious cider, and about the young people. One thing she left out was Jake Byler, but Hannah figured he was not important.

When it was done, she signed, "Yours truly, Hannah Miller," the letters of the words running together in gentle loops and circles on top of each other on her name.

For Jake Byler, the days passed slowly. The mountains still awed him, yet he was bored. Looking out his window at the surroundings, he was sure they were not the cause. Something else was going on, so that now even the silence and the waiting were not as enjoyable as they had been for him before.

It was tonight that Jake finally sat down to try to figure it out. Fidgeting on the chair, he sat by the kitchen table, his meager supper over. Maybe his mother's cooking was what he missed.

*No*, Jake grinned to himself, it was more than that.

Then it occurred to him that he had just laughed at himself. This was something new, since it had been a long time since he had been able to do that. Normally, for what seemed like years now, such a cloud had hung over him that any mirth seemed too heavy a burden to bear.

*I just laughed at myself.* He pondered this fact and then reached the startling conclusion: he was healing. Jake was sure that was what it was, and the more he thought about the issue, the more sure he became. No contrary opinion presented itself.

Although Jake told himself that healing takes place with the passage of time, it had not been that long. However, somewhere in these mountains or in this cabin, the pain was becoming less.

Jake could still envision her face, but now it was harder to see, and the emotions no longer stirred within him. Without a question, there was still some anger there, anger at her, at his cousin, and at the unfairness of it all.

Yet, without his permission or even his seeking it, the healing must have begun. Jake had come here to get away from it all, and now he was getting away from it, although not in a way he had supposed.

Did he like this turn of events? Jake thought about that for a while and he concluded that he really did not. It seemed almost sacrilege to him since he had looked to her as a central part of his life for so long. Could he just let it slip away without protest?

Jake had come here so that the pain might be bearable, not that he might lose her entirely. He now knew the memory of her was still a part he was hanging on to, and, yet, he felt it slipping away. Although this was happening unintentionally, he had somehow caused or at least aided the process by his actions in coming here. This he now saw clearly.

Suddenly, these mountains no longer looked as much like his friends as they had only moments before. They were, in fact, stealing the last remnants of her from him. Jake grimaced as if in pain. What was he to do?

Could he hold on to what they used to have, even as a memory? He now doubted it. Should he leave for home then, now that he knew what was happening? That solution seemed a little strange to him. Why go back to where the pain had come from?

Must he let go then? Jake thought about that, and a great sorrow rolled over him at the thought of it. Yet he knew deep down inside of him that it was the right answer. Sitting there he contemplated the situation and what it really meant. If he let go she would really be gone.

Placing his head on the kitchen table, sobs racked his

body for the first time since she had told him it was over that Sunday evening. He cried in anger and then for the pain and, finally, in sorrow. Through his tears, the memory of her was becoming less and less a part of him. It really was over.

Finally calm came over him, though not exactly peace, but a cessation of emotion. Jake walked to the window and looked out. Full darkness was only half an hour away, with the sun already below the horizon. Shadows were already in the valley, reaching out as if with long bands to hold the earth in their grip for the night.

Over the top of the mountain behind him, sunlight still streamed through the sky, highlighting the contrast between itself and the darkness below. Jake pondered the sight and sighed in resignation.

Maybe he really was among friends who were helping him. Though the help had not been asked for, it might have been necessary. Yes, Jake decided, that is what it was. Although this knowledge did not make the reality easier to bear, it did give his choice meaning.

Turning away from the window, a question occurred to him. Where was he to go from here? Was there another girl for him? The very thought that would have seemed unthinkable not that long ago now presented itself for an answer.

The fact that Jake could answer this without feeling like a transgression was being committed against something sacred surprised him. Yet there it was, and he knew that he now could. What would it be then? Was there to be another girl?

That question produced another question, almost in

concert, before the first was answered. Could it be Hannah? Hannah was so different from her. Would this not be the way to go? A fresh start, a new beginning that might have a chance of ending differently?

The thought intrigued him at the same time that a firm "No" formed itself in his heart. It was simply not fair to Hannah. No, Jake wouldn't do it. A friend — now that was a possibility. Was that not what they shared at the volleyball game on Saturday night?

Jake concluded that it was. So that is what it would be. They were a natural at it. He would keep it so. This new direction of his would not need to have the same goal as before, that of marriage, but simply something more manageable.

Jake walked over to the kitchen table, picked up his dirty dishes and headed for the sink. The summer lay before him, and he would enjoy it, freely and without regret. That was his decision and next week would be a good time to start. Was it not? He saw no reason to think otherwise.

## CHAPTER TWENTY-THREE

MORE THAN A week later on a Saturday afternoon, Hannah could not have been more astonished to see Jake Byler being dropped off at the end of Betty and Steve's driveway.

Hannah was brushing Prince and Mandy down with the intention of turning them out to pasture for the weekend. The last riders for the day had just left, going up the trail with the other two horses.

It had been a long and somewhat trying day. The first riders of the day had brought their child with them. Hannah figured the young boy was about six. His name was Jared, his mother said. The sign out at the end of the driveway that said *Horse Back Riding* did advertise in smaller letters underneath *Will Babysit While You Ride*, so childcare was expected.

The young boy was what was unexpected. He would not listen to anything Hannah told him to do. Instead, he ran all over the barn into places that were dangerous for him. She decided definitely that he was not safe in barns like normal Amish children seemed to be. Everywhere he went, she had to follow him around. Jared wanted to see what was in all the corners of the barn, in the upper levels of the hay mow, and in the feed bags he came across.

"What's this?" he asked, sticking his hand into a bag of oats she kept for feeding the horse.

"It's oats," Hannah told him.

"What's that?" he wanted to know, as he pulled out his hand clutching a handful of fresh oats and let it all fall on the floor.

"It's for the horses," she told him.

"I never saw horses eat this on television," he said. "It must not be any good." Jared then proceeded to follow the natural course of his conclusion by deliberately tipping over the bag of oats so that the upper portions of the bag spilled out onto the floor.

"Don't do that!" Hannah protested. "It costs a lot of money."

"But if it's not good for the horses you should throw it away."

"It is good for the horses," Hannah told him. "Television doesn't show everything."

"Yes, it does," he informed her. "I watch it all the time."

So it went, from one end of the barn to the other. When his parents came back from the ride, Hannah sighed in relief, only to have the next couple also bring along their child.

This time it was little Louise, and although she was not nearly as naughty as Jared, she did pull the cat's tail and managed to get herself scratched on the hand. This produced loud weeping on the part of Louise that never completely subsided until her parents returned.

It also required an explanation to Louise's mother that became more involved the longer Hannah talked. That was because Hannah could tell it was not having the effect that she was used to seeing from explanations.

"You have some first aid bandages?" the mother finally asked.

"Ah, yes," Hannah told her, "they are in the house." Since it was such a small scratch, she had not thought to bandage it, but now went to get the kit Betty kept in the kitchen pantry.

With the hand bandaged, Louise's mother wanted to examine the offending cat. Hannah was afraid this demand would be hard to comply with, now that kitty's tail had been pulled, but kitty proved amicable. He purred in Hannah's arms after she had caught him behind the horse stable. The cat was then examined carefully by the mother as Hannah held him, although he cast a disdainful eye in Louise's direction from his elevated perch.

The mother petted him, and he offered no resistance, and even arched his neck as her hand crossed over his head. "Nice kitty," the mother told him, Hannah thought more for her own assurance than as a statement about kitty's condition.

"He's usually just fine," Hannah said to add weight to the assessment of the cat's innocence. She thought of adding, "Louise did pull his tail," but decided against it.

"I guess it'll be okay," the mother finally ventured, gathering up Louise to go. "Maybe you ought to watch the cat in the future, though," she commented to Hannah.

Hannah nodded. What else was there to do? She would be watching kitty in the future, to be sure, if for no other reason than to keep him away from any future babysitting charges she might have.

So the day had gone, and now Jake Byler was coming up the driveway. He walked with his head erect, and Hannah had to admit that he was an attractive boy. She shoved the thought away, although that seemed to trigger other unbidden thoughts.

*Surely Jake was not up to what he seemed to be.* If he was, she would have nothing of it. There was simply no reason for this. Hannah had given Jake no encouragement of this sort, not even an indication in this direction at either the volleyball game or on Sunday night.

Preparing herself, Hannah waited.

"Hi," Jake said when he got close enough for her to hear him. "How's your day going?"

Hannah shrugged, not wanting to go into it with him. "The last riders are on the trail," she finally offered.

"You have an opening for one more?" he asked.

Startled, she glanced at him.

Jake chuckled at the look on Hannah's face. "I know, it's strange, but I get lonesome not being around horses. I thought this would be a good way to get some riding in, and it's a good way to get some exercise."

"You want to ride?" she asked, completely uncertain that she had heard him right.

"Yes," he said. "How much is it for an hour?"

Shaking her head, she told him.

"That sounds fine," Jake said.

Hannah, however, was not done yet. "You, an Amish boy, are paying to ride a horse?"

"Why not?" Jake asked. "The Forest Service pays me well enough. Why not spend some of it on a worthwhile cause?"

"Okay," Hannah said, although she was not convinced.

She was sure there must be more to it than this, and she looked at him anticipating the dropping of the other shoe.

"So which horse will it be?" Jake asked, apparently seeing her question, but undeterred.

Forcing herself to think, Hannah said, "Prince, I guess. He's a wonderful horse."

"You like him?" he wanted to know.

"Yes," she said, indignant that he should guess.

"Then that is what it will be," Jake said, as if that ended the matter.

"This is Prince," Hannah told him as she stroked the horse's neck. I just got him brushed down, but I can do it again when you come back."

"Don't worry," Jake told her, "I'll do it. It's not like my Saturday afternoons are that full."

*Here it comes*, she thought.

"Where's the saddle?" Jake wanted to know.

Embarrassed to catch her mind wandering in that direction, Hannah pointed towards the barn. "I'll get it, if you lead him over closer."

"No, you lead him," Jake said firmly. "I'll get the saddle. Which one is it?"

Hannah took the reins from him without looking at his face, not wanting this to go anywhere. There was just no way that it could. She was writing, and that was the way it would stay. Another Peter was not on her list of things to do.

"It's the one on the first hook. The big leather one."

Jake headed towards the barn as Hannah followed with Prince. Expertly he threw on the saddle, fastened the cinches, mounted and was off. "I'll be back in an hour," he called over his shoulder.

As Hannah watched him ride up the trail, Jake did not look back. His hands were expertly handling Prince's reins, his body gently flowing with the rhythm of Prince's trot. Hannah was impressed.

It was then that Hannah became aware of Betty's presence behind her, or maybe it was her voice asking, "What is Jake Byler doing here on a Saturday afternoon?"

Hannah turned around startled. "I don't know. He was just dropped off by his ride and walked up to me, asking for a horse to ride."

Betty was not convinced.

"He's paying just like the rest," Hannah offered quickly, trying to make her case.

"He is?" Betty was still skeptical. "An Amish boy?"

"Jake said he needed to be around horses, and he wanted the exercise, too," Hannah assured her. "He's paying for an hour."

"There's nothing else going on?" Betty lowered her eyebrows. "You know how your mother would feel about you quitting Sam over another boy."

"I'm not doing that," Hannah replied, "and don't go telling Jake that I'm writing. It would just insult him, I'm sure. He's not after me."

"Are you after him?" Betty asked.

"I'm not," Hannah told her determinedly.

Betty seemed satisfied. "Well, I was just checking. How's your day going?"

Hannah sighed deeply. "Not too well. I seem to be making all kinds of mistakes all day."

"Really?" Betty was quite concerned.

Starting with Jared and Louise, Hannah told Betty the

whole story. Betty was completely sympathetic and encouraging. "We have some of those days at times. Just be thankful, as I am, that God has given us protection for another day. Be extra careful with the children, though. They aren't like Amish children it seems."

"You can say that," Hannah told her, "and I am thankful. Louise's mother had me scared."

"God helped us," Betty was quick to say. "But we must also do our part in whatever way we can. I wouldn't let the children play with the pets anymore."

Hannah nodded her head in agreement. "I'll be more careful in the future.

With that, Betty returned to the house. The last riders returned soon after that and had no more than gone when Jake came down the trail, his face all smiles. "That's quite some horse you have here."

"He's wonderful," Hannah agreed.

"That he is," Jake said as he dismounted. Handing the reins to her, he undid the cinches and carried the saddle back into the barn. Pulling out his wallet he paid her and told her that he would have to do this more often.

"No problem," she told him. "I'll be here with the horses as far as I know."

"When are you returning to Indiana?" Jake wanted to know.

"The end of the summer, maybe the last of August," Hannah told him. "What about you?"

"I don't know yet," he answered. "The fire season needs to be over first. I guess that varies with how dry it is from year to year. When that's done, I'll be going back."

Jake cleared his throat.

Hannah stiffened. *Don't do it. The answer will be no.*

"I thought maybe the young people from the community could come up some Saturday morning for a hike past my station. It's quite some view up there," Jake explained. "If it's on the Saturday that I come down, I could go back with you then."

"Oh." Hannah cleared her throat. "I guess so. You would have to ask some of the others. I just do what they do."

"I suppose so," Jake allowed. "I'll see what Bishop Nisley says about it. He should know how to schedule something like that, or if they are even interested."

Hannah nodded, and then Jake was gone.

~

"There's a letter from Hannah on the living room table," Laura told Sam when he walked in for supper.

Sam headed for the letter but Laura stopped him. "Clean up first, and if your father is still not in, you can look at it then."

Hesitating, Sam wrinkled up his face before heading for the sink in the laundry entrance.

Laura watched him go, the realization growing on her that her youngest son was no longer a baby. *My, they all grow big so fast, especially the last ones.* She sighed and her eyes misted over a little.

Sam's broad back disappeared into the laundry room, his red hair dusted with the hay he had been putting up all day. Laura herself had only gotten into the house from helping in time to make supper.

*Getting jumpy, like Enos said, in my old age. Maybe that's why I'm worrying about him so much. What if he gets the wrong girl, though?* The question made her catch her breath. That seemed so impossible in her world. Once married there was no longer any question of whether it was wrong or not. Was that why she was so worried now? Yet Sam was so certain about her.

"How's it going with Hannah?" she inquired when Sam came back out, still wiping the water from his hands. He leaned back at the laundry room door to toss the towel back in.

The glow on his face said it all. "She writes wonderful letters," he told his mother.

"When is she coming back home?" Laura wanted to know.

"She hasn't said yet," he replied, heading for the living room and his letter, since his father was not in yet.

Laura heard Sam tear open the envelope as Enos slammed the door as he came in from the outside. "Is supper ready?" he wanted to know.

"As soon as you wash up," she told him.

Sam was back at his place at the kitchen table before his father finished washing up, with a smile on his face that lasted all through suppertime.

*I sure hope he knows what he's doing,* Laura thought as supper proceeded in silence, their tiredness making conversation seem unnecessary.

## CHAPTER TWENTY-FOUR

BISHOP NISLEY AGREED readily to Jake's suggestion for a hike into the mountains for the young people in the near future. On Sunday morning the bishop made inquiries among several of the men about the matter. He could not talk to all of those concerned, since it would have been inappropriate to step too far out of the line of men standing around the barn where church was being held.

He could talk to several of them, those on either side of him and the next ones down the line, without causing any undue commotion. In this way he gained sufficient information to arrive at a conclusion. There would be no objections to such an outing. If a date were set, those who could come would do so. Bishop Nisley expected this included most of the young boys. There were not that many activities going on among their Amish youth to compete with this.

During the following week he asked Elizabeth to make further inquires among the women. There were no negative reactions. So it was that he made the announcement after his youth Sunday school class the next Sunday. The news of the planned event was greeted with nodding heads.

"When will it be?" Ben Stoll wanted to know. Seated across the room from him, Hannah could not help wondering how he got so many scars on his arm. It was a question that had never been answered for her. She supposed she could ask Betty, but that might look like she was too interested in him, so she dropped the idea.

"Maybe the first Saturday in July," Bishop Nisley was saying in response to Ben's question. "We've planned it for then at least. If it doesn't suit someone, if you'd let me know today after church, maybe we can move the date. Jake is not here today, of course, but I think about any time suits him."

Again heads nodded, and after church no objections were made to the bishop.

That was how it happened that at eight o'clock on the first Saturday morning in July, Hannah was waiting for her ride into the mountains.

Originally talk had been to use the buggies since the Cabinet Mountains were within sight of the Amish community. That was until Ben Stoll got an offer from the English boy he worked with on the logging crew. The offer was the use of his driving services and his pickup truck if he could go along.

"It's an Amish youth group," Ben had told him.

"No problem," Scott told him. "Hey, I work with Amish, right?"

"I guess so," Ben responded. "Do you like hiking?"

"Love it," Scott told him. "It would be a great chance to get into the Cabinet Mountains."

"You're not after one of our girls, are you?" Ben wanted to know.

Scott laughed at this. "Why would I do that?" he asked.

"We don't have that many," Ben glared at him. "Besides, she already writes to someone."

"Hey, it's fine with me," Scott told him. "I already have a girlfriend."

Ben then suggested to Scott, "Well, you could bring her along then."

"We'll see," Scott told him. "I'll ask."

Watching from the living room window, Hannah saw the pickup truck pull into the driveway. She knew it was her ride by the Amish boys seated in the back. An English boy, who she assumed was Scott, was driving with a girl in the front seat with him.

"There's only Amish boys in the back," Hannah protested to Betty, who had stepped out of the kitchen. "I don't want to be the only girl!"

"John and Elizabeth are going along, too," Betty told her quickly. "They probably haven't picked them up yet."

"Are you sure about that?" Hannah asked before giving her approval to this arrangement.

"I'm sure," Betty said, and Hannah then headed out the door.

"Good morning," she said upon arriving at the pickup truck.

Bales of hay were stacked in the bed of the pickup truck as seats. She was offered a comfortable spot towards the back as well as nods of "Good Morning" from the seated boys.

Settling in, Hannah hung on as Scott turned left at the driveway towards Bishop Nisley's place. Not used to riding in the back of pickup trucks, she soon learned to face the other way from the front of the truck. The wind took her breath away once Scott got up to cruising speed.

John and Elizabeth were waiting at the end of their

driveway. Hannah made room for them beside her seat on the straw bale.

"You like the ride?" Elizabeth asked her.

"So far," Hannah told her, making a motion of hanging on to the top of her head.

Elizabeth chuckled, "Imagine they don't do this much back East."

"No," Hannah agreed, "but I like it."

Scott made a U-turn and headed back towards Troy and turned south in town towards the Cabinet Mountains. When he came to where the road started to climb, he stopped and hollered back out of his window.

"How far are we driving up?"

"To Jake's cabin," John told him. "We'll get out and hike the rest of the way from there."

"You know where the cabin is?" Scott called back, getting the pickup to start off again.

"Jake said about three-quarters of the way up. It's the only outpost on this side so we should be able to find it easily."

"Good enough," Scott nodded his head as he started.

They climbed slowly, the pickup truck starting to groan under its load as the grade became steeper.

"Going to make it?" John asked.

Scott didn't hear him, or else he decided to keep his mind on his driving.

"We can get out and push if necessary," Ben offered.

The pickup truck kept going up another grade, the view opening up once they reached the top. Hugging the cliff's edge the road leveled out for a few hundred yards before turning right and up again.

Below them lay their first good view of the valley and the town of Libby in the background.

"Beautiful," John commented.

"It is nice," Elisabeth agreed, turning in her seat on the straw bale for a better view. "God's handiwork is so wonderful. He really worked his best in these mountains."

Hannah agreed fully, soaking in the sight below them. The next turn, the scene was repeated only higher up, enhanced by the freshness of the morning mountain air on their senses. They rode in silence, watching for fresh views of the valley, until a cabin and an obvious lookout tower came into view.

"We're here," Scott announced as he pulled the pickup truck into the designated parking space.

Dropping the tailgate, John hopped down and the others followed. Hannah brushed straw from her dress as Elisabeth did the same. It was an instinctual reaction, but Hannah had a deeper reason.

*He's here,* she thought, then told herself to stop. *There's no reason for this.*

Jake had been stopping by on his weekends down for church. He would take Prince out for a ride and come back refreshed and smiling each time. Their relationship had settled into a routine comfortable for both of them.

Hannah had stopped worrying that he would try to make it something more since that would require her saying no. Jake never did and gave no indication that he ever would. For this she was glad, yet at moments like this, her mind still wandered. He was a nice boy, Hannah could not help but thinking.

The door to the cabin opened and Jake appeared. Grinning, he asked John, "Are you driving all the way to the top?"

"No," John told him, "we want to hike from here."

"You want to climb the tower first?" he asked, including all of them.

This was agreeable so Jake led the way to the tower. There they had to wait until another group came back down.

"I have off all day," Jake told them as another ranger stepped off the platform to greet them.

Jake did not add that this avoided having to be seen by them in his English uniform. The best part, though, of being off for the day was that he could join them on the hike.

A younger couple was making their way down the winding staircase as the Amish group waited to enter the observation platform.

"Girls first," Jake announced when the couple had made their way down and headed up the trail. Motioning with his hand, Elizabeth and John went first. "You next," he told Hannah and then followed her up.

She felt no nervousness at this turn of events. Her friendly relationship with Jake was already well established with the others, and she got no strange vibes from any of them for it. This helped a lot, particularly because the opinion of what others held of one in such a close community often had as much weight as what the actual situation might be.

To them Jake was her friend, almost like her brother. So they were allowed to do things others could not have done without being thought of as having a romantic relationship. This would then have come with all the associated deference. Hannah wanted none of that. Now, the atmosphere was comfortable, both from their point of view as well as from Hannah's perspective.

Hannah glanced back at Jake climbing behind her. He grinned at her. "Some view, huh?"

Indeed it was. Glancing out over the valley she asked him, "They pay you to work here?"

"It doesn't seem right," he chuckled, "but they do."

Reaching the top, Hannah stood there looking at the view. "It's beautiful," she said softly.

Jake silently agreed as he stood beside her. "Time to go down," he said a moment later. "We have to keep it moving. Lots of people come through on a Saturday."

John led the way down with Elizabeth following him. Hannah followed her, and Jake brought up the rear. Half way down Hannah glanced over her shoulder back up towards Jake. For the first time she caught a gleam in his eye that she had never seen before.

Quickly, Hannah looked back down at the stairs and her heart felt like it skipped a beat. *Oh, no,* she groaned on the inside, hoping she was not turning red. *This is bad.*

Collecting herself by the time she reached the bottom, Hannah kept her eyes away from Jake's face as she walked over to the railing to look at the valley again. The other half of the group was heading up the metal stairs above her.

"You ever think about moving out here?" Elizabeth asked from beside her. Hannah had been so distracted she had not noticed her approach.

"It's a wonderful country," she replied as soon as she could think of what to say. "But moving, I'm not sure. I'm still an Indiana girl."

"We're always looking for new people," Elizabeth told her. "Young couples especially. It seems like they are more resilient to new things than older people."

Hannah decided it was time to reestablish things as quickly as possible. "Sam's inheriting the farm on the home place," she said.

"Oh, you're that serious then?" Elizabeth raised her eyebrows.

Now Hannah did blush, which only served to answer the question before she spoke. Her words said differently, but Elizabeth chose to go with the look. "No, no," Hannah said quickly. "We're just writing."

"He must be a nice boy," Elizabeth observed.

Hannah nodded, not trusting her voice. *Yes,* she thought, *in many ways he is. At least, my mom thinks so. If Sam's mouth just wouldn't fall open all the time.*

Elizabeth took her silence as consent.

Moments later the group got under way again and reached the top of the Cabinet Mountains an hour later. Back down was much quicker. Jake seemed to be making a point of staying out of Hannah's way the rest of the afternoon. Even on the way home, he sat on the back end of the pickup truck, with Hannah in the front of the line of hay bales.

Hannah was dropped off first at the end of Betty and Steve's driveway. She walked in to Betty's cheerful greeting, "Did you have a good day?'

"Wonderful," Hannah told her. "The valley looks lovely from up there."

"Any problems?"

"No," Hannah told her, as there were none of the kind to

which Betty was referring. Heart problems were on another plane.

Hannah resolved once again to keep her dreams in check. Hopefully Jake would make things easy for her. After that look on the tower today, she was no longer sure.

## CHAPTER TWENTY-FIVE

THAT EVENING AFTER retiring to her room, Hannah made a valiant effort to stem the tide of her feelings. They seemed to be coming in waves out of nowhere. She shut her eyes in an attempt to block them and this seemed to help.

Hannah then took out paper and a pen to write. She wondered whether a letter to Sam would help get her focused again. She decided it would.

"Dear Sam," she wrote on the fresh sheet of paper, after copying the date carefully on the top.

"We went up to the mountain today on a youth outing. The view of the valley was really something." Lifting her pen, she pondered what else to write and then settled on more details of the day, with tidbits of her past week of handling riders. Coming to the end, she told him, "I know it's still only the first part of July, but already my thoughts go towards coming home at the end of August. As fast as the time has been going out here, it will come soon enough." She closed with, "I will see you then, I guess. Love, Hannah."

Slipping the letter into an envelope, she sealed it for Monday's mail and wrote Sam's address on the outside. "There," she said out loud, "that's done."

*Now stay off the dreaming*, Hannah told herself as she prepared for the night and hopefully some sleep. Dropping off to sleep, her hopes were not disappointed — that is, until towards morning.

Drifting between sleep and awakening, she dreamed. It was Peter's car again she was riding in, gravel crunching under its tires. They were traveling at a great rate of speed, and she could not see who was driving the car. That it was Peter's car she was sure because the handle by the window she was hanging onto was definitely the one she remembered. That memory was seared in her mind.

Passing through the darkness and then under the yard light of some residence along the road, she caught a glimpse of the driver's face. It was Jake Byler. She was sure of it. The face was focused and intent, just like Jake's face. Now the light from the yard light was gone, and she could not see anymore. In the darkness she hung onto the handle as horror swept over her. She was disobeying again. How had this happened without her knowing it?

Scenes kept flashing in front of her eyes as the car slowed and it finally stopped somewhere although she wasn't sure where. A flash of light came through the car revealing the driver's face again. It was Jake. She was even more sure this time.

As darkness filled the car again, the first notes began. Jake was singing the Praise Song, just like he had done at church, only by himself now. Its rising and falling melody had never in all her life sounded so haunting or out of place.

Reaching deep within her Hannah tried with all her strength to wake up. Her muscles strained with the efforts and it seemed as if nothing moved. Her left arm was pasted to her side and the one clutching the handle by the window would not let go.

She filled her mouth with air and screamed. At least she thought she did. Finally waking up, her body chilled with sweat under the covers. The whole house was silent. She waited for footsteps in the hall of someone come to see what the problem was. There was only silence.

If Hannah had screamed, wouldn't she have awakened someone? She waited, trembled and listened in the dim light of her room. Still, no one seemed to be stirring anywhere else in the house.

Finally her breathing slowed and she relaxed enough to think about falling asleep again. Hannah's last thought before dropping off to sleep was a fresh resolution to hold her dreaming heart in check. She must stay away from Jake Byler. That much was clear. Her heart could not be trusted to do the right thing.

In the morning Betty said nothing about hearing any screaming, so Hannah figured that must have been a dream, too. At church the next morning, she kept her eyes on the floor whenever Jake Byler was in her line of vision. Sunday night at the Hymn Singing, she made a point of sitting on the second bench. All of these things she undertook in her attempt to avoid Jake.

Hannah crawled into bed that evening impressed with her own efforts, yet troubled with the distinct feeling that they had only made matters worse. How that could be, she was not sure, but that it was so she was certain.

By the end of the week, Sam got his letter from Hannah. Happening to be around the house when the mail came, he was the one who got to the mailbox first. Now he was reading it, one page dangling in the air on the walk back to the house.

What he was reading could not have pleased him more. Hannah's hard work with the horse riding at Steve and Betty's place continued to impress him. She was quite a businesswoman. This could not but help matters immensely with his parents' feeling about her. He smiled to himself, his eyes still firmly on the page, his feet hitting the gravel when the lane became uneven. Too concentrated in his attention to the letter to notice, Sam kept from falling only by subconscious intervention.

Also, Hannah had said she would soon be coming home and would be seeing him then. Not that they had ever said it in so many words, but it had been somehow implied. But it now was official. Of this Sam was sure. Hannah would be his steady in the true sense of the word. Not just letters, but in his buggy on Sunday nights for the ride home.

The whole world would know that he, Sam Knepp, was doing well for himself. Gone would be the stigma he had often felt since the last few years of Amish grade school. Now, with such a girl as Hannah by his side, all would be right.

Sam held his chin firm as he walked up the lane towards the house, his letter still in his hand. This was a moment to enjoy fully. Remembering in time, he kept his mouth shut, even though he could feel it want to fall open from sheer joy. Such things must now be changed also, he felt strongly. He was writing to Hannah Miller and would soon be formally dating her. The world was truly on his side, he was certain.

"Another letter?" his mother asked him when he stuck his head in the kitchen door to deliver the rest of the mail.

He grinned, his face revealing the answer before he shut the door.

She watched him leave, and as he walked towards the house, a worried look came to her face. *Why am I worrying?* she finally asked herself. *He's old enough to make his own decisions.*

⤜

The next week a letter arrived from Sam. Hannah stuck it in her drawer after reading it. She intended to get it back out, but by Saturday morning she had forgotten it even existed. It was Jake's scheduled weekend down from the mountain.

The regular number of riders was coming through. As of yet, there had been no unruly children, but her nerves were still on edge for another reason. It was none of her business, she kept telling herself, but she still was wondering. Was Jake coming down today? If he did come, how was he going to be?

No amount of pondering seemed to help provide solutions, nor did her resolutions to keep her feelings in check give her much comfort. At three, she got her last group of riders ready and had just sent them off down the trail when a car stopped by the road. She turned to look who it was, her hand flying to her mouth. Jake Byler was climbing out, and while she stood there dumbfounded, he was coming towards her, his form erect and confident.

Hannah still thought he looked like Peter, only different in every other way. Jake was more mature, conscientious, clean, wholesome, and, she was sure, godly. Jake would never be driving a car or trying to steal a kiss from her.

*Please God, help me,* she prayed silently, as she glanced around her. *I am not a strong person like I need to be. You will have to save me.*

"Hi," Jake said, as he approached her. "Are your riders about done?"

Hannah took a deep breath, *so far so good.* He seemed like he always had been before. Maybe she was just imagining things with her *dummkopp* ways. That was what it was, she decided. She was jumping to conclusions when there really were none to jump to.

"The last ones," she told him, looking into his eyes. They looked like they always did. She relaxed. "Do you want Prince today again?"

"I think so," he told her, then paused before asking softly, "Why don't you come riding with me?"

*Oh no,* she screamed on the inside, *I was not imagining things. He's going to ask if he can bring me home on Sunday afternoon. What am I going to say?*

He was looking at her with a question on his face and she was unable to find her voice. "You love to ride," Jake told her. "I thought we might go together. You probably don't have much chance anymore."

"Ah, yes, no," Hannah said fumbling around for the right answer. "I mean, I don't get much chance anymore."

"Then it suits," he said, as if that decided it.

She tried, but the words didn't come. "No" stuck somewhere down in her stomach and refused to come out. *I'll say no if he asks me about Sunday,* she decided. It produced a small measure of comfort, but not much.

"Is Prince in?" Jake asked. "I didn't think that was him going out with your last group of riders."

"No," Hannah told him, "both he and Mandy are tied inside the barn.

"So you were waiting for me?" he asked grinning at her.

"No, yes. I mean, I expected you to come, yes. You normally stop by on your Saturdays down."

"Well," he said, "let's get going then, or do you have to wait for your group to come back?"

"Someone has to," she said, the thought occurring to her that telling Betty about the ride with Jake now would be much easier than when she came back. Why not ask her to take care of the group when they returned and break the news using that conversation?

"I'll ask Betty," Hannah told him, making as if to start towards the house.

"Whatever you say," Jake shrugged his shoulders.

When Hannah got to the house, Betty was sitting on the living room couch folding a clean pile of washed clothing.

Opening the front door, Hannah asked as calmly as she could muster, "Could you take care of the last group of riders when they come back?"

Betty looked strangely at her. "You're not going to be here?"

"Jake asked me to ride with him," she said, sure her cheeks were red but hoping Betty thought it due to the outdoor weather.

"No," Betty told her firmly from the couch, "you can't do that. You're writing."

"It's not like that," Hannah assured her. "If he asks for anything like bringing me home on Sunday night, I'll say no right away. This is just a ride. I think it would be rude not to go with him."

Betty did not look convinced, but with another barrage of Hannah's logic about not wanting to hurt Jake's feelings, and that she got to ride little of late, Betty guessed it did make sense. *The girl is trying hard*, she thought. *I suppose she has enough sense to handle herself. They have always been just friends.*

"Well, I guess," she said out loud. "I'll take care of your group of riders, but don't get ideas about Jake. Okay?"

Hannah nodded, glad that Betty was being reasonable because there was every reason to, she told herself.

When Hannah returned, Jake had both horses ready and gave her the reins to Mandy as he then climbed onto Prince. Hannah followed by mounting her horse.

Together they rode out with Jake leading the way. At the river they met the other riders coming back. Hannah told them about the arrangement with Betty, to which they happily agreed.

Both of them had grins on their faces as if they knew more was going on than Hannah was telling.

*There is nothing going on*, Hannah said firmly under her breath, wishing she could say it out loud, but that would just make matters worse.

Turning, she followed Jake, who was already heading down to the river. They would just have to think what they wanted to. She was going to be good girl. Of this, she was determined.

"Let's go," Jake yelled over his shoulder, already at the

open stretch by the river. He waited momentarily until she caught up on Mandy, then he let the reins out on Prince.

Jake was assuming a lot, Hannah thought as they raced along the river. How did he know she could ride this well? She had never ridden with him before, nor mentioned it. Yet the fact that he felt she was that good was also obvious by his actions. Only glancing back once, Jake was now in a wide-open gallop with Prince.

Hannah kicked Mandy lightly in the ribs, thrills running up and down her spine. It was not just the speed they were going by now, nor the rhythm of a horse under her. She knew it was more than that as the wind whistled through her hair. It was Jake. That was what it was.

To be with him, to see him riding in front of her, or to see him bend double over the saddle to cut down on the wind resistance with his hair flying out behind him, all of these things were thrilling. Hannah knew what it was, and, at the same time, knew she could never admit it. Not to herself, not to God, and especially not to Jake. Jake was forbidden to her by forces beyond her control. There was a line that could not be crossed.

Yet the memory of her dream and the desires it stirred in her came back with great force. When Jake pulled Prince in, Hannah did the same with Mandy, coming to a stop just behind him. It was more than the wind which gave her watery eyes, but she forced herself to look at him.

"Wow, that was something!" he exclaimed. "You do know how to ride."

Hannah shrugged her shoulders, not trusting her voice at the moment.

"Where did you learn to ride like that?" Jake asked her.

"I've had a pony since I was small," she told him, then added for the sake of conversation: "I fell off of him once and broke my collarbone. I guess those things help you learn."

"That's interesting," Jake told her. "How did it happen?"

"The pony stepped into a groundhog hole," Hannah said, almost adding that Sam was there. But that would not do. My how things had changed! Jake would not understand. She was to be married to Sam, the same Sam who had been standing there by the fence with his mouth hanging open, watching her. She was to be Sam's wife, and here she was riding with Jake, her heart pounding. Things were strange, indeed, in how they worked out. Hannah supposed it would all be okay once she was married. It seemed to be for others once they said "Yes" to the bishop's questions. Maybe then all this heart pounding would cease, and she could be what she was supposed to be: obedient to her parents and a good wife who had stopped all this dreaming.

"Did it hurt the pony?" Jake had asked the question twice already, but she had not noticed.

"Oh, no," Hannah told Jake, her face blushing. What if he knew what she had been thinking?

"How did he keep from breaking his leg?" Jake's face looked at her questioningly.

Hannah willed her brain to stop spinning, trying to form words that made sense. "He, I don't know, it happened so fast. But I think we weren't going fast enough so that he had time to pull it out."

"Still he was going fast enough to break your collarbone?"

"Yes," she said, "he threw me against a fence post. It

doesn't take much speed when you add in the fall." That Sam was standing there she left out again.

"I guess so," Jake shrugged his shoulders. "I'm glad you weren't too hurt."

Hannah nodded her thanks.

"Should we get back?" Jake wanted to know.

Hannah nodded again, and they rode back to the barn in silence.

Betty said nothing about the subject that night, and Hannah ignored Jake in church the next morning. Hannah again got the distinct feeling that that was just making things worse, but there seemed to be little she could do about it.

## Chapter Twenty-Six

WITH JULY FAST fading, Hannah knew that there were only a few more weeks left of her stay in Montana. Her baptism would be on the last Sunday she was here.

A sorrow formed at the thought of leaving this place: its mountains, its peace, its brisk air, and the people she had come to know. At the bottom of it all, though, she admitted it once and then quickly shoved the thought away, was not seeing Jake anymore.

There were two Saturdays yet when he would stop in at Betty and Steve's place to ride. At least she assumed he would. If he didn't, that would certainly solve some problems, but deep down she hoped he would.

Sitting down to write Sam on Friday night, Hannah told him all the news she could think of: the riders, the horses, their children, how beautiful the approach of fall weather was here, and of her planned trip home. Jake did not make the list.

In the morning Hannah got up early to start the day, but the riders were slow in coming right from the start. "It's getting to the end of summer," Betty told her when she went back in the house at ten o'clock. "We always slow down about this time of the year."

Hannah had little to do after lunch and was glad when Jake came early. He said little to her, other than "Hi," and took off down the trail on Prince. She watched him go, emotions throbbing through her. *He's mad at me. I just know he is.* Then she realized what she was doing and changed tactics. *Stop it, stop it,* she told herself firmly. *It doesn't matter. It's none of your business how he's feeling. It could just be his work.*

Startled to hear the kitchen door opening at the house, Hannah glanced up. It was just Betty, who looked out for a moment. Seeing Hannah standing by the barn door, she went back inside. The gesture was unmistakable. Betty was checking up on her.

Thoughts flashed through her mind. *Oh, she doesn't trust me anymore. She thought I was going riding with Jake again and was up to something. Am I that bad? How do I know? I don't even know myself anymore. How can I know if I am or not?*

Pressing her hand against her head, Hannah willed the turmoil to cease. To distract herself, she went into the barn and brushed Mandy down before releasing her into the pasture for the weekend.

Not wanting to go inside, Hannah waited out of sight from the house until the sound of Prince's hooves came back down the trail.

"It's getting a little chilly," Jake commented as he dismounted. "Fall comes early in this country." He was not looking at her.

"That's what Betty said," Hannah commented, feelings of desperation flowing through her. She wished he would look at her. How was she going to stand it if Jake was mad at her for some reason?

"Well, I should be going," he half muttered. "John has

some work for me to do yet before dark."

With that Jake was gone and she watched his back retreating slowly down the lane and then down the road. It was a full ten minutes before Hannah could move again. Her face ashen, she found her way to the house. Betty could not help but notice when she got in.

"You okay?" she asked.

Hannah nodded her head unconvincingly.

"Was there a problem with the horses?" Betty probed.

Hannah shook her head. "No, they are fine."

"What is it then? You look positively white."

Not trusting her voice lest the tears come, Hannah simply sat down on the couch. The house was silent as Betty looked at her.

"It's Jake," she finally concluded correctly. "You haven't agreed to see him, have you?"

Hannah shook her head.

"Did he ask?"

"No," Hannah managed to say.

Betty was still looking at her. "I thought you two were just friends. You know that you are writing to someone, and what your mother thinks about it, don't you?"

Hannah nodded.

"This is not moving into something it should not, is it?" Betty's eyes bored into hers.

"I don't think so," Hannah ventured.

Betty was not convinced. "I think your heart is straying again. That's really what's happening. You must stop this, Hannah. You know that, don't you?"

Hannah nodded numbly. She did know it but seemed helpless to do anything about it.

"Well, I'm glad to hear you say it." Betty's voice reached her as if from a great distance. "Thankfully, there are only two more weeks to go and then this thing will be over. I want to get you safely home to your mother. Okay?"

Hannah tried to smile but the effort was not very successful. It satisfied Betty, though, who patted Hannah on the head as if she were her own mother and Hannah her five-year old.

"I'll try real hard," Hannah told her. "And I am looking forward to getting back home, but I will really miss this place and the people out here."

Betty smiled now. "That's nice of you to say. We will miss you, too, and maybe that's part of your problem. Leaving and going home like this. Well, you can always come back for a visit."

"It's pretty far," Hannah told her. "And it is expensive, too."

"That it is, but we will just have to see. Well, I must get busy. Sunday's coming on fast. Are you ready? What about packing? Is there something that needs to be started already?"

"No," Hannah shook her head. "I'll wait till the last week, I think. There should be plenty of time then."

Betty showed her agreement by heading for the kitchen and her work. Hannah soon followed her, tackling the stack of dishes on the countertop without being told. The splash of the water and the slush of the soap soon joined her thoughts of Jake in one mixed up, jumbled mess.

It was the next morning sitting on the church bench facing the line of teenage boys, with Jake all the way over on the end, that Hannah knew she was losing it. She could not keep her eyes from straying in his direction. All her resolve to control her feelings and to obey her parents were waving like a stalk of wheat standing by itself in the wind.

When Jake finally looked at her, the dam broke. Hannah let him see every feeling she had for him. Every desire that her dream had inspired passed from her eyes to his. And she knew there was no taking it back. Jake now knew.

What she expected next she was not certain. The feelings of guilt mounted up in her, but she couldn't help herself. Jake would now ask her, of that she was sure. When or how did not matter.

What Hannah also knew was that the answer would be "Yes."

That would involve so many things, confessions to Betty and to her mother and seeing their disappointed faces. It also meant writing Sam, or maybe telling him when she got back home. The thought of his mouth dropping open caused no joy in her; instead the sorrow increased. How could life get so sad? And how could one be doing something one knew was not right, but could not stop it?

*Maybe God will help me yet,* Hannah thought. That brightened her spirits up a little. He always had before, had He not? Yes, that's what she would do. She would pray and ask for help. Surely the Almighty God in heaven who knew so much and could run the whole world could figure this all out.

*But does He have time?* The thought startled her with its insistent clarity. Hannah had no idea what the answer was.

Suppose He didn't and she was on her own. Panic struck her, filling her heart with terror. *Oh, please God,* she breathed, *help me, because I can't help myself.*

Around her, the church service continued. Bishop John was having the main sermon, and she tried to focus her attention on it. The desire to look at Jake was completely gone, now that she knew he knew. Only the fear of what was coming and when was still with her.

Whether Jake was paying attention to her or not, she felt no desire to know. It was only a matter of time now, and then she would say yes. Beyond that the world looked far more fearful than she would ever have thought possible. *Why, oh why don't I stop dreaming?* she asked herself. Then Hannah found comfort in the thought that she had tried as hard as she could. The rest was now in the hands of God.

When there was no sign of Jake the rest of the day, peace still stayed with her. God would surely supply help in some way because Jake was going to ask. Of this she was still certain.

Up in his cabin on the Cabinet Mountains, Jake was going through his own plans for leaving and packing. In the background was the greater turmoil of Hannah. That she had gotten to him, he now knew for certain.

Gone was his notion that he was not being fair to Hannah because she did not look like her. Sunday had been the watershed. Jake had been suspicious of it for some time but now he knew. Hannah wanted him to ask her for a date as much as he wanted to ask her.

But could he? That was the problem. Anger still seethed in him for what the other girl had done. No doubt by this time they were talking marriage, and that to Jake's first cousin. His cousin was the one now looking into the blue eyes that Jake had once thought he would be spending a lifetime looking into. Now the two of them would be together and that in front of him for the rest of his life.

But the pain was no longer as sharp as it once was. Maybe, Jake thought, it had been for the best. Hannah gave him a completely new vision of what a girl could be, and he found himself admitting that he liked it better. That seemed at first like a betrayal of the one he had once so loved, but then Jake knew that it was not.

Jake started arranging things to leave that week but didn't start packing until Thursday of the next week. There was not that much to pack that could not be thrown into his duffel bag. On Friday he hitched a ride down to town for his last check.

Now the question was whether he should stay at the Nisleys for one more weekend or return home now. The Nisleys would think nothing of his early departure and his parents would be glad to see him.

The answer, Jake knew without thinking too much about it, was already clear to him. He would go back for one more weekend, and he would ask Hannah. The thought brought a smile to his face. How wonderful God was, and his ways were truly mysterious. Here Jake had thought the world had ended when his love had betrayed him, but, instead, it had just begun in a completely fresh and new way.

Visions of writing to Hannah and perhaps visiting her community arose in Jake's mind. Suddenly he remembered that he was not quite certain where that was. Indiana, he knew, but the Indiana Amish community was vast. He would have to ask her this along with the many other things that needed to be talked about.

Squaring his shoulders and feeling like a man, Jake stood along Highway Two to hitch a ride. The second car pulled over on the shoulder. Twenty minutes later he was standing beneath the *Horse Rides* sign with *Will Take Care of Children* in smaller letters under it.

## CHAPTER TWENTY-SEVEN

Hannah saw him from the living room where she had been sitting on the couch. There had been no riders all day except for one at eleven. Now that the Saturday housework had been caught up with her help, she and Betty were resting for a moment as they savored their last few hours together. Sunday would be the baptismal, and Monday morning would find her on the Greyhound returning to Indiana.

"It's Jake," Hannah said, startling Betty who could not see out the window.

"I was wondering if he'd stop by," Betty commented dryly. "It's his last weekend also, I think."

"He probably wants to ride Prince for one last time," Hannah volunteered, and she began feeling guilty all over again. That there was more he wanted, Hannah saw no need to tell Betty.

"Let him get Prince by himself," Betty told her. "He's capable."

"I should be out there," Hannah insisted. "It's the last weekend."

Betty shrugged her shoulders. "I guess it can do no harm."

Hannah was out of the door in a flash, leaving Betty with a puzzled look on her face. "That girl's up to something, now don't tell me she isn't," Betty told herself as she watched Hannah's retreating figure heading towards the barn. "I just wonder what."

"Hi," Hannah told Jake, who was standing by the barn door waiting.

"Hi," Jake replied, meeting her eyes. They were warm and soft and the world seemed right to him.

Hannah melted on the inside as she looked towards the ground. Her feelings had been correct. He was going to ask her before he left. Wasn't that why he was here? The confirmation came quickly.

"You want to ride with me?" Jake asked, still looking at her.

She nodded, glancing back up at him before going to get the horses.

Jake insisted on saddling both Prince and Mandy, even when Hannah protested. She found it a little awkward, standing there, doing nothing, but decided to enjoy it. Later would come the guilt feelings, but they just would have to come. Somehow, this would all be straightened out. It was simply out of her power to do it.

Mounting the horses, Jake and Hannah rode up the trail. Betty saw them go and frowned. "She's up to no good. I know she is." But for the moment there was nothing to be done about it.

Reaching the river, Jake turned to her. "One last gallop for the summer?" he asked.

Hannah nodded, her heart swelling with emotion. What a boy he was, so alive and full of life! Bending slightly forward, she made ready to follow his lead. He laughed out loud as he urged Prince forward, a sound so musical and manly at the same time she could hardly believe such a sound existed.

Together they raced along the river plain, two hearts beating as one as the horses' hooves beat in rhythm. The mountains filled Hannah's vision as the wind stung her eyes. It was all a little too much, and she was afraid there would really be a flow of tears, but she managed to control her emotions.

Pulling Prince up, Jake threw his head back in sheer joy. "Whee!! That was something. I sure will miss it."

Hannah pulled up beside him, feeling the same, but saying nothing. The moment had come, she was sure.

Jake sat there on Prince looking off into the distance, as if pondering the deeper things of life, seeming to be oblivious of her. Hannah was just getting ready to say something to break into his thoughts when the cat screamed.

The sound came from the wood's edge just to the west of them, piercing and unearthly. Both horses reared and neighed in panic, their nostrils flaring in fear. Jake kept his mount, but Hannah slid off backwards, although she managed to use the saddle and Mandy's haunch to keep herself upright before hitting the ground.

Jake yelled in anger when he saw her hit the ground. First directing his attention to the mountain lion now standing in plain view at the edge of the woods, Jake moved towards it. He dismounted from Prince, who was jerking his head violently back and forth, grabbed Mandy's reins and held both in one hand.

Reaching down, Jake found the rock he was looking for

and hurled it in the direction of the cat. It hissed as the stone went past it into the woods and then vanished as suddenly as it had appeared.

Holding both reins of the horses, Jake went immediately over to where Hannah was still on the ground. "Are you hurt?" he asked, concern written all over his face.

She moved what body parts she could feel, and then slowly rose from the ground. "Everything works," she commented without much confidence.

"There's blood coming down on your foot," he told her.

Hannah quickly found the spot just above the ankle where a small gash had been cut. "I probably cut it on a stone," she told him.

"It needs to be looked at," Jake told her. "It needs to be disinfected if nothing else."

Hannah agreed.

"Can you ride?" Jake asked her.

"I think so," she told him, heading towards Mandy while he held the reins. Mounting proved no problem, and they were soon on their way. They rode in silence until they arrived at the house. Betty saw them coming and knew that something was wrong by Hannah's dirty dress.

She met them halfway across the lawn. "What happened? Are you hurt?"

"It was a mountain lion," Jake told her. "It screamed at us, and the horses reared. Mandy threw Hannah off."

"Are you hurt bad?" Betty wanted to know. "Come down off that horse right away so I can check."

"I think it's just a little scratch on my foot," Hannah volunteered. "Other than that, I don't think I got hurt from the fall."

"Let's look at your foot then. Come down and we can go into the house."

Hannah complied, slowly sliding off the saddle.

"I'll put the horses away and then check on her," Jake told Betty. "I think I know where things go."

Betty nodded, distracted at the moment with getting Hannah into the house. "I'll tell Steve about this tonight," she said on the way in. "He can get the game warden on this right away. We can't be having a big cat wandering around here."

Hannah was not paying that much attention. When Betty got Hannah inside, she grabbed the first aid packet and together they went up to Hannah's room. After she was certain Hannah could move all her limbs without pain, Betty concluded there really was nothing more serious than the cut on Hannah's leg. With that bandaged up, Betty went back downstairs, leaving Hannah to get cleaned up.

Betty found Jake on the living room couch waiting. "Is she okay?" he wanted to know.

"Yes, just the cut," Betty told him.

"That's good," Jake said, then pointed towards the small lamp stand beside the couch. "Who's that from?"

Betty looked over to where he was pointing. Hannah had left one of her letters from Sam lying there, unread, from the morning's mail. "Oh," she said, without thinking, and then was glad Jake had noticed. It was high time this thing was brought to an end. "That's from the boy Hannah's writing to."

Jake's face went white, his lips moving. "Writing?" He barely got the words out.

"Oh, yes," Betty told him, "all summer. I think they

were sweet on each other already before she came out here in the spring. Her mother is really for it."

She thought for sure the boy would pass out, right then and there in her living room. Betty reached out as if to steady him, but Jake got himself under control before she reached him. "Well, I must be going," Jake said. "I'm glad it was just a little cut."

"Yeah, I am, too," said Betty as she watched him disappear out the door. *Well, that's taken care of,* she told herself.

Jake walked out to the end of the lane, hitched a ride back to Libby, and was on the Greyhound Bus bound for Iowa three hours later.

Hannah found her way downstairs, expecting to find Jake waiting, but he was not. "Where's Jake?" she asked Betty.

"He's gone," she told her.

Hannah's face asked why.

"Jake saw your letter from Sam," Betty told her, "and I told him."

Hannah took the news without any outward signs of emotion. Her first thoughts were that God had come through for her and saved her. There was hope after all. But that night once the house was quiet and still and with the stars twinkling in her window, Hannah cried like a baby, muffling her sobs with her pillow.

≫

When Sunday morning came it produced the planned baptismal, but when she saw no Jake on the boy's row at church, Hannah knew for sure that he was gone. Until then, there was still the niggling hope that maybe he would be there, climbing out of the Nisleys' buggy.

*It's for the best*, Hannah told herself, knowing full well that her mind would not be able to convince her heart. Another night of crying was ahead, she was sure.

꿈

As the Greyhound bus pulled through Billings, Montana, after driving all night, Jake was aching from the tight quarters on the seat. Other things were hurting also, such as his heart. Tempering that though was his anger at Hannah.

So all girls were the same? Jake now knew for sure, even if they didn't look the same. They were all treacherous beings who smiled at you while cutting your heart out.

*So she was writing, all that time, all summer, in fact. Writing to someone, while leading him on with those deep brown eyes.* How could be fall for this again, after being through it the first time? Jake beat the seat in front of him out of sheer frustration.

"Would you quit beating my seat?" a voice protested. A twenty-something girl stuck her frowning face around the corner of the seat.

Upon seeing him, she brightened. "Oh, I didn't know it was you. I'm sorry. I didn't intend to snap at you." Her blue eyes sparkled. "My name's Clara. What's yours?"

*Why not?* Jake asked himself. *Talk to her. Sure she's English, but maybe they are better than your own people. Sneaky girls they produce.* "Hi," he said, returning her greeting. "It's Jake."

"Well, hi, Jake," Clara said. "It's good to meet you. Are you heading home?"

"Yes, I am," he told her, surprised that she knew. "Where are you going?"

"Nowhere in particular at the moment."

*That's a strange answer,* Jake thought. *Everyone is going somewhere.* Aloud, he said with a sudden urge to share, the words spilling out, "Really? Well, I'm going home, after being gone all summer. Home to the farm and working the soil I guess. I've always been a farmer and I guess I always will be."

"Ugh," Clara replied, making a face. "Dirt. Who wants dirt and soil, and working in the sun?" Her face disappeared back around the edge of the seat. From the sounds of settling in that followed there was no doubt that her face was not coming back around the back of her seat.

Jake was now completely confused as he looked out of his window at the passing scenery. *Well,* he guessed he would just stay that way. *Girls are obviously a complete mystery. Even English girls don't want to talk to me.* He supposed it was just always going to be that way.

When he got back home, some twenty-six hours later, Jake decided he would stay there, probably forever. There was one thing, though, of which he was certain: he would never trust girls again.

## Chapter Twenty-Eight

At first, the whine of the Greyhound Bus she was on helped soothe Hannah's nerves. It was only later during this long trip home that it got on her nerves. It had been some time since anything had seemed so endless to her. Town after town, stop after stop, and still the bus moved on slowly.

By dusk of the third day they pulled into the Nappanee bus station. Coming in from the west on Highway six, the sight of Amish Acres sharply brought back the fact that she was home. Hannah was not sure she was ready for this again, this semi-flat land with houses everywhere. Certainly it was not Montana.

Hannah saw her mother before the bus came completely to a halt. Kathy was standing outside the station, her white head covering and plain dress standing out from the small crowd waiting for the bus.

At the sight of her mother, the first stirrings of joy rose up in her. It was just that Hannah was not looking forward to seeing Sam. Thankfully he was not at the station waiting for her. His mouth hanging open was not a sight that she wished to see just yet. The time would come, she thought, but a little more space between them at the moment would help.

Stepping off the bus, Hannah saw her mother's face light up. She waved and then came over. "It's so good to see you!" Kathy exclaimed. "How was the trip?"

"Whiny," Hannah said, laughing. "It sounded good for a while, but three days of it is a lot to bear."

"Oh, you mean the bus whining?" Kathy chuckled. "I didn't know what you meant for a moment. Yes, I remember how it was, although it's been a while since I rode on the Greyhound. So how was everything at Betty's?"

Kathy was eager for information about her sister, even while they were walking towards the buggy. Hannah knew she should start talking, but was not sure how to begin. "Let's see," Hannah finally said, "Betty said to tell you hi, and that they are really happy you let me come out for the summer."

"Did it go well with the horse riding?" Kathy asked.

Hannah grinned, "I think so. I enjoyed it, and I think they made gobs of money. Betty never said how much, but it must have been lots."

"Well, we are glad to help," Kathy told her. "They can certainly use it. In the west it is harder to make money than here in the industrial east."

"But it's so beautiful out there!" Hannah gushed. "The mountains, the rivers, and just the air are wonderful."

"I see you fell in love with the country," Kathy smiled at her, "and you fell in love with someone else, too?"

Her mother was still smiling at her while Hannah was sure she was turning white, instead of blushing red as was expected of her. "We've been writing all summer," Hannah said quickly, hoping that was all her mother knew.

"Oh, not too sure of it, are we?" Kathy raised her eyebrows. "What do you think of him by now?"

Hannah felt her face drain even more of its blood. She must not disappoint her mother now. Not after all she had been through. God had helped her out, and she must now do her part. "Well, we've just been writing," she said quietly. "I've not seen him since I've been away."

Kathy was still smiling, for which Hannah was thankful. "I guess that will change now that you are back. Has Sam asked to see you?"

Hannah nodded. "He wants me to be his steady."

"And?" Kathy raised her eyebrows.

"I said yes."

"Well, Sam's a nice boy," Kathy told her. "Your dad has always liked him, so I'm glad to hear it."

Hannah nodded her head again, trying not to look too glum. It would get better, she told herself.

Arriving home, there was the flurry of meeting all the brothers and sisters and getting settled into her room again.

Her father seemed pleased to see her and asked for details about Steve's logging in Montana. He was even more pleased when Hannah told him that Sam had asked her to be his steady.

"I'm glad to hear you are going with such a solid boy," Roy told her. "If it comes to something more serious, Sam is well placed financially and comes from a good family."

Now Hannah did blush, which added the exact touch needed at the moment for both Kathy and Roy. They were glad to see her on solid ground after the Peter episode.

Later that evening after Hannah had gone upstairs to her room and the other children were already in bed, Kathy asked Roy, "Are you sure about Sam? He seems not quite the right match for her."

"He'll do fine," Roy reassured her. "Sam's of good quality. We don't have to worry about it at all."

"But he seems mismatched to her, somehow," Kathy continued.

"It's not for us to pick her husband," Roy told her. "We can just guide her, that's all."

"I guess," Kathy sighed. "I just hope she's happy. After Peter, this is quite a switch, don't you think?"

"It does seem like it," Roy acknowledged. "But something needed to be switched somewhere. If this is what it is, then we should be happy about it."

"I suppose so," she said quietly. "May God have His way in this."

Hannah was upstairs standing by her window. The new moon hung just above the horizon to the west, its little sliver glittering in the sky with the faint circle of the rest of its body surrounding it.

In front of her, Hannah saw the back porch roof with the tree still standing beside it. The long limb that had overhung the roof was gone, she noticed. For this she was glad. It would not have been a temptation to ever climb its branches again, but it was still good to see it gone.

That was how her old life seemed to her now — gone. Peter was no more, now his memory would be gone, too. God had helped her get away from Jake when her own strength had failed her. Now she was going to be a good girl while the opportunity presented itself.

It was not even such a hard choice to make, now that Hannah was here. Sam was a good boy, a hard worker, and he was inheriting the farm. Why not take the blessings God was giving to her, and be happy? There seemed no reason not to. The road was clear and the bumps had been removed by all appearances. For this she was finally glad. God was helping her, and she would now help herself. She got into bed and slept a soundless sleep all night.

Hannah got up in the morning ready for the day, and was eager to get into the swing of things. Kathy stopped her after breakfast and insisted on one thing before they began the day's housework. "We have to talk about something," she said.

Hannah was not sure what that was, but sat down on the kitchen table bench to see what was coming. She had already made up her mind about Sam, so surely there could not be anything else she was doing wrong.

Kathy sat down in front of her. "I want to talk about Sam," Kathy began.

Hannah nodded her head.

"I just want to make sure that you understand that we are not pushing you into anything just because of your mistakes with Peter."

Hannah was not sure what to say, but nodded her head.

"This should be your own decision, and even though your father likes Sam a lot, you are the one who has to live with him."

"Yes," Hannah said resolutely, "but I have made up my own mind on it."

"Well, then I wouldn't want to interfere, but you shouldn't do it just because you might think someone else wants you to."

Surprised at her mother's words, Hannah looked at her. "I am trying to make up my own mind," Hannah said. "I went through a lot out in Montana, and this seems to be the thing to do."

"I'm sure you did."

"Now the way is clear, and I want to follow God and His direction for me."

"Is this it, then?" Kathy wanted to know.

Running the thoughts of the past few months through her head, Hannah sat on the kitchen bench thinking it over. Kathy waited patiently across from her. Her resolutions passed in front of her, and the fact that Betty said her mother wanted her to write Sam. Was this still true? Yet she was not going to put her mother on the spot by asking if she had or still did. That would simply not be fair, and then God had given her a way out of the situation with Jake, just when she was ready to give in.

"Yes," she said out loud, "the way seems clear on what I am to do."

"Then I hope for the best," Kathy smiled at her. "Shall we get to work?"

Hannah nodded, glad that this was decided and over with. Now life could go on the way it was supposed to. She would be seeing Sam on Sunday, and God would be with her, she was sure.

Sam would be a better person for knowing her, Hannah decided. Even his mouth dropping open could possibly be cured if a person tried hard enough. She was sure of that, and smiled at the thought.

❧

Jake was home in time to help with the oat shocking,

already in full swing in preparation for the fall threshing season. The teams of Amish men and boys helping each other took turns at each other's places in some order that depended on the need and the weather.

Jake simply helped each day in the fields, his arms itching from the scratchy bundles dropped by the binder. Each bundle had to be gathered by hand and set up with its companions in a precise sequence. When done right, charming little shocks resembling miniature tents dotted the fields. When done wrong, they blew down with the wind or simply fell from their own weight.

At lunchtime there was a huge meal served at the place they happened to be that day. Usually this was out underneath the shade trees, or in the house if there was enough room. Mostly, it was outside, to keep things cleaner in the house, he figured. That many men and boys with straw hanging off of them defied cleaning off completely and were sure to leave traces wherever they went.

Jake was glad to be home. However, evenings and nights were another matter. Forgetting Hannah was much harder than he thought it would be, and yet there was no hope. She had been writing to someone else, had she not? It was just the way it was. The same way it was when the first Sunday came around and he saw *her* with his cousin.

They were to be married in November, his mother had told him, watching him carefully when she told him the news. "I thought someone should tell you," she said gently.

Jake nodded his head and took shelter in silence. It was safer there. Whenever someone wanted to talk about his summer in Montana, he gave the simple basics and no more.

Bishop Andy talked to Jake after church the second Sunday he was home, wanting details of his stay in Montana. What he really wanted to know, Jake told him without being asked directly, giving him Bishop Nisley's name and address. Beyond that there was little use of saying anything on his own behalf. Letters would follow between the two bishops, and that was just the way it was.

By the end of the next month, Jake had heard nothing from Bishop Andy and figured he must be safe. If anything serious had been discovered, the deacon would have been by to visit him on one of the Saturday nights for sure.

God would help him, Jake decided. Girls were simply beyond him, and he settled down to bear his sorrow on the flat Iowa plains in silence.

## CHAPTER TWENTY-NINE

O<small>N HER FIRST</small> Saturday night home, buggy wheels sounded on the driveway just before dark. Hannah thought she knew who it would be, and her mother confirmed it by saying, "Look who's here."

Not wanting him to come inside, Hannah went out on the porch and waited for Sam to swing around to the hitching post. Walking out, she surprised him before he had a chance to climb down. He opened his buggy door to find her standing there.

Astonishment was clearly written on his face, but his mouth stayed shut. Used to seeing him otherwise from their school days onward, Hannah smiled in delight. Already, this was a good sign. She was, indeed, having an excellent effect on him. Was this not what wives and future wives were supposed to do? She was sure that it was.

"Good evening," she said. "I thought you might stop by."

Sam still had not come fully to terms with this sudden turn of affairs. First of all, Hannah had consented to write to him, and now she was standing there, perfectly friendly, obviously willing to have him stop by. He now found it hard to find his voice. "Good evening," he finally managed. "I just thought I'd stop by and see you before Sunday."

She nodded her head, waiting for him to go on.

"Those were awful nice letters," Sam ventured. "I just wanted to be sure that I could take you home on Sunday evening. I know we said so in the letters, but I wanted to be sure."

"I understand," Hannah smiled at him. "Yes, that will be fine."

"Okay then," Sam half smiled, embarrassed, she could tell. "I'll see you then. I really have to be going. There are still chores to do at the farm."

Hannah nodded, stepping aside so he could swing his buggy around and out the lane again. As he left, she stood there watching his buggy drive away, a queasy feeling coming over her. *My, what did I just do? Was it the right thing?* she asked and then told herself just as quickly: *He's already improving his manners by so much. God is surely giving me signs to point the way.*

Slightly comforted, Hannah walked back inside.

"Seeing him on Sunday night?" Kathy asked.

Hannah nodded and then went up to her room. Morning was going to come soon enough, and her new life would be beginning in earnest. It would take a lot of rest, she thought, to keep up with it.

Hannah now had the strong impression that being a farmer's wife was not an easy matter. This realization came from seeing Sam again in person. Just the sight of him smelled of hard work, and she knew she would be expected to keep up. *With God's help*, she told herself, as she was falling asleep. *I can do it.*

On Sunday morning, Mary, her friend from school days, found time to talk with her out in the entrance for a moment before church started. "How was Montana?" she asked, leaning over closely to Hannah.

"Beautiful," Hannah whispered quietly, using a one-word explanation because that did capture it all for her.

"I haven't seen your aunt Betty in years," Mary commented. "Ever since they moved out there."

"She's doing okay," Hannah told her. "The little group that they belong to has struggles, I think, but they were all nice to me."

"Was there a large young people's group?" Mary asked.

"No," Hannah told her, making a face. "Just boys."

Mary grinned. "I'm surprised you didn't find one out there, instead of writing to Sam. You surprise me, Hannah."

"I guess it was just meant to be."

"Well, I guess our school day's relationship has lasted, too, so it does happen."

"When's the date?" Hannah asked, hoping she would say.

"I can't tell you," Mary told her, "you know that. Laverne will be helping on the new construction crew out at Miller's. I can tell you that much."

"So it's soon then?" Hannah raised her eyebrows, visions of the good-looking Laverne flashing in her mind. *It's not fair,* her mind sent her signals. *Why should Mary have someone like Laverne and you just have Sam?* She shoved the thought aside.

Mary demurred, "You know how it is. It takes money nowadays to run a household. A good job helps."

"So when is it?" Hannah insisted, forcing herself to stay with the subject at hand.

"I can't tell you!" Mary repeated, laughing. "But don't be surprised, I can tell you that much."

"So it is soon then?" Hannah concluded.

Mary just laughed again. "We should join the others," she said, motioning slightly with her hand towards the larger group of women. "It's just you and Sam that surprises me. I never could figure it out when you picked him out in the eighth grade, but I guess he does need a good wife."

Hannah said nothing as they walked over to the others.

As church started, Hannah could clearly see the line of boys including Sam. He did not pay her much attention during the service, which was fine with her. The evening was coming soon enough.

After church let out, there was no dinner, since it was the off Sunday. Hannah spent the afternoon in her room reading and getting ready for life back in Indiana. She also spent time getting ready for the evening. This was going to be a new world, a new start, and she wanted to be prepared for it.

Conversation was a big thing on her mind. *What were they going to talk about? Would Sam stay till twelve? Should she mention anything about what time might be appropriate? What time would that be?* Hannah sighed, deciding that things would just have to be taken as they came. Not that she was nervous, just concerned.

Nor was she afraid that it would fail, as she supposed she ought to be, but then she had to stop thinking about what could be and think about what was. That was the answer, she was sure. If it were up to her, this would work, even though she wondered how it could not work.

Certainly Sam would not stop it. Would she stop it? That was the question that wanted to be asked, but she was not going to let it be asked. The road was simply too clear, too certain, the signposts too staked out to be mistaken. Life was not meant to be lived in a dream world, but with real people. *Yes*, Hannah thought that was what it was, and she would do her part in making it work.

Yes, she would. Once she said "yes," in front of the bishop, the world would certainly be right and things would go the way they were supposed to go. Getting there was going to be the hard part, but she would make it. Of this she was certain.

The evening arrived soon enough, and with it the familiar singing. It was good being back among so many young people. Most of the faces were familiar to her. Those that were not, she assumed, came from neighboring districts. With such a large settlement the back and forth visiting was very common.

After it was over, figuring out which was Sam's buggy proved a little harder than she had anticipated. It would not do to ask, so she must make the selection on her own. In the just fallen dusk she headed down the walks, hoping against hope it wasn't some strange boy when she opened the buggy door.

It was Sam's freckled face that greeted her, lit dimly by the lantern inside the kitchen she just came from. If she missed that, his red hair glowed softly. Her feelings of relief soon translated into a comfortable silence as they headed out the driveway. He said little until they arrived at her place, and she left it at that. A farmer's wife spoke little, she assumed, and it might as well begin like that.

Hannah offered Sam a glass of orange juice, a fitting gesture, she figured, to a healthy start to their relationship. Of course, it had already started in writing to each other, but this was the first in-person start.

Sam proved to have little to say, which translated into Hannah talking more. Thus it was that Hannah first of all talked about Montana. Sam joined in, mostly on subjects that involved work and business. It was his casual comments about obscure points that surprised her. He wanted to know in great detail the amount she had charged for rides, how many rides were given in each day and so on.

Her information then produced moments of silence in which Sam did muttered calculations, followed by looks of delight on his face. "That was pretty good money," he told her.

"I suppose so," Hannah allowed, although that had not been the point of the story.

"I wonder if someone could do something like that around here?" Sam wondered out loud.

"There are no mountains," she suggested. "That seems to be what really drew the people."

"Tourists, in other words," Sam stated.

She nodded.

"Then tourists are tourists," he said. "They are really all the same. They all want to see things. In Montana they are there to see the countryside, but here they are here to see us."

"I suppose," Hannah conceded, not entirely liking the idea, like she might be a monkey at the zoo.

"It's really something." Sam was fully enthusiastic now. "That's valuable experience you gained. Kind of a surprise, I would say. I never thought people out west could teach us anything." He shrugged his shoulders in sympathy and at the same time, dismissal. "We being the much more industrialist east. We have the factories, the hotels, the big lumberyards, and Amish acres. But I guess it goes to prove that surprises are possible everywhere."

"I think people around here probably already know about giving horseback rides," Hannah told him, raising her eyebrows.

"Could be," Sam allowed. "I had just never heard of it. Anyway," he brightened again as his train of thought continued, "you still have had the experience of doing it, or something like it. That's very valuable. Not too many women can do that."

"I think they can," Hannah objected. "It wasn't that hard."

"Well," Sam commented again, "I think it's good that you can. About the others, I don't know. I know my mother can, and," he blushed a little, "and it's important that you can."

A distinct feeling that she was passing some kind of test, like common merchandise, passed through Hannah's mind, but she suppressed it. It was okay, she decided. She needed to learn to be the proper wife, and this was how that learning happened, apparently. It never happened the way it had in her dreams. Of that she was sure, so why not follow this path? It did appear to her the thing to do.

"I am glad you like it," Hannah said out loud.

Sam grinned from ear to ear, but his mouth stayed shut, about which she was greatly pleased and impressed. It was a continued sign to her of God's direction on her journey. She felt she was having a very positive influence on Sam.

"You should have seen the countryside down by the river," she started to tell him in the following silence. "The land ran on a flat plateau on a long stretch beside the river. There were mountains all around you, with the air blowing across the water. We used to gallop," she caught herself in horror, but there was no taking the words back. *What if Sam asked with whom?* Hannah continued, hoping against hope he had missed it, "along the river bank. Mostly in the evenings." She looked at his face to see where she was. He was saying nothing one way or the other, just listening, nor did he ask who had been with her.

Hannah quickly continued, "Sometimes there were sunsets. You couldn't see them too well with the mountains and the sun just drops behind them. But one night one did develop that was beautiful."

Hannah glanced at Sam. He was looking at her, but showed no signs of interest. "That's an interesting story," he said.

That was why she did not tell him about the mountain lion. That and the danger of where it might lead made her keep those details to herself.

"Well, I had better be going," Sam announced, glancing at the clock. "We have to be up early in the morning milking, and then the fall plowing starts right after the oats are shocked."

So he was going to be leaving early. In a way Hannah was glad, but aloud she said, "You can't stay any later?"

"Maybe next time, although I doubt it. I don't like staying up too late."

Again Hannah was glad.

Sam cleared his throat, a half embarrassed smile crossing his face. "I guess there will be another time?" he asked.

"If you want to," Hannah said, knowing full well that he wanted there to be another time.

"I do," he said, his mouth staying shut. "Until next Sunday then. Maybe we can see each other on Sunday afternoon after awhile?"

"Would you like that better?" Hannah asked him.

"I think so," Sam said. "Not always maybe, but sometimes. I could take you over to our place then. For those Sundays," he explained.

Her mind twirled trying to keep track of this. It was a little unusual, but Hannah figured it made sense. "But you do the chores then?" she asked him.

Sam nodded. "I could take you straight home from church, we could talk some in the afternoon, and you could help chore. I would take you back to the singing then."

She raised her eyebrows. "Not every Sunday, though."

"No," Sam allowed, "not every Sunday."

"Okay then. We'll decide as we go along. Next Sunday at the singing, right?"

"Right," Sam said, and disappeared out the door. The sound of his buggy wheels soon sounded on the gravel outside.

"My first date," Hannah said aloud. "And I'm not dreaming. Isn't that good? Just good, old, practical, sensible human living. That's a good girl."

Going upstairs she stopped by her window before

climbing in bed. A momentary sadness passed over her at the passing of a certain memory through her mind, but then it was gone.

"I am a new person now," Hannah said into the night. "It is a new and a better start."

## CHAPTER THIRTY

"So how did your evening go?" Kathy wanted to know the next morning.

"Okay, I guess," Hannah told her, to the rattle of dishes in the kitchen sink. "He's a farmer. He wants to have me over to his place on a Sunday afternoon sometime."

"That's not too unusual. Are you going to help chore then?"

"I think that's the plan," Hannah told her. "He probably wants to see if I meet the grade."

Kathy wrinkled up her face. "Maybe you shouldn't jump to conclusions too quickly. Sam seems quite smitten with you. I doubt if you doing chores has anything to do with it."

"Whether I can do them may have, though," Hannah said as she kept her eyes on the dishes in the sink, the soap suds clinging to them wherever they broke the surface of the water.

Kathy chuckled.

"It's not funny, Mom. Life shouldn't be this hard. I shouldn't have to prove myself. It makes no sense at all. I thought love was supposed to just come, all by itself."

"Now, now," Kathy tried to soothe Hannah with her

voice. "First of all you don't know if that is what it is, and even if it is, that's not too bad. You can't blame Sam, can you? He does have to keep that farm up he's getting from his father."

"I guess," Hannah sighed in resignation. "I'll try. Not that I don't like cows, but it just doesn't seem right."

"There is still time to say no," Kathy said without looking up. "That's what courtship is all about, is it not?"

"I can't do that," Hannah told her. "It would be like walking away because it's too hard. I don't want to do that."

"Well, love is hard sometimes," Kathy agreed. "Life throws all kinds of things at us, and some are not too pleasant."

"It does seem that way." Hannah lifted the last of the dishes out of the soapy water, rinsing a plate before placing it on the rack. Taking a towel out of the drawer she started wiping the plates dry.

"It'll all work out for the best," Kathy assured her. "It always does when we trust God. He knows what is best."

Hannah nodded her head, hoping against hope her mother was right.

≈

On Sunday night, as expected, Sam raised the question whether Hannah could come over the following Sunday afternoon. That was how she found herself a week later in Sam's buggy at two-thirty after church. The sun was shinning brightly, a little disconcerting, she thought, to be with a boy in a buggy without it being dark outside. Just another thing to get used to, she assured herself. Married people were together at all times of the day.

"Did you get a chance to read the book I gave you?" Hannah asked Sam, making conversation, since he was not saying anything.

"I tried to," he said. "Pilgrim's Progress was great to read, my dad said, but I didn't get very far. It's pretty heavy stuff."

"Not really," Hannah told him, thinking that it was not, and also because she thought he needed all the encouragement he could get. Reading books was one of the things she thought he was in great need of. From her school days, she could never remember seeing him reading anything, as most of the other boys did. This was part of how she would do him good, Hannah had decided.

"I got as far as when Christian fell into the swamp," Sam told her, a silly grin forming on his face. "I thought that was pretty stupid of him. If he had just stopped to look there was a perfectly good set of steps to use across. That evangelist, whoever that was, pointed it out to him after pulling him out of the mire."

"It's supposed to teach a lesson," Hannah told him. "A spiritual lesson, of course, about what happens when we have sin strapped to our shoulders."

"So why doesn't the story just come out and say that?"

"Because it's more interesting this way."

"It wasn't to me," he told her. "That's the problem with books. They don't just say what they want to say. You have to think and figure it out for yourself. It makes no sense to me to even bother. If I have to figure it out anyway, why not just figure it out without the books?"

If it had been dark, Hannah would have looked at him, but since it wasn't she kept looking straight ahead. Her look of dismay would have simply been too obvious and there was no use letting him see it. Clearly another tack was needed for this effort to be successful.

"Have you ever read any books that you liked?" Hannah asked, looking at him and feeling sure that her face was now in proper order.

Sam shook his head, his freckles moving with his face, causing her eyes to hurt from trying to focus on the sudden movement. *Freckles, no, nothing can be done about that*, she told herself.

"Have you heard of *Tom Sawyer* and *Huckleberry Finn*?" she asked him.

"No," he said, pulling up on the horse's reins as they were approaching the Knepp driveway.

"I will give them to you next Sunday night," Hannah stated resolutely. "Every boy ought to love those. Not that they have much value, but they are interesting, shall we say?"

"Are they fit for married men to read?" Sam asked.

"But you're not married," Hannah told him.

Sam blushed, becoming even redder in his face than his freckles already were. "That's what Dad says is a good standard," he explained. "He never said it about books, but about other things. If a married man should do it, then it is probably good."

Hannah shrugged her shoulders. "I have never heard that one before. Anyway, let's see what you think about Tom Sawyer, okay?"

"Was it in the school library?" Sam wanted to know.

"No," Hannah said, "it wasn't. Why do you ask?"

"I can't remember seeing anything like that anyway,"

he told her. "I looked at all the books there once, but none of them interested me."

"Well, maybe these will," Hannah told him.

Pulling up to the barn, Sam got out to unhitch. She helped him undo the traces, then waited while he went into the barn with the horse. He would leave the harness on until the evening, she knew, when they would leave again for the singing.

Walking into the house, Sam reached out to open the kitchen door, letting her in first. "We can go into the living room," he told her.

Taking her bonnet off, but uncertain where to put it, Hannah carried it with her. Half expecting it, she was still surprised to find both of his parents in the living room. Enos nodded at her from where he was seated on the couch reading *The Budget*. "Hi," he said.

Hannah nodded in return, looking back over her shoulder to see where Sam was.

It was Laura who saved her from further embarrassment, getting up out of her rocker after laying her crocheting on the floor. "Sam said you were coming," she told Hannah, reaching out for the bonnet Hannah was still holding in her hand. "Let me take that for you."

Wondering where Sam was, Hannah looked back towards the kitchen again. "He's probably looking to see if the popcorn is ready," Laura offered as explanation, seeing Hannah's look. "Just take a seat. He'll be out when he finds it's not made yet."

True to her word, Sam appeared at the kitchen doorway. "Where's the popcorn?" he asked.

"It's not made yet," his mother told him. Then she asked,

JERRY EICHER

"What are you two going to be doing this afternoon?"

Sam grinned. "Why don't we play a game of backgammon with you and Dad? You can have the popcorn done later then."

"But only two can play," Laura told him.

"We can take turns," Sam insisted. "Two watch and two play."

"Are you up to it, Enos?" Laura asked him.

"I guess," he grunted from the couch. "I haven't played it in a while."

"I know it's been just me and the children now that they are big. But you and I used to play it a lot," Laura told him. "Get your old bones up here and try your hand again."

Enos chuckled. "Well, where are we playing?"

"Out in the kitchen," Laura said, going in that direction. The others followed.

Pulling up a chair, Hannah got into one so that her back was against the wall. This was going to be interesting. "Who goes first?" Enos asked.

"You and Mom," Sam announced. "Then Hannah and me. The winners play winners."

"Sounds good," Enos grunted. "We need to get this done before the chores, though."

"And the popcorn," Sam said quickly.

"Let's start then." Laura opened the playing boards, the brown and tan checkers sliding across the table. Hannah still said nothing. She was just watching.

Arranging the checkers in their proper places, Enos led out. Sam watched intently, Hannah noticed, giving advice freely to his mother. "You just be quiet," she finally told him. "I usually beat you anyway."

"Not always," Sam said grinning, "just sometimes."

The match was a close one with Laura seeming to be ahead. But then Enos pulled off a string of double sixes right at the end. "That's not fair," Laura protested.

"It's just a game," Enos told her.

"It's still not fair," she replied as he moved his last piece home.

"Now I get to play the winner," he pronounced triumphantly.

Laura smiled as she got the new game ready. "Now it's Sam and Hannah's turn."

Letting Sam lead, Hannah threw her dice carefully. It was not even close, as she brought her last checker home quickly.

"That's good," Laura told her.

"Okay, now it's us two." Enos looked cautiously at Hannah. "You seem to know what you're doing."

"Just throw the row of sixes again," Laura said sarcastically. "Just to be fair, you know."

"I'll try," Enos assured her.

This time Hannah led. Again as with Sam, it was not even close. "Where are your sixes?" Laura rubbed it in, halfway through the game. "Hannah is beating you."

"She must have played this a lot," Enos suggested.

"Not really," Hannah said. "Maybe it's just luck."

Enos just grunted as she moved her last piece home.

Glancing at the clock, Laura pronounced that there was still time for popcorn before chores at four.

"I hope so," Sam said. "I wouldn't want to miss that on a Sunday afternoon."

Hannah mentally noted the fact of what would be

JERRY EICHER

expected in the future. Not too difficult she decided, just a tradition she had not really planned would be in her future.

At four Enos and Sam left for the barn to get the cows in. Thirty minutes later, Laura announced that it was time to go also. Hannah followed, having changed to some old clothing Laura offered to her.

In the barn the cows were already lined up in their stanchions, licking at the little dash of feed placed in front of them. A mere tidbit, it was soon gone.

"You'll just watch," Laura told her, "since you've probably never milked before."

"I have milked by hand," Hannah said to redeem herself, since she actually had.

"This is different," Laura told her. "This is milking with machines."

"Is there something I can do?" Hannah asked her.

Thinking for a moment, Laura suggested that she might be able to wash utters. "Not a pleasant job," she puckered up her face to make the point, "but something you could do."

Hannah figured the moment of truth had come, and that she had better jump if she was to survive. "Sure, I'll try," she said.

Laura offered her the bucket of water and gave instructions.

Taking the cloth, Hannah started, leaning carefully against the first cow's hindquarters. A sharp kick would do her in, she figured, but the thing had to be done. Leaning down she took her wet washcloth and closely followed instructions she had been given. Pieces of dirt and manure fell off before her intruding hand and her shoulder slipped on something slimy. Yet when it was done she knew it had been done right.

Laura's smile proved the point. "That's right," she said, "just move on to the next one now."

Twenty cows later, Hannah had fully mastered the technique. She also now smelled like a cow. Seeing Sam's concerned face when he passed by her, she was gratified at his interest in her plight until he smiled at his mother's words. "She's doing real well."

Then Hannah felt sure Sam was just concerned that she might not be up to the job. A little disappointed, she concentrated on telling herself, *I can do it. You just did it, now keep it up.*

After the chores had been done and the popcorn eaten, they left together on the way back to the singing. Sam seemed in high spirits, humming to himself in the buggy with her. That was another thing that would need work on, she decided. Humming in other people's presence was not good manners. But that would all come later, she supposed. The day had been full enough already.

"We are doing the last of the shocking next week," Sam interrupted her thoughts.

"Yes," Hannah said, assuming he meant the threshing crew.

"I was wondering if you could come over in the afternoon to help?"

She looked at him in bewilderment. "But the threshing crew does that."

"Oh," Sam said, "they were already there. This is just a small field that wasn't yet ready. We have to do it ourselves, and all the help we can get would be appreciated."

Hannah's head was spinning. Was he going to pick her up or how was she going to get there? Apparently she was getting there herself. It might seem like a weakness to ask for a ride. So she asked instead, "What time?"

"Soon after lunch on Thursday," Sam told her.

"Okay, I'll be there, if Mom doesn't object," Hannah said.

Sam nodded his head.

After the singing he simply took her home and dropped her off at the front door. Hannah stood listening to his buggy wheels fade into the night. So this was the way life was going to be. Well, it might not be too bad. At least he knew how to play games. She would have to work hard, but there were worse things, she told herself as she headed upstairs for bed.

Taking *Tom Sawyer* off of her little bookshelf, she laid it on the dresser for future use. "He'd better like it," she muttered before falling asleep.

# Chapter Thirty-One

It was the following week and Kathy had no objections to the requested help. "They probably do need the extra hand," she offered as explanation to Hannah.

"They are just making it hard on me," Hannah insisted. "It had better be over with soon or I can't make it."

"Are you thinking about quitting him?" Kathy raised her eyebrows.

Remembering her resolutions quickly, Hannah assured her mother, "No, no, that's not what I'll do at all. I just hope they decide I'm capable before too long."

"It might just be what life is like with him," Kathy told her solemnly. "You can't say you aren't being warned."

"I can make it." Hannah straightened her chin. "I'm capable and strong enough for anything a farmer's wife is supposed to be. They'll see."

"Whatever," Kathy shrugged her shoulders. "How are you getting over there?"

"Will you let me drive your horse?"

"I guess so. No one else is using him. Just be back before too late, as your dad might want him for the evening."

With that, Hannah was off, hitching the horse up right after lunch on Thursday and heading down the road. It was a beautiful day as she drove along and it reminded her of Montana. *What a distant place,* she mused.

Already it seemed so far away, and then the thought of Jake jerked through her like a shock. She hadn't thought of Jake for a long time. That was a good sign, was it not? Slapping the reins Hannah assured herself that it was, then settled back into the buggy seat and let the memories of that far away place flood through her.

Betty and Steve, the horses, the mountains, the plain by the river, and riding there with Jake. She had come so close to saying yes to Jake. She could hardly believe it now. Where would that have led her? No doubt someplace wrong, so God had intervened for her when she could not help herself.

That's what had happened, Hannah was certain. Now she was living the life He had planned for her — clopping along here, heading to Sam's house, and a life as a farmer's wife. She just wished there was more excitement in it, but was that not exactly what had always gotten her into trouble before? *It was,* she decided firmly. *No more of that.*

Slapping the reins again, Hannah urged the old family driving horse on. When she got in sight of the Knepp place, already a small cloud of straw dust was in the air beside the barn. The threshing of the afternoon had started.

Laura waved at her from on top of the wagon as she drove in. Heading in that direction after she tied the horse, Hannah wondered exactly what she was supposed to do. Laura solved that question by offering her another pitchfork. "Come up and help me," she hollered above the racket made by the chugging tractor running the threshing machine.

Climbing up on the wagon from the front, with its tiered

sideboards, she stood shakily on the top. "Don't fall off," Laura said, seeing her unsteadiness. "Grab the fork and use that to keep your balance."

Hannah did that, wondering at the same time how she was supposed to do anything else. "Have you ever done this before?" Laura wanted to know.

Hannah shook her head.

"Be careful then." Laura was quite concerned. "You pick up the bundles one at a time and throw them into the hopper."

Hannah looked at the hopper, its yawning hole staring back at her. Out of the hole came rotating sets of iron teeth reaching as if to grab whatever was there and pull it in. Hannah shuddered at the sight and the thought of what damage those teeth could do.

"We need bundles," a voice hollered from around the corner of the threshing machine.

Hannah did not recognize the voice above the roar of the machinery. Only later would she recognize Enos's father when he stepped away from running the threshing machine.

"We'd better get to work," Laura said grimly. "Hang on tight, and throw when you're ready." She demonstrated how it was done and Hannah followed her lead. One by one, the bundles of oats hit the spinning iron teeth, with a roar and a groan each time by the threshing machine.

Hannah was scared she was going to miss the hopper on her first try, but she succeeded, to her own great pleasure. "That's good," Laura said from beside her. They cast down the bundles one after the other until the wagon was empty.

A full wagon was already waiting behind them when they were done. Sam, who was driving the team, looked sweaty and dirty, as she assumed she herself did. "I would have offered to help," he hollered above all the racket, "but you're already done."

"Hang on," Laura hollered, "I'm moving the wagon."

Hannah knew how to do that, balancing herself on the empty wagon bed as it lurched forward. Sam immediately pulled his wagon into place in front of the threshing machine and began throwing bundles into the hopper.

"We'd better take over," Laura told Hannah. "He needs to go back for another load."

She nodded, following Laura up the side of the wagon.

"Hi," Sam said, when she got to the top. "How's it going?"

"Okay, I guess," she told him, forcing herself to smile. "It's dusty work."

"She's doing just great," Laura told him, which seemed to be the answer he was looking for.

"Two more loads," Sam said before heading down the side of the wagon. "We should be done before dark."

"I can't stay too late," Hannah told Laura when Sam had left, his wagon bouncing noisily down the lane to their back fields. "Dad might need the horse tonight."

"You just go when you need to," Laura told her. "I think we'll be done before Sam thinks. He always overestimates the time it takes."

Swinging away at the bundles, the wagon was soon empty again. Laura offered her a glass of water while they waited for Sam to return from the field.

"Only another half a load," Sam announced when he

returned. "We'll have it loaded in no time."

"What about unloading it," Laura groaned. "The life of a farmer's wife." She looked at Hannah. "What do you think of this life?"

"I think I can do it," Hannah forced herself to smile again.

"Just thought I'd warn you," Laura told her.

Hannah nodded. It seemed that her mother had said something like that not too long ago, also. *I can do it,* she told herself firmly, grabbing the fork again and swinging the bundles into the hopper.

"You are good at this," Laura finally told her, "for never having done it before."

"I'm trying," Hannah said as she heaved another bundle into the air.

By the time the next load was off, she excused herself, happy that she had lasted for the whole thing. Stopping at her buggy she returned to give Laura the copy of *Tom Sawyer* for Sam she had forgotten to give him, and then she headed home.

*I can make it,* Hannah told herself that evening before falling into a solid sleep. *Life as a farmer is a good life.*

❦

Apparently Sam thought she could make it, too, because he proposed that winter. It was one of those winter Sunday afternoons with a blizzard threatening from the west. Talk had been of calling off the singing, but the young folks had braved it. Now with still no snow coming down, Sam was sitting in her living room.

"You will marry me?" Sam asked simply and directly. "That is what this has all been about, has it not?"

"Well, yes," Hannah said slowly, suddenly confronted with his question. She thought she had been ready for it, but seeing it face to face was still a little different than she had imagined.

*You have stopped dreaming,* she told herself, but there was still one more sign she needed. "What did you think of *Tom Sawyer?*" Hannah asked Sam.

Sam looked puzzled as if wondering what that had to do with it. She supposed it didn't have anything to do with it, but it must still be asked. This might not be exactly a sign from God, but she wanted to know.

Seeing her obviously waiting, Sam finally said, "My dad said it wasn't worth reading when he saw it, but because you gave it to me I read it anyway." He chuckled, "It was funny."

"So you liked it?" Hannah asked him.

"Yes," Sam said, still puzzled. "I think it's the first book I really liked."

"Oh," she said feeling a sense of accomplishment. Now sure that she was on the right path, she added, "The answer is yes."

"Yes, to what?" Sam asked, now completely puzzled.

"To marrying you," Hannah told him.

"You will?" he asked, astonishment coming into his voice. "That's so wonderful." He stared at her, his mouth shut, a tear threatening to come out of one eye.

"So when will it be?" Hannah asked, embarrassed that he was so touched.

He thought for a moment as if contemplating whether

to say it or not. The tear still hung there going nowhere. Then his face became firm and certain again, as if he had arrived at a firm conclusion. "How about in spring?"

"That soon?" she asked him, her mind spinning. "How do we make plans that fast?"

"It can be done, if you want to," Sam assured her. "Dad already started their *dawdy* house. It might be done in time; if not we can stay upstairs in the big house until Mom and Dad leave."

"Oh," Hannah said again and then brightened. The signs were right and the way was clear, *Why not?* "Why not?" Hannah said out loud, smiling at him.

Sam dropped his eyes. "Spring it will be then."

And in spring it was. The day dawned perfect for a wedding. Kathy had been in a perfect tizzy at first when she heard the news, but it had been pulled off. The pies were baked, the potatoes done, the casseroles stirred, and the fruit set out.

Roy's cousin lent them his place, the house for the ceremony and the pole barn for the reception afterwards. The home place simply was not large enough for an Amish wedding. Hannah picked out her colors, dark rose for a wedding dress and a lighter shade for the attendants.

Rows and rows of tables now stood in the pole barn. They were covered with white paper tablecloth, and matching silverware had already been laid out. Betty had arrived by Greyhound on Monday. Steve was unable to come, but Betty said she would not have missed this for the world, having had a hand of sorts in the matter.

Relatives came in from the neighboring states, usually arriving the day prior, and were put up in whatever homes were available. Kathy had people in every room of the house, stacked in at times it seemed when the situation warranted.

Laura insisted that their entire upstairs be kept empty out of respect for the soon-to-be-couple. Plans were that they would be spending their first night together there and the weeks ahead. The relatives knowingly nodded their heads and took no offense when they had to stay at some other place.

Bishop Knepp from Holmes County would be presiding over the ceremony. Hannah understood that he was more than just an uncle of the family. Apparently he was also someone who was pretty important. Although the exact cause had never been made entirely clear, she sensed this was the case mainly from the tone of their voices when they spoke of him. Hannah accepted that. An important bishop must be respected whoever he was.

At nine sharp they all filed in to take their seats. Hannah and Sam sat up front very prim and proper in their starched wedding outfits. Sam had on a brand new black suit Laura had ordered for him from a top seamstress who lived around the Goshen area.

It was when the men filed in that the first fright caught Hannah by surprise. Where it came from, she never could figure out. But it was suddenly there, just out of the blue, with the force of a hurricane in her chest. Terror gripped her. *What if this was the wrong thing to do?*

*Stop, dumm kopp, you can't doubt this now.* Although Hannah told herself this firmly, she was sure her face must be growing white. She glanced at Sam although she knew this was not really the proper thing to do at that moment. Amish brides-to-be are supposed to keep their eyes on the floor. But Hannah just had to know if Sam was noticing.

Sam had not noticed. His eyes looked calmly in the minister's direction as if he did not have a care in the world.

*If he's okay, I'm okay,* Hannah told herself, slowly calming down.

The singing started and, with it, her breathing returned to normal. They had to leave to follow the ministers upstairs to receive final instructions. She managed that without embarrassing herself, and followed Sam quietly back downstairs when the instruction time was over.

Ten minutes later the ministers themselves came back down and the preaching started. What then seemed like ten minutes later, although she knew it was more like at least an hour and a half later, she heard the voice of Bishop Knepp faintly reaching her.

*"Wenn diese unser geliebter Bruder und Schwester wünschen noch, in der heiligen Ehe vereinigt zu werden, sie würde sich zu ihren Füßen erheben."*

(If these, our beloved brother and sister, still desire to be united in holy matrimony, would they rise to their feet.)

Hannah rose to her feet after Sam had gotten up, the hurricane having returned in full force. Her heart pounded so hard her head hurt, but the ceremony was going on. Turning to Sam, Bishop Knepp asked him:

*"Tun Sie Sie gestehen vor dem Gott und der Kirche, die dieser unserer geliebten Schwester Hannah Ihnen in der Ehe durch den Willen des Gottes gegeben wird?"*

(Do you confess before God and the church, that this

our beloved Sister Hannah is given to you in marriage, by the will of God?)

Sam said "Yes" in a loud and clear voice.

Bishop Knepp had now turned to her, his hand already preparing to reach out and join the two of theirs together.

*"Tun Sie Sie gestehen vor dem Gott und der Kirche, die diesem unserem geliebten Bruder Sam Ihnen in der Ehe durch den Willen des Gottes gegeben wird?"*

(Do you confess before God and the church, that this, our beloved Brother Sam, is given to you in marriage by the will of God?)

Hannah could not have gotten a sound out if she had tried, and she was not trying. *By the will of God?* Horror was flowing through her. *What was she doing?* In desperation she reached for sanity and resolution, but found nothing.

Bishop Knepp was looking at her, a kind expression on his face. No doubt he had seen fright-stricken Amish brides before and was sympathetic to their plight. It crossed Hannah's mind with absolute certainty that all she had to do was nod, and Bishop Knepp would accept it.

Instead, she shook her head.

*"Die Schwester sagt nein?"* (The sister says no?) The Bishop asked out loud in sheer astonishment.

Hannah nodded her head firmly.

Bishop Knepp seemed rooted to his spot, unable to move. Clearly this was out of the routine. Finally he simply motioned to Sam to seat himself and signaled for the service to proceed. The song leader led in the closing hymn, the one they always sang as people looked at each other with questions in their eyes. Had they seen what they actually saw?

## Chapter Thirty-Two

N UMBLY THE CONGREGATION sat there, uncertain what to do, as the last notes of the singing died away. Hannah could have burst out bawling right then and there, but it would not do to lose control in public. What was going to happen next was beyond her imagination.

A rustle of feet in front of her sounded, with a man clearing his throat. Hannah hardly dared look as the voice of her father began speaking: "The meal is already prepared, and will proceed as normal," he said simply and then sat back down.

That was all the direction that was needed. A frightened bride might have freaked out, but they would all discuss that later. Food was prepared and must be eaten. That much could easily be understood and followed.

There was one remaining problem, though, since the bridal party was to lead the way. Custom was ingrained deeply, and Sam was not moving, his face tight and turned towards the floor. Neither did anyone else dare make the first move.

Hannah dared not move a muscle, sheer numbness slowly filling her body. She was now much more than a *dumm kopp* in the eyes of everyone. It was clearly a mental sanity question going through everyone's mind. The pity and compassion could almost be felt.

Kathy solved the logjam by rising to her feet. Women in all cultures are, in moments of crisis, given the most latitude for their actions. She walked over in front of everyone to where the bridal party was seated. Placing her hand on Hannah's shoulder, she shook it gently.

When Hannah managed to raise her head, she motioned for her to come. Taking her by the hand, she led her into the kitchen and then into the small sewing room off of that. No one followed except Betty, but the problem was now solved. Sam got to his feet and headed outside. Going straight to the barn, he got his horse and, with the help of several of the sympathetic younger boys, was on his way by the time the yard was just filling with people.

None of the adults stared, as that would have been considered severely impolite. A man must be given his privacy, even in public, for his time of grief.

In the bathroom, Hannah had dissolved into uncontrollable sobs. Lest her cries extend beyond the sewing room door, Kathy pressed one of the towels lying there against Hannah's face. Betty stood there helplessly, endlessly repeating to herself, *"Oh, Gott im Himmel, Oh, Gott im Himmel, helfen Sie uns."*

There was only one thing to do. Hannah had to be taken home. This could not be hidden for long, and there were no signs she could be brought under control any time soon. But how was she to be gotten out of the house without causing a great scene?

"Tell Roy to get the buggy," Kathy whispered to Betty. "Have him pull it up to the end of the walks."

Betty nodded her head and disappeared out of the sewing room door, closing it gently behind her. There was no lock on the knob, but the crowd of women around the exterior could be trusted not to intrude.

Giving no explanation, Betty stepped outside. Finding no sign of Roy in the yard, she headed out to the pole barn. He was there, directing people to their seats. Seeing Betty and the look on her face he came over to her.

"Kathy wants the buggy brought up to the walks," Betty told him.

"I'm not leaving," he told her. "These people have to be taken care of."

"You don't have to," Betty told him. "Kathy and I will take her home."

"What about the food and managing that?"

"There are plenty of cooks around," Betty told him. "We are not needed. They can manage."

"What went wrong with that girl?" Roy now asked, his voice lowered even lower than it was before. "She's lost it completely now."

"I don't know," Betty shrugged her shoulders. "We'll talk to her."

"I may do more than that," Roy said, his face tense. "We have been completely embarrassed in front of everyone. No one can hide this."

Betty shrugged again, mainly because she didn't know what to say.

"I'll get the buggy," Roy finally told her.

She nodded and went back towards the sewing room. As she came in the door, the circle of women parted to let her through.

She quietly went in to where Kathy now held the still-weeping Hannah against her.

"He's coming," Betty whispered.

"Keep a look out," Kathy told her, knowing Betty would know what that meant.

Betty did and she slipped outside to watch by the kitchen window. When Roy jumped into the buggy out by the barn, she came back in to tell Kathy to come.

Kathy dried Hannah's tears the best she could and gave her a stern look. Hannah ceased crying. With Betty in the lead, they exited.

Eyes all around them were cast to the ground out of respect for the moment. Women stepped aside and held open the front door for them. Down the walks they went, to the gawking of the smaller children standing around. No one said anything.

"I'll take it from here," Kathy told Roy who was standing by the horse's head waiting.

He simply nodded and let go once they were all inside the buggy.

On the way home, Hannah broke out into fresh wails of agony.

Arriving home, Kathy marched Hannah into the house while Betty tied the horse. By the time Betty could make it in, Kathy already had Hannah on the couch and was demanding explanations. "So what are you trying to prove?" Kathy stood, her arms on her hips. "That was quite a show to put on for nothing. Now your father has all that wedding to pay for, and you are not even married."

Hannah felt like wailing even louder, but gathered her

thoughts together. "I thought you wanted me to marry him," she said numbly.

"Wanted you to marry him?" Kathy was incredulous. "What has that got to do with it?"

"After Peter, I wanted to be a good girl for once," Hannah muttered.

Kathy was still. "I never wanted you to marry Sam. Where did that come from? You said you were making up your own mind. I told you to do that."

"Betty said you did," Hannah indicated Betty.

"She did?" Kathy waited. "Betty told you I wanted you to marry Sam?"

"Yes," Hannah said, emphasizing her point by slightly nodding her head.

"So what is this all about?" Kathy wanted to know as she turned to Betty.

"Well, I thought so," Betty protested. "I forget exactly why, but I kind of put two and two together with why you sent her out there. That is what I came up with. She was trying to get away from Sam, and you wanted her to be with him. Was that not why he wrote right after she came out to us? Your letter said you gave him Hannah's address, or rather our address where Hannah was."

Kathy took a deep breath and took a seat on the couch. "Maybe you had better start at the beginning and tell me everything that went on while Hannah was with you."

Betty shrugged her shoulders. "Sure, I have nothing to hide."

"Okay, start then," Kathy told her, exhaling deeply. "This has turned into a pretty mess. I may have some things to tell you also when you are done."

So Betty did, starting from the first day Hannah came until she chased Jake off by revealing to him that Hannah was writing to Sam.

Hannah listened with an open mouth.

"Now it's your turn," Betty concluded.

"I guess it is," Kathy told her. "I just wish we had done this sooner."

"I am waiting," Betty insisted. "You made me tell everything."

Kathy sighed deeply. "There was Peter," she began and wrapped up thirty minutes with the funeral and their decision to send Hannah out west.

Betty had her hand over her mouth and Hannah was close to open wails again. "Oh, my life is all messed up now!" she said in horror.

"I would say so," Kathy agreed. "How are we going to get it all untangled? Now you've walked at your own wedding. You know people are never going to forget that. What are we going to do?"

"This is all my fault, this is all my fault," Betty was repeating rapidly to herself as if her mind were stuck on that one refrain.

"Oh, I'm ruined," Hannah wailed. "No one will marry me now. I was going to tell Sam about Jake, but now it's too late forever." She covered her face in her hands in total despair.

"So what do you think?" Kathy finally asked Betty, searching for sanity.

"Oh, my, oh my!" Betty was beside herself. "I've messed things up so badly, I don't know."

"Well, maybe if we talk to each other like sisters are supposed to, we can keep this thing straight from now on."

Betty nodded her head, thinking fast. "I think Hannah should come back out with me. I can leave tomorrow. We can tell people she is going with me to get her well out there, which she is of course. That will make sense to everyone, and with a little time, this thing will blow over."

"It won't blow over for me," Hannah muttered. "I'm really messed up now."

Kathy ignored her. "That makes sense. Let me tell Steve about it when he comes home and we will go from there. For now, Hannah, go up to your room, get out of that dress, and start packing as if you are going."

Hannah nodded glumly as she went upstairs.

Steve was told the story that evening, from beginning to the end, Betty filling in whatever details Kathy had left out. "I never heard of something so stupid in a long time!" he proclaimed. "I guess it takes a woman to straighten out what a woman messes up."

"Can Hannah go then?" Kathy wanted to know.

"Yes," Steve said, "but she's paying for her next wedding herself."

"Just be thankful if there is another one," Kathy told him. "She's pretty shook up."

"Oh, there will be one," he said grimly. "Girls always figure out how to do that."

"This one will take God's help," Kathy assured him.

❧

The whine of the Greyhound bus was getting on Hannah's nerves again. She heard that whining between her occasional outbursts of tears and Betty's silence. Her talkative aunt was saying little. It was somewhere on the plains of Nebraska, around Omaha, that Hannah finally asked her, "What about my dreams? I was trying to stop and do the right thing. How did I go so wrong?"

Betty continued looking out the window until Hannah was sure she was not going to answer. *She's mad, too,* Hannah thought. *The whole world hates me now.*

Betty turned back from the window towards Hannah. "It's this way," she began. "Dreams are just to show us the way, to give us courage when the road gets hard, to give us hope when we find the thorns. They are not evil or to be rejected."

"But I did," Hannah said, tears filling her eyes again. "I can never undo that."

"You can open your heart again," Betty told her, and she turned back to looking out the window.

"But it hurts." Hannah stifled a little sob.

"I know," Betty nodded, "but it's the way to sanity."

"But it may never happen," Hannah insisted.

"Then we must let that hurt, too," Betty said. "But that is where God will walk with us."

Hannah said nothing, simply letting the tears flow freely.

They switched buses in Sioux Falls about five that evening, climbing out to claim their luggage and hauling it over to the next bus. Being a connecting bus, some passengers were already aboard, their dim silhouettes visible through the high windows.

After stashing their luggage underneath, Betty led the way onto the bus, holding on to her small carry-on bag. Hannah followed her. Betty stopped abruptly mid-way back. Hannah almost bumped into her. "Jake!" Betty exclaimed. "Jake Byler, what are you doing here?"

Jake stared grimly at the two of them. Hannah, now white in the face, was silent.

"Maybe you should answer that question first," Jake told Betty, glaring at her.

Then to Jake's great surprise, Betty took the empty seat behind him, motioning Hannah in first. "I think I should, too," she stated flatly. "And I will start right now."

Hannah was too frightened to get a sound out. Jake was mad.

A white-haired older lady was seated in front of Jake's seat, her head visible when she turned towards the window. Behind Betty and Hannah was a younger couple, holding sandwiches they must have purchased during the stopover. None of this stopped Betty, because she could speak Pennsylvania Dutch, and so could Jake and Hannah. It was a great tool if one wanted to speak in public without being understood by most.

Right there, Betty launched into her side of the entire story, concluding with the result, Hannah's botched wedding. "Really?" Jake said, fire still in his eyes, but they were softer now, Hannah thought.

It gave her courage when Betty turned to her: "Now it's your turn."

She did, starting with Peter and why she agreed to write to Sam, how she was going to tell him that evening the mountain lion had screamed at them, how she took his leaving as a sign from God, and then all the rest. Finally she said how sorry she was.

Glancing at Jake she was astonished to see an even softer glow in his eyes.

"I guess I have some things to say, too," he told them.

Then he held them spellbound for the next twenty minutes with his own story.

When he was done, the older lady in front of him turned around in her seat and stuck her head around the corner. "Oh, that was the sweetest thing I have heard in a long time. You people sure make a mess of things, but it looks like God is looking out for you."

Betty was aghast. "But we were speaking in German! How did you understand?"

"*Ach*," she chuckled, "*Ich bin Deutscher*. (I am a German.) You were speaking some dialect, but I understood it real well. It's such a wonderful story."

"I see." Betty recovered herself rather quickly. Then she turned back to Jake. "So where are you going, Jake? You never answered my question."

"I guess to Montana," Jake said shyly, glancing at Hannah.

"You were wandering again, weren't you?" Betty looked sharply at him.

"Well," Jake began sheepishly, "I had a thirty-day ticket on the Greyhound. Maybe I would have stopped in Montana, but I wasn't expecting to find this."

Hannah smiled at him through her tears.

"Oh," Betty said ecstatically, "is it too much to hope for? A wedding out there? Maybe you'll even live there."

The other two were saying nothing but simply looking at each other. Betty looked sharply at them. "Oh!" she exclaimed after one glance. "It is true. I am not dreaming."

"Let's not mention anything about dreaming right now," Hannah told her.

"That's because we don't have to," Jake added. "We are living it."

"By God's grace, by God's grace we are," Betty repeated fervently.

"That's right," Jake agreed still looking at Hannah. Hannah simply nodded her head.

It was a moonless Sunday night some weeks later outside of Nappanee, Indiana, fifteen minutes after the singing had dismissed at nine. Girls were standing around the front door, watchful and waiting for their rides. The group stiffened when she walked out. Her brother's buggy was not next in line.

"So soon?" one of them wondered after she was out the door and out of earshot.

"Someone's in a hurry," the one closest to her responded, and the buzz began.

"Good evening," she told him as she hopped in gracefully, her dress not even brushing his buggy wheel.

"Good evening," he responded. Letting out the reins of his horse, they drove out of the driveway in silence.

She gathered herself to say it. Her hands were clasped tightly in her lap. The quiet of the night gave her strength. No more was she the clumsy, blushing girl from her school days. Years of waiting and sorrow had tempered her soul. Now she would take the chance given to her and not let it slip away.

She cleared her throat. "That was not nice what she did to you, Sam, you know that."

Sam said nothing, holding onto the reins as his horse pulled hard.

"I am glad, though," she said into the darkness.

"Really, Annie?" he asked, his voice trembling slightly.

She said nothing for a moment, then told him: "I think God has kept you. You do not know how thankful I am for that. That day of the wedding was really a miracle for me and I hope for us."

There was no light penetrating the buggy at that moment, nor could much of anything be seen. If there had been light, one could have seen that while his hands were still on the reins of his horse, his mouth was hanging wide open.

Jerry Eicher and his wife were raised and married Amish. They live in central Virginia with their four children.